7/14

My Faire Lady

My Faire Lady

Laura Wettersten

SIMON & SCHUSTER BFYR

NEW YORK LONDON TORONTO SYDNEY NEW DELHI

SIMON & SCHUSTER BFYR

An imprint of Simon & Schuster Children's Publishing Division
1230 Avenue of the Americas, New York, New York 10020

SIMON & SCHUSTER BFYR is a trademark of Simon & Schuster, Inc.
For information about special discounts for bulk purchases, please contact Simon &
Schuster Special Sales at 1-866-506-1949 or business@simonandschuster.com.
The Simon & Schuster Speakers Bureau can bring authors to your live event.
For more information or to book an event,
contact the Simon & Schuster Speakers Bureau at 1-866-248-3049
or visit our website at www.simonspeakers.com.
Jacket design by Chloë Foglia
Interior design by Hilary Zarycky
The text for this book is set in New Caledonia.
Manufactured in the United States of America
2 4 6 8 10 9 7 5 3 1
Library of Congress Cataloging-in-Publication Data
Wettersten, Laura.
My faire lady / Laura Wettersten.—First edition.
pages cm
Summary: After breaking up with her boyfriend, seventeen-year-old Rowena
takes an out-of-town summer job at a Renaissance fair, but romantic
entanglements soon follow.
ISBN 978-1-4424-8933-2 (hardcover)
ISBN 978-1-4424-8935-6 (eBook)
[1. Renaissance fairs—Fiction. 2. Dating (Social customs)—Fiction. 3. Love—
Fiction. 4. Summer employment—Fiction.] I. Title. II. Title: My fair lady.
PZ7.W5335My 2014
[Fic]—dc23
2013021542

FIRST
EDITION

To Andy, my real-life knight in shining armor

My
Faire
Lady

1

FRIDAY

"Rowena! Are you home?"

Normally, the sound of my mother's voice would have been enough motivation to get me to turn off the talk show I was watching and get off of the couch. Normally, I would have grabbed a book or picked up some sort of cleaning supply and acted like I was busy learning or making myself useful around the house.

Today there's no reason to even fake it, though. I haven't moved since this morning. I'm still in the pajamas I wore to sleep, I haven't bothered to run a brush through my hair, and the bowl of cereal my mother set in front of me before leaving for work is untouched. The multigrain rings have swollen up to three times their normal size. There's a disgusting amount of used tissues scattered all around me—evidence of the many times I've burst into tears today.

I lift my head but don't move my eyes from the TV. "In here."

My mom appears in the doorway. She's impeccable as always, with her curls pinned back into a tight chignon and a suit that I'm sure looked impressive to the members of the jury she spoke in front of today. Out of the corner of my eye I see her shoulders sink.

"Ro . . . this is the fourth day you haven't moved from that couch."

Yep. Four long, horrible days since finding out my boyfriend was cheating on me with another girl. A *freshman* girl. Dante may have failed to mention it, but finding out your boyfriend is cheating on you with a freshman is definitely the Tenth Circle of Hell.

"You're home early," I say, half annoyed and half glad.

"The case got postponed."

Just then a fight breaks out on screen and I point at it. A woman is getting in a man's face, screaming about what a liar he is. The show's security guard has moved behind them, at the ready if it should come to blows. "This girl's boyfriend cheated on her, too." My mother doesn't move to look at the TV, so I feel the need to show my solidarity. I shake my fist at the screen. "That's right! Tell him what a scumbag he is!"

My mother sighs so loudly that it sounds like she's deflating. Then she walks into the room, plucks the remote from the coffee table, and turns the TV off.

"Rowena," she begins, sitting on the couch, close to my head. "I know he hurt you, but lying here watching trash isn't going to help. You need to get out. Hang out with Meg and Kara. See a movie. Head to the mall."

I let out a frustrated groan and do my best to bury my head, ostrich style, in the pillows of the couch. "I can't go to the mall. Kyle will be there. With *her*."

"Even better," my mother says brightly. She pets my head. "It's like your father always says. You can't keep a Duncan down. Do your hair and put on a cute top and go have a good time. Show him that you're just fine without him."

I look up at my mother. "But I'm not just fine without him."

My mother's smile is pitying, and she takes a moment before she responds, her voice soft. "I know. But sometimes we have to pretend until it's true. Besides, lying on the couch for four days is—"

"Undignified?" I finish for her, thinking of another thing my father always says: A Duncan is always polite and dignified.

"Unhealthy," Mom says. "And I hate to say it, but you start at TK's next week. You're going to have to face the mall sooner or later."

TK's. That elicits another groan. I'd totally forgotten about TK's, my summer job. Before the rumor that wrecked my life, and consequently, the confirmation of said rumor from my now ex-boyfriend, TK's seemed like the best job ever. Just like last summer, I am going to be a waitress for the tiki-themed restaurant where the only uniform is jeans, a Hawaiian shirt, and a lei. The problem is that TK's is inside the mall, and there's no way I won't run into Kyle there all summer long. Our town is small and mostly quiet, so the only places for us to hang out are the mall, the beach, and sometimes, just for a little variety, the parking lot of the mall, if we don't get in trouble for loitering. And TK's is popular as well. There's a luau every Friday night, and loads of people come in to see the ukelele player and drink sugary drinks out of fake coconuts.

The thought of seeing Kyle with his new girlfriend, Lacey, makes my stomach do an unsettling flip, and I look up at my mom. "Do I have to work this summer?"

"You know the Deal. You've got to pitch in for college."

The Deal, all part of my father's great plan to instill me with some sort of work ethic. I nod to my mother, but allow myself one last indulgent whine. "I just don't want to see him with her . . ."

"I know how much you liked the Anderson boy, Ro, but there are other fish in the sea."

With that statement, my mother confirms exactly how much she doesn't know what she's talking about. He's not just the "Anderson boy," the son of the town's pharmacist, he was my boyfriend for over a year. He was the romantic boy who asked permission before our first kiss, the thoughtful boy who would whisper with me on the phone until the early morning so we wouldn't wake our parents, the cute lacrosse player who took me to junior prom. He was so, so much more than just "the Anderson boy."

I guess now, he's also the first boy to break my heart.

My mother jolts me out of my thoughts with a pat on my arm. "Come on, Ro. Get up. Shower. When you're finished, you can help me start dinner for tonight."

When I don't immediately move, my mom issues a threat. "If you don't, I'm going to call Kara and Meg and have them come over and get you up."

Talk about motivation. Kara and Meg are my two best friends in the world, but their methods are devious. They'd come over and be as obnoxious as possible to get me off this couch, and they are gold medalists in being obnoxious. I'm up and moving so fast that I practically knock my mother off the couch. I hear her chuckling to herself as I head up the stairs to the shower.

The shower washes away the funk I've been accumulating for the past few days, and a good portion of my sour mood, too. It's not enough to make me want to do my hair and head to the mall, but it's enough that I continue my effort to look a little better. I take out my giant box of nail polishes and open it, sinking back into the big pillows on my bed.

Before a particular shade can catch my eye, an instant message dings on my laptop, which is sitting on my desk. I flip over onto my stomach and pull the laptop toward me.

Briansgurl: how are you? we're worried.

I smile at Kara's message and type back.

CrazyCurls27: I'm ok.

Briansgurl: are you lying?

CrazyCurls27: Is Meg with you?

Briansgurl: this IS meg! i've taken over Kara's computer. don't avoid the question. are you lying or not?

CrazyCurls27: Not lying.

Briansgurl: then you should come out tonight. we haven't seen you since you broke up with Jerkface McGee.

CrazyCurls27: Nah. I'm helping Mom with dinner later. You guys have fun. I'm going to paint my toenails. I know. I'm super exciting.

Briansgurl: OK, but mall monday? it's our last day of freedom before we become TK slaves!

CrazyCurls27: No mall. NO. I would freak if I saw them.

Briansgurl: um . . .

CrazyCurls27: What?

There's a pause in our conversation.

CrazyCurls27: WHAT Meg???

Briansgurl: kyle's taking HER to six flags monday. but that means the mall's safe!

I blink at the screen. I don't know how many times I suggested to Kyle that we go to Six Flags together, and every time he had some excuse. He had practice, he had to work for his dad, it was too cold, it was too hot.

Funny how all those things don't seem to matter now. I clench my teeth and type back to Meg.

CrazyCurls27: OK. Mall. Monday. See you then!

I log off before she can type back, and push the computer

away, my gaze drifting back to the nail polish colors in my box. A perky bubblegum pink catches my eye, so I start with my big toe, jabbing the brush at it a little angrily. As a result, the paint job looks bad when I'm done. Kind of awful, really, as if I've forgotten every single lesson Mrs. Robertson ever taught me in art class. She'd probably be appalled that my brushstrokes look so jagged, but that's how I've felt since Kyle said, "I'm sorry, Ro. I like someone else." Jagged. Like all my edges are rough and sharp.

I look back to my big toe and the awesomely bad job I've done painting it. Maybe pink isn't my color. Red is more suited to my current emotional state. As in, "When Rowena Duncan heard that her boyfriend had been seeing a freshman cheerleader behind her back, she saw red."

Yep, red is the way to go.

I pick out a garish candy-apple color from my box and move on to the next toe, whispering to myself, "A freshman. She's not even that pretty."

I wiggle my toes and admire my handiwork. The red looks much better than the pink, as far as technique goes. The two colors look good next to each other, too. Like a valentine.

Which of course makes me think of Kyle. Last Valentine's Day he sent me pink roses during school, so I got to carry them around all day, bragging about what an excellent boyfriend he was. What a lie that turned out to be.

Okay, so maybe I should throw in a different color so my toes don't look like Valentine's Day threw up on them. Perhaps something that won't remind me all about the cheating loser who ruined my life. But as I'm picking out a blue from my toolbox of nail polish, I think, "Why stop there?" and dig out more bright shades. A whole rainbow of colors on my feet. If that won't make me smile, nothing will.

Though I love every color I choose, my favorite is a bold orange I found in the bargain bin at Target after Halloween last year. Orange always makes a statement, or so Mrs. Robertson says. It can be angry, or joyful, or passionate. It can be calm or restless, cautious or dangerous.

"Colors can speak louder than words, Rowena," she told me during my first art class. "And they can invoke as much emotion as music." If that's true, then I bet Mrs. Robertson would love this color therapy I've got going on with my toes.

I lift my feet and admire the result: a whole palette of color on my feet, each nail a different, bright hue. It will look really awesome at the beach, maybe when I get a little more tanned.

That thought punches me in the gut. The beach. That was also part of the summer plan. Working at TK's, hanging out at the mall, going to Kara's parents' beach house on the weekend. All of it was supposed to be spent with Kyle, but now everything's messed up. Not just because we aren't together anymore, but because Kyle is part of our group. Kara's boyfriend, Brian, is Kyle's best friend. Now the whole group will be awkward, or *she'll* be along with him, and I just can't take it. I don't want to see them together. I don't want to see him kiss her the way he used to kiss me, or wrap his arm around her waist, or put sunscreen on her back. Lacey gets all of that now, I suppose, and every time I think about it I get this horrible, cold feeling in my chest. That's the worst of all of it: I miss him.

There's just no way I can face a summer filled with seeing Kyle but not being *with* Kyle. But I have to work. It's part of the Deal.

Although . . . my parents never said I had to work at TK's. Just that I had to work.

Inspired, I grab my laptop, where I have the entire World Wide Web and Google at my disposal. All it takes is a couple of clicks of the mouse and I have options for my summer.

Most of the summer job postings leave something to be desired. There are openings for tutoring (too boring), house cleaning (too dirty), lawn mowing (too sweaty), and canoe instructing (too many flesh-eating bacteria scenarios). But there are a few openings I might like. I'm about to click on a roller-skating waitressing gig when something else catches my interest.

Body art specialist, the ad reads. I frown. What on earth is body art? And how do you specialize in it?

I read on.

. . . for a remote community of artists in the woods.

Now that has merit. Remote? Woods? Ha. It's just about perfect. Goodness knows, Lacey doesn't seem like the outdoorsy type, what with her perfectly straightened hair, her designer skinny jeans, and her penchant for heels. I bet she takes one look at a tree, smacks the wad of bubble gum in her mouth, and goes, "Oh my god. You can't, like, be serious. Nature is SO LAME." There's no way she and Kyle would show up out there. No way, no how.

I'm pretty qualified, too. At least for the art part. The body part . . . well, even if I knew what exactly that meant, I'm sure I don't have experience in it. But art I can handle.

I look around my room for a minute. Nearly every wall has a painting that I've done, either for my art classes or on my own time. I even have a few finished paintings leaned up against the walls because there's not enough space to hang them. They're decent, really, even if I don't always get the shading right, or my brushstrokes aren't as skillful as they could be.

That's when I decide: Whatever a "body art specialist" is, I can do it. Especially if it's truly a *remote* community of artists, far away from Kyle and Lacey and their sickening new romance.

I look at the website again and gasp so loudly that I'm sure my mom hears me downstairs. *In-person interview required. Deadline, June 1.*

"Today is June first!" I exclaim to nobody in particular, and grab my phone.

I punch the number in and cradle the phone against my shoulder as it rings. It rings so long that by the time someone picks up, the sudden human voice in my ear makes me jump. I miss his entire greeting because of this surprise, and because his voice is heavily accented. It sounds . . . British, maybe, but not quite.

"I just saw your ad," I explain. "About a body art specialist? If it's not too late, I'd like to interview."

The accented voice tells me, distractedly, that I can still interview but I need to get there before four o'clock. Then he mumbles something obviously not meant for me that I could swear sounds like, "Make sure the swords look sharp" before rattling off an address. I'm about to ask exactly what a body art specialist is, and why the swords need to look sharp, and why there are swords at all, but then there's just silence in my ear.

For a moment I keep the phone pressed to my ear, as if the silence can somehow soothe the uneasy feeling in my gut. I may be desperate to get away for the summer, but I'm not sure I want to spend it with people who have sharp swords, and goodness only knows what they mean by body art. Especially if it's truly remote, as in far enough from civilization that no one could hear my screams.

Curious, I take out my laptop again and type in the address the man gave me. Google finds it for me and shows me a map. The end point, the little thumbtack-looking destination, is right smack-dab in the middle of a huge patch of nothing but green. The only thing close to it that even mildly resembles civilization is a creek and a rest area a mile or two north of it.

"Well, Ro, you *did* want to be in the middle of nowhere," I whisper to myself, and click on the driving directions.

I let out a curse when I realize that if I want to get there by four, I have to leave in ten minutes, because this place is a full hour away and it's nearly three.

The next few minutes rush by in a frantic blur as I cram in all I have to do. I print out my resume and the job info. While that's printing, I throw on a green V-neck tee and a long, flowing skirt—the only skirt I own that doesn't require ironing. After that I apply a coat of mascara, brush my teeth, comb my hair, and spray on a metric ton of body spray. Then I slip my feet into my nicest pair of sandals, grab my resume from the printer, and dash toward the front door.

"Rowena?" My mother appears in the front hallway. She's changed out of her power lawyer suit and is wearing jeans and a T-shirt with a lighthouse on it, with an apron over that. My mother is the only woman in the world, aside from Martha Stewart, who actually wears an apron. "Where are you going?" she asks.

"I'm going to go see about a job," I say, hoping that will suffice. There are too many follow-up questions I don't want to answer. Questions like, Where is it? What will you be doing? And what about TK's fine Hawaiian dining?

Somehow, miracle of miracles, she's distracted by another thought entirely. "You said you'd help with dinner."

"I'll be back in a few hours, I promise," I say, which seems to appease my mother, and I'm out the door and in my car before she has time to remind me that the Duncan family dinner is at seven p.m. sharp.

I'm almost to the interstate before I put the address into my GPS, but it's a no-brainer that I'll have to use the interstate to get there. You can't get anywhere from my dinky little town without using the interstate. I just don't remember whether Google said it was north or south.

North it is, or so says the snooty British voice of my GPS as she commands me to turn on to the on-ramp. I obey. Although the voice is usually good with giving me clear directions, she's terrible at reminding me about those other pesky details involved in driving. I forget to check my mirrors and try to merge straight into an eighteen-wheeler's lane, and nothing, I mean *nothing*, will get your attention like the deep, frantic honk of a huge truck.

I grab the wheel and swerve out of his lane with a drastic, tire-squealing curve to the right, until I can safely put my car in park on the shoulder. It's not until the truck whizzes by me, still honking, that I finally scream.

I'm shaking, my elbows like jelly on the steering wheel, my leg barely able to keep the brake pedal down. I rest my head against the window and try to breathe. In and out, in and out.

"Get a grip, Ro," I whisper to myself after a few minutes. I glance at the rearview mirror and see that I still look terrified, with wide eyes and a line of sweat on my brow. I've had my license for a year and I pride myself on being a good driver, an aware driver, but today there's too much going on in my brain. It's too filled with thoughts of getting the heck out of town, and Kyle's cheating and Kyle's everything else.

Somehow, the thoughts of him strengthen my resolve. I will get this job. I will spend my summer in the middle of nowhere. I will get over Kyle.

I smooth down my hair, take a deep breath, and ease the car back onto the road, taking care to check all mirrors before I merge. It's as if my GPS senses my newfound determination, as she gives me what must pass for words of encouragement in her little world. "In one half mile, veer right onto County Road 4."

Once again I do what she says, and I find myself on a wandering country road with quaint old farmhouses and ancient-looking trees.

Soon I start seeing fewer and fewer houses, and more and more trees. Pretty soon I'm also the only car on the road, and there's no sign of civilization anywhere. I'm still on track according to the GPS, though, so I keep driving, but it's unnerving feeling like I'm the only one out here, and it seems as if I've been driving for days. Probably because the road is so curvy, I can't go any faster than thirty miles per hour. Finally, Snooty British GPS tells me to turn right, and my only option is a dirt road, which can't be it.

But then my eyes fall on something strange. It's a wooden post about three feet high that might have had a mailbox on top of it at one point. In place of a mailbox, however, sits a little troll.

Not a real troll, obviously. I'm not hallucinating or anything. It's a wooden one, and it's charming in the way all trolls are charming—ugly enough to be cute. Its arms tuck under its fat belly, its legs bow in so that its knees touch, and it has the funkiest looking beard I've ever seen.

I take the weird little guy as a sign and turn down the road. After all, the ad did say remote. Maybe these artists don't want to be disturbed.

My car rumbles and shakes along the dirt road, kicking up a cloud of dust as I go. A canopy of trees arches over my head, and the sun flashes through gaps in the leaves, bright and golden. The colors blur like watercolors as I drive, and I long to be able to capture them with a brush and canvas. I'm grinning like an idiot, thinking about how beautiful the woods are, when they suddenly stop. I'm so startled at the sudden change that I slam on my brakes.

In front of me, stretching as far as I can see in either direction, is a wide open field cut into the forest. And in this field, like glistening sequins, hundreds of cars are parked in neat rows. To my right is a tall pole with a large painted wooden sign that points to the left. I read it desperately, trying to get my bearings.

THIS WAY TO THE FIFTEENTH CENTURY, it says. *What?*

I stare at it some more, as if the words will somehow make more sense if I just give them more time. A knock at my window makes me yelp in terror. A guy in a leather vest and a billowy shirt motions at me to roll my window down. I do.

He flashes a smile that, in any other situation, might be handsome. Right now I just find it confusing. "Good morrow, my lady. May I be of assistance?"

All I can do at this point is hold the printout of the ad in front of his face and make some sort of weird noise meant to ask a question. His smile becomes an amused smirk.

"Aye, my lady. You have come to the right place. If you would allow me the honor, I can escort you to the king myself. If you would kindly park your carriage, I will assist you anon." I stare in response, which makes him clear his throat, possibly to cover a chuckle. He motions toward an empty parking spot at the end of one of the long rows, politely telling me to get a move on. In my rearview I can see that I'm holding up a line; a few cars have appeared behind me, and the driver of the one directly in back is tapping his steering wheel impatiently.

I ignore him and turn back to the guy at my window, finally finding my voice to ask, "But what is this place?"

The guy dips his head in a slight bow, eyes twinkling at mine as they connect. "My lady . . . Welcome to King Geoffrey's Faire!"

2

FRIDAY

As soon as I step out of the car I hear strange music off in the distance. It sounds like an Irish jig, with some sort of flute and a low-pitched drum. Those who have parked their cars close to mine climb out with smiles on their faces and walk assuredly toward an arch on the other side of the field. The fancy block letters painted on it are big enough to read and confirm that this is, indeed, King Geoffrey's Faire. That's good. The dude in the leather vest might be crazy, but at least he tells the truth.

He appears at my side with another slight bow and I can't help but let out a startled laugh.

"So King Geoffrey's Faire is . . . ?"

"A Renaissance Faire, my lady." He sticks out his hand. "I'm Will."

"Rowena. Ro." I shake his offered hand, his callouses

scratching against my palm lightly, tickling. His grip is gentle, not at all like my father's I'm-a-Duncan-and-I-mean-business handshake. I squint at him. "So a body art specialist would be . . . ?"

"Ah, you've come to be our new face painter?"

Face painting. I let out a relieved breath. Sure, some of the possibilities my imagination conjured seemed interesting, maybe even exciting, but other possibilities had been just plain disturbing. Face painting I can do. Just little kids and glittery butterflies and stuff, right? Has to be easy.

"I guess," I say to Will. "I didn't really know what I was applying for. I just, um . . ."

"You just . . . ," Will prods, leaning in toward me slightly.

"Wanted a place to get away," I finish, embarrassed, and Will nods as if he understands completely.

"Nothing wrong with that. That's why we're all here." I look back up at him and he's got that kind smile on his face again. He's dropped the fancy talk and the slight accent he was using. His real voice is slightly less robust, and warmer as well. "That, and we're all sort of geeky history buffs. Or people who believe in dragons. Take your pick."

He laughs at that and starts walking, and I can only assume I'm supposed to follow. He's not going toward the arch like everyone else, though. He's veering off to the right.

"But isn't—"

"We're taking the back way," he says, angling his head at me. "Jeff—that is, King Geoffrey—runs his whole kingdom from a luxurious trailer in the campgrounds. We can't let the peasants see that."

"I see," I say, even though I really don't.

There is a wall around King Geoffrey's Faire that is made entirely of logs standing upright, twice my height and whittled to points on the tops like sharpened pencils. It extends out from the front gates on either side, disappearing into a forest to the left. We head into the forest, keeping next to the wall. I can't see much of the faire in the small gaps between the logs as I'm walking by, which makes me wonder why the fence is so high and the tops are so sharp. Are they trying to keep people out, or keep people in?

Just as I'm wondering it, Will stops at a section of the wall, lifts up a bolt that I hadn't noticed, and a dwarf-size door swings open. He grins at me. "The back way."

As I duck through the door, I feel like the air around us has changed somehow, like now that I'm inside the wall, I'm in on some sort of secret. The trail is just narrow enough that two grown people can't fit side by side, so Will walks slightly ahead, leading the way. It's heavily wooded and I try to keep up with his surefooted stride, carefully avoiding tree roots and stones as I go. I steal a few looks at him when I can, because he seems like maybe he could be kind of cute, though it's hard to tell in that getup. What I can tell is that he's got a nice build, and he manages to show it in spite of his oddly puffy shirt and pants. He's wearing a feathered cap now, which he produced from his back pocket like magic. It hides most of his golden brown hair, and what's visible curls up around the hat, as if out of habit.

The woods thin out, and I can tell we're near the faire. The music is louder now, and I can hear voices talking and laughing, some as robust as Will's and using the same accent and old-fashioned language. We pass the back sides of buildings, and I feel like I'm walking through some ancient alleyway.

"What is all of this?" I ask.

Will merely shrugs. "The butcher, the baker, the candlestick maker."

"Seriously?"

Will snorts. "No. Not seriously." He makes a wide, sweeping motion to indicate all the buildings in the row. "These are the shops. Anything you could possibly want from a Renaissance Faire is all right here at your fingertips. Costumes, dolls, figurines, weapons . . ."

I feel my eyes widen. "Weapons?"

"What's a knight without a sword, my lady?"

Knights. Of course there are knights here. How silly of me to forget the knights.

"And speaking of the knights, this is what we call the backstage for the joust."

I look where Will is pointing. The forest has thinned out even more, though the big trees that remain provide plenty of shade. The knights' backstage looks so much like the set of an epic war movie I can hardly believe it. There are swords and spears and shields, all in racks or haphazardly leaning against trees or strewn about on the ground. There are horses everywhere as well, but not just any horses. These horses are huge, with hooves as big as my head, and they're draped in gorgeous quilts of bold jewel tones.

By far, though, the most impressive thing in the camp are the knights themselves. They're sitting proudly on their steeds, all clad in armor of shining bright silver that creaks every time one of their horses makes a move. Though they don't have their helmets on yet, they're still impressive. Bigger than I thought possible, like how my jock friends look when they have all their football pads on. They talk with one another, laughing and gesturing as though the armor doesn't weight them down at all. Behind them, at the edge of the trees, is a huge gate, much like the wall that surrounds the faire, with tall logs and sharp points.

"It's almost showtime," Will says, leaning close to me. He points to the gates and I understand: On the other side, an audience awaits.

"Hey, Indy!" one of the knights yells, and Will waves. I turn in the direction of the voice, and realize for the first time that one of the knights is a girl.

She clucks her tongue at her horse and races over, armor clanging the whole way. She's got bright red hair that's cut in chunky spikes. It reminds me of fire. Will beams at her. "Going to win today?"

"Oh yeah. Big Red's itching to move. Grant's going *down*," Sage says loudly and over her shoulder so that the knights behind her can hear her trash talk. She turns back, looks me over, then asks Will, "Who's the newbie?"

"Sage, this is Ro. Ro, Sage." Sage bends down and shakes my hand rather enthusiastically, and she rolls her eyes as another knight rides up, his horse bumping into Sage's. The animals give each other an annoyed glance, one that their owners give each other at the exact same time.

"This is Grant," Sage says to me as if it's an apology. "He's about to get his ass kicked."

"Keep dreaming."

"Please," Sage says to him with a laugh. "You're just sore that a woman can handle a jousting lance better than you."

Grant looks at Will, more amused than ashamed. "Gotta love a woman who knows what she's doing with a big stick."

Sage huffs but I let out an unladylike guffaw at that, and Will looks at me, approval stamped all over his face. "I think you're going to fit in just fine around here, Ro."

"I haven't got the job yet."

"Aye," Will agrees, though it's not in his fake accent. I wonder if it's just habit at this point. His gaze shifts to something over my shoulder, and he speaks to Sage out of the corner of his mouth. "Richard's coming."

"Crap. The old man's been on a rampage lately . . ."

Sage and Grant have just enough time to wince at each other before a booming voice calls out, "Sage! Grant! I swear, if you're late for the show again, I'll put you in the stocks and let the tourists throw rotten tomatoes at you!"

"Somehow, I don't think he's kidding," Grant whispers.

"Roger that." Sage pulls on the reins and turns her horse. "See ya, Indy!"

We watch Sage and Grant ride off, racing each other to the edge of the forest, where an impatient and burly older man gestures angrily at them.

Will snorts. "Richard runs a tight ship. He's nearly as bad as Jeff."

My stomach tightens into a nervous knot, and it must show on my face because Will says, "Don't worry. Jeff's not awful, he's just . . . a stickler for the rules. All you have to do is pretend that the last five hundred years didn't exist and you're golden."

"Oh, it's that easy, huh?" I quip, and Will's mouth twitches into a smile.

"Come on. Let's cut through the backstage."

I follow Will as he moves deftly around the trees and swords and other various knight equipment. We pass the knights who are ready to go out and perform, and I see Sage look through the logs to peek at the crowd. She has her helmet on, and the only reason I know it's her is because of her horse's green quilt.

When I turn my gaze back to the path, there's another horse coming our way with a knight on top. He's straight-backed and broad-shouldered, clearly confident and comfortable with himself. He already has his helmet on, and the beautiful white horse he's riding is decorated with a quilt in a velvety deep blue. A design in silver stitching decorates the quilt as well, and as the knight nears us I realize it forms the profile of a wolf. The detail and artistry of it make me stare in awe. Not that any of the other knights look shabby, but this one looks like royalty.

Will greets him, and I note that it's not with the same warmth he had for Sage. "Christian."

"Will," the knight says, and pulls off his helmet.

It takes every scrap of willpower I possess not to gasp. The knight is, quite possibly, the hottest boy I've ever seen. He's got thick black hair that hangs just past his ears, tanned skin, and eyes that match the deep blue of his horse's quilt. Against his skin and dark hair, they almost glow. He turns them on me and smiles in a way that makes my legs feel absolutely useless.

Holy crap. I've just met Prince Charming.

"My lady," he says and dips his head at me.

The urge to curtsey in response is nearly irresistible. I bow my head back instead, because it seems like the more appropriate thing to do. "Sir."

I feel his gaze roam down my whole body, from my V-neck (which I just realized is a bit low cut) to my rainbow toes and back up. Normally I'd whack a guy upside the head for that kind of ogling, but with Prince Charming I find myself hoping that he likes what he sees.

Well. Isn't this a pleasant surprise? Who knew a geeky history buff who lives out in the woods could look like *that*? I have seriously underestimated this so-called community of artists.

I'm picturing Kyle in a jealous rage, trying to challenge a knight for my honor, when Christian says to Will with a grin, "I think I'd rather have your job today, Fuller."

"You couldn't handle my job, Christian."

Christian's gaze settles on me again, and his eyes are definitely not on my face. "I think I could handle it just fine."

He tips his head at me again, this time making such intense eye contact that I feel like maybe someone should ready the smelling salts. Then he gives his pretty horse a kick in the ribs and is gone, the clomping of hooves growing fainter and fainter. I watch until he disappears through the gates and the crowd behind them roars.

I turn to Will. "Is he the best knight or something?"

"He's . . ." Will looks upward, as if the right words are printed on the leaves overhead, then he says, "He's the most popular. Come on, Jeff's trailer is way in the back."

I can't tell if his tone is resigned or simply irritated. Either way I don't question him any further about Christian. We walk on until we've arrived at a small trailer, the old-fashioned metal kind that people used to pull behind their trucks for camping trips. There are a few plastic chairs under a retractable awning, one of them occupied by a girl with dreads and a huge ring in her nose that goes well with her bull-like glare.

"Your competition is a little scary," Will muses quietly, and I nod, suppressing a nervous giggle. Then he clears his throat and says in a louder voice, the one he used in the parking lot, "Well, fair lady, I bid you good fortune."

He dips down in a bow before he leaves, and just for fun, I curtsey back, pulling my skirt out wide. I find myself smiling as he walks away. I'm still smiling when I sit down next to the girl with the dreads, but she wipes the smile clean off of my face with her dagger-like stare. She clutches a giant leather portfolio closer to her body, as if she suspects I want to steal it.

I try to put her at ease. "I'm Ro," I say, and extend a hand.

She does not shake it. Nor does she offer her name. I clear my throat and try again.

"So what do you do?"

She continues to stare at me suspiciously, as if small talk is the work of the devil or something. "Art."

Needless to say, I'm relieved when a middle-aged guy peeks his head out of the trailer and asks for the next candidate. Scary Art Girl gets up and stalks into the office, throwing me another vicious glance.

Jeff gives me an apologetic smile. "Hi. I'm Jeff. I'll be right with you, um . . ."

"Rowena Duncan," I supply and smile brightly back. "I called earlier. You said if I made it by four o'clock—"

"Ah. Right, right," Jeff says. "I'll be with you in a few."

His office door slams and I'm alone with my thoughts. I hear horse hooves galloping in the distance and the cheers of a crowd, and I wonder if Prince Charming—I mean, Christian— is jousting right now.

Beyond that, though, all I can hear is the sound of the

breeze rustling the leaves overhead and the occasional bird singing its song. It's pleasant. Peaceful. Sure, if I stay here all summer, I'll miss Meg and Kara, but I'll have some quiet time to myself. No honking cars. No TVs. No gum-smacking freshman girls. Best of all? No chance of running into Kyle.

Yeah. I have to get this job.

I fidget in my seat, suddenly afraid that I might not. Scary Art Girl has been in there for a while, and she had the fore-thought to bring a portfolio. That doesn't bode well for my chances. By the time she exits the trailer and Jeff motions me in, I've chewed the nail on my pinkie down to the quick.

"Sorry about your wait," he mumbles as he leads me into a shabby little room that's decorated with cheap wood panel-ing, a few old file cabinets, and a small bowl with a beta fish in it. He catches me eyeing it. "That's Merlin."

I laugh loudly at that, and when he quirks a brow at me, I offer an explanation. "I used to have a guinea pig when I was little. I called it Dumbledore."

Jeff looks amused by that. "Two of the greatest wizards of all time. Please, have a seat."

As we sit in our respective seats, I take the opportunity to study his outfit. He is dressed for the job, like Will, only his outfit is truly fit for a king, in hues of luxurious gold and bur-gundy. His sleeves are so puffy it's almost comical, and though he's not overweight, a bit of gut spills out over a braided gold belt. Behind him, on a hook on the wall, is a cape and what looks to be a genuine metal crown glittering with rhinestones.

If he is going for a Henry the Eighth look, he's certainly achieved it.

Jeff shuffles some papers on his desk and holds his hand out. It takes me a second to realize he's asking for my resume, which in spite of everything, I'm still carrying. I hand it over.

"I'm surprised anyone showed up at all, the way that ad was worded. It sounded creepy. Totally my fault. Didn't even read it over before I put it on the website, but I had no time. Our last girl was poached by some weird sort of artsy circus and it had to be quick." Jeff lifts a brow at me. "You do realize this is for face painting and not for something freakier, right?"

I try hard not to laugh. "Right."

He sighs and looks at my resume, reading parts of it out loud. "Babysitting . . . waitressing . . . Do you have any actual art experience?"

"Not paid, but I've been taking art classes at school for years. I . . ." I stop talking because I can't really offer any excuse for my lack of work experience. Instead, I do the only thing I can: I take out my phone and pull up pictures of my paintings. I lean across the desk so I can give him a view of my screen.

"I started my freshman year, because I needed an art credit and it was that or choir, and there's no way I should ever sing in public." Jeff snorts at that, but his attention is all on my phone, on the still life of a fruit bowl that was my first painting. "It turned out I had some talent for it, and Mrs. Robertson, that's my art teacher, has been helping me ever since. I go in and paint during study hall, and sometimes even lunch. So I've been doing this for three years."

I don't know if three years of art classes and giving up my free time to practice really impresses Jeff, but when I flip to a recent sketch I did of Kara, his eyes take it in eagerly. I am rather proud of that sketch. I somehow got the light in her eyes just right so it looks like she's about to laugh, or maybe even about to spill some juicy gossip.

After a moment of staring at it, Jeff turns his chair around and begins to rifle through a filing cabinet. When he speaks, his voice is all business.

"Food and board is included in this gig, as you'll be living on the grounds. You are not allowed inside the faire in plain clothes and you must be in character at all times. No exceptions. King Geoffrey's Faire prides itself on creating the illusion that our guests have traveled back in time, and any disturbance of that illusion is not looked on kindly. You will speak like you are from the Renaissance, you will act like you are from the Renaissance, you will dress like you are from the Renaissance. Can you handle that?"

I trip over my words. "So . . . I got the job?"

Jeff places a form on the desk in front of me. "I prefer that my staff be . . . how should I put this? *Personable.* Your competition looked like she'd rather eat the children than laugh with them. So yes, you got the job. As long as you can duplicate the pictures in the sample book, you're good enough."

I straighten. Good enough? I can do better than good enough.

"I can do that," I promise. "I can wait tables too. I've got plenty of waitressing experience."

Jeff studies me, rubbing his mouth. "Yeah, you'd make a good serving wench, and we have a shift open, so it's a deal."

Jeff taps the form he put in front of me, and I notice that it's an employee contract of sorts. In addition to all the rules he laid out about keeping the illusion alive, it also states what food and board is expected to be, and my hourly wage, plus tips. I suck in a breath. With tips I'd be making way more than I ever did at TK's.

"Have your parents sign the release form, since you'll be under our watch over the next few weeks," Jeff continues. "The faire is closed on Mondays, so you'll start Tuesday. Welcome to King Geoffrey's Faire, Rowena."

It's the second time I've heard those words today, and I'm starting to really like the sound of them. I thank Jeff and shake his hand, running out of the trailer with a lightness I haven't felt for nearly a week. My summer is going to be awesome. Painting, the woods, and boys calling me "lady."

All of that happiness deflates like a balloon when I realize there's one big roadblock standing in the way of me and my fantastic summer: I still have to convince my parents.

FRIDAY

"How'd it go?"

Will's voice surprises me so much that I whirl around at the sound of it, managing, somehow, to twist my feet around themselves so that I trip and fly face first into the grass.

"Whoa there," Will says, coming over to offer me a hand. "Walking can be a tricky thing, what with gravity and all."

I take his hand and he pulls, and then I spend a few seconds brushing myself off and avoiding eye contact. I muster some pride. "Shuddup. You scared me. Were you waiting out here the whole time?"

"Well, I couldn't leave not knowing who I'd be working with all summer." Will's eyes widen dramatically. "You or the psychopath."

"Me, not the psychopath."

"Aw. That's too bad. I was looking forward to learning all about dark magic from her."

Will laughs at himself and then there's a weird, static squawk and his pocket says, "Fuller, make sure our new girl gets back to the parking lot without incident, will you?"

I blink. "Did your pocket just order you to take me to the parking lot?"

Will pulls out a walkie-talkie that's covered in leather with what looks like the plans for some sort of machine sketched all over it. "Behold, the Renaissance talk box. One of da Vinci's lesser-known inventions." He holds it up to his mouth and presses a button. "Aye, King Geoffrey. And good morrow to you, my lord."

The "talk box" squeaks to life. "Kiss-ass."

Will chuckles and pockets the walkie-talkie. "I'm clearly his favorite. Want to see a little of the faire on the way back?"

Will takes my grin as a yes and we begin to walk, Will leading and jabbering a mile a minute. "So the faire has games, entertainment, shopping, food. Especially food. If you're hungry, we've got fried cheese on a stick, steak on a stick—we call it steak on a stake, ha—baked potato on a stick, corn dogs—"

"Is there anything at King Geoffrey's Faire that isn't served on a stick?"

Will thinks for a while. "Turkey legs. Those are technically on a bone, not a stick."

I briefly wonder if this summer is going to make me gain forty pounds. "Sounds like I'm going to need a corset."

"We sell those here too."

"Of course you do."

"Actually, you'll need some clothes. You can't wear flip-flops and shorts around here, you know. Not very Renaissance-y."

Will leads us behind the shops again, and once more my ears fill with the sounds of music and swords clashing. This time, however, I notice something else. A pleasant sound. A hum, a buzzing, like a busy hive full of enthusiastic bees.

I turn to Will and he's grinning a very satisfied grin. "The post-joust rush. Seems like everyone and their mother gets hungry after a good fight. It starts at four p.m. on the dot, and it's chaos until about six. So we're right in the thick of it. Come on, follow me."

Will jogs off between two of the shops. We come out onto a dusty street, and I feel like I've truly gone back in time. Both sides of the street are lined with Tudor-style cottages and buildings, doors thrown open wide, shopkeepers beckoning the crowds to come in and explore. Hundreds, possibly thousands of people in modern clothes walk around slowly, fascinated, trying to take it all in.

I can understand that. For a moment I stop and just stare.

Somewhere to my right, a pair of acrobats does a routine in the middle of the street, one leaping from her partner's shoulders to the ground with a somersault and a flourish. Onlookers clap as they stretch and pose and go into another tumble. A woman hangs out of the window of a shop, looking very scantily clad for the Renaissance period, in not much more than a corset and an underskirt. She winks at a woman passerby, suggesting she come in to pick up something to wear for her husband later that night. Next to her shop is a store called The Bone Needle, and leather goods hang outside on displays and in the windows. I can smell the leather, tangy and sweet, even from this distance. Farther down, I spy a beautifully scripted sign reading MICHELANGELO'S GALLERY, which piques my curiosity. I'll have to check it out later and see what kind of art they have for sale there.

My gaze travels down the street and back up. There have to be about twenty different shops, stages, or work areas, and about twenty more of what look to be food tents. The smell of grilled meat and fried potatoes is inescapable, and so is the enthusiasm.

A young couple passes me and I catch them teasing each other about how many turkey legs they can eat. A little boy dashes by, waving a wooden sword as his father trails behind, calling his name. A handful of people dressed in velvet robes pass as well, and they look at me with an intense gaze, like they're trying to cast a spell. Everyone in that group has plastic elf ears, making them look like something other than humans, and I find myself walking a little closer to Will.

"We always get some Ringers," he says as he eyes them too. I raise a brow in question. "*Lord of the Rings* fans," he explains.

I grimace. "You're serious, aren't you?"

"Unfortunately."

Ringers. I'm going to be spending my summer with people who dress up like *Lord of the Rings* characters.

I stop right there in the middle of the busy street and start laughing. Probably from the shock of it all. It's the kind of laughing that won't quit, but rather snowballs until it's completely out of control and there's nothing you can do to stop it. I double over, clutching my stomach, and simply let it all out while Will watches in confusion.

"Are you okay? We do have a cart that takes away people like you, you know. The mad ones. The deeply disturbed ones. Takes them right off to the looney bin. I mean, it's fake, but I'm sure we could get you somewhere for help."

I hold up my hand, my laughter finally petering out. "I think I might need that cart. I'm sorry. This just isn't what I expected at all. I was going to have a nice, normal summer. The beach. The mall. Working at a stupid themed restaurant. Not working at a place where I have to speak old English and talk to hobbits."

"They were elves, actually." Will winces. "And let's just ignore the fact that I knew the difference. Anyway, it might not be normal, Ro, but it's fun. I promise. You'll like it here."

Will looks at me. There's still a hint of laughter in his eyes, maybe even a twinkle of mischief, but his voice is sincere. It's not an empty promise, not in the slightest, and it fills me with something warm that feels a lot like hope.

Yeah, this place isn't even close to normal, but maybe I could use a little abnormality in my life.

I'm about to say so when a group of little girls runs by me, talking to one another in high-pitched, excited voices. They're all wearing crowns of flowers on their heads, and they run toward a shop that has beautiful dresses and dolls in the window.

Will watches them too, then turns to me. The seriousness is still there, though he grins wide and impish. "Looks like they're onto something. Let's follow them."

We head toward the shop, following the girls in. They take off in all directions, darting around to the back, where I can see that there's a whole other room just for children. It's filled with dolls and small dresses.

The door closes behind us with the jingle of sleigh bells and I lose myself in my new surroundings. There are racks and racks of dresses in every color, material, and style you could imagine, and they all look like they could be straight out of the Renaissance. There are plain gowns, everyday gowns for everyday people. There are gorgeous layered dresses of gold and blue and purple, fit for royalty. There are dresses made of Scottish tartan, with leather vests and scabbards, for the girls who feel a bit more rebellious, for the warriors. There are also wedding dresses, for the ladies who have found their lords, I suppose.

A woman steps out from behind one of the racks. Her ash

blond hair is pulled into a loose updo, and her hazel eyes have deep laugh lines around them. "Will, how are you, love?"

I watch as Will embraces her, curious.

"Can't complain," Will answers. "Showing our new face painter the ropes. Ro, this is Lindy, the fairy doll maker and resident seamstress. She can make anything—dolls, dresses, quilts. She's the one who does the fancy stuff on the knights' horse blankets."

Lindy steps back from Will and studies me. It's a bit like how Kyle's mother looked at me the first time I met her, like she was searching for my flaws. I stand up a little straighter and speak clearly.

"These dresses are beautiful."

"Thank you, dear. I've been at this almost twenty-five years now."

"Lindy's a lifer," Will says to me, and I look to him, hoping he'll explain. He does. "Been in a Renaissance Faire all her life."

"Born at a faire, raised at a faire. Hope to die at a faire." Lindy studies me again, and I don't know exactly what test she's putting me through, but I find myself really wanting to pass. "You'll need clothes, then. I'm surprised Jeff hasn't issued some sort of demerit to you already."

Lindy stalks back to a desk in the corner of the shop and snatches a tape measure and a pincushion full of pins from the top of it. She stands in front of me, head tilted to one side, staring.

"What are you, about five-four?"

With this question, I finally understand why she's been studying me so much—she's trying to dress me. Relieved, I breathe out an answer. "Yes, exactly five-four."

Lindy makes a sound of agreement and gestures vaguely to my arms. Because I've been fitted for a formal dress before (prom and all the homecoming dances, thank you) I know what she's asking for, and I lift my arms out so my body makes a T. She starts measuring. Hips first, my waist, finally my bust.

"Hmnm, a B cup, then?"

I glance over at Will, who is staring intently at a doll on the windowsill, but I see the corner of his mouth twitch and I know he's heard. I whisper back to Lindy, hoping she'll get the hint.

"Um, yeah."

Lindy hums again and steps back, staring at me like a sculptor might stare at a slab of stone. "Well, my daughter, Susannah, has a few dresses that don't fit her anymore. They would do if I take them in for you."

"Really?" I ask. That seems like a lot of work, and we barely know each other.

"Oh, sure. Won't take me any time at all." Lindy drapes the tape measure around her neck. "So what do your parents think of you running off to join the circus?"

"I haven't told them yet. Jeff just gave me the job today." I can only imagine what my parents will say when I tell them

I want to spend my summer out here, surrounded by people who talk funny and wear elf ears and eat steak on a stake. I grimace. "My parents are very . . . practical people."

Lindy nods as if that explains everything. "Well, if you'd like me to chat with them, give them an adult's perspective, I'd be happy to."

That's the second time she's offered to do something nice for a complete stranger and I am completely amazed and humbled by that. "Thank you," I say.

Lindy merely waves me away. "Not a problem. Good luck breaking the news to your practical parents."

I give her a smile, even though my stomach flips at the thought. Ted and Louise might just blow a gasket over this. "Speaking of, do you know what time it is? I promised my mom I'd be home by dinner."

Both Lindy and Will glance out the shop window, but it's Will who answers. "Nearly six."

There's no clock outside that I can see, and it takes me nearly a whole moment to understand that they were looking at the shadows of the buildings to tell the time.

Telling time by the sun's position? They really take this whole historical accuracy thing a little too seriously. I hope vainly that I won't be expected to do that, or to navigate by using the stars or something.

"I'd better get back then," I tell them. "It took me nearly an hour to get here."

"Then let's make haste, my lady," Will says with a gentlemanly, if not a little mocking, bow.

I thank Lindy again as we head out the door of her shop. I follow Will through a large crowd who all seem to be heading in the opposite direction like a herd of sheep. They're in a hurry too, and Will's far more capable of crowd dodging than I am.

"Where are all these people going?" I yell to Will over the noise.

"It's time for the joust," he says, slowing to make sure I'm right next to him. I elbow my way through the crowd, a salmon swimming upstream.

"Didn't they already have a joust?"

"There's one every two hours," Will explains. "It's a whole scripted thing about a tournament to find the kingdom's best knight."

"Oh, so they know who will win?"

Will puts a hand on my arm and guides me to the side of the street, out of the way of most of the crowd. He keeps his voice low, secretive. "Yeah, it has to be, otherwise someone might get hurt. The whole thing's fake. Choreographed right down to the lances they use. They only look like they're getting hit. Kind of like a magician's sleight of hand."

I think of Christian and I don't know whether to be disappointed by this revelation or thankful that no one's truly in danger.

"You'll have to see it Tuesday. It's a good show, even if you know what's really going on."

We're nearing the main gates, which are designed to look like the Tower of London. There are four stone archways with ticket-takers standing under each, and a tall stone tower in the center. It rises almost a full story over the tallest store in the village, and it boasts a huge clock with vine-like, wrought iron hands.

Thank goodness, there's a clock. Hopefully, I can use it to tell time instead of getting to know the shadows of the buildings intimately.

Will nods to the ticket-taker as we pass through an arch, and even though I can't tell one row of cars from the next, Will easily finds my vehicle. He opens the door for me with another slight bow.

"Your carriage, my lady."

I chuckle. "Thank you, Will. And thanks for making sure I didn't get lost."

"I'd be happy to show you around more Tuesday, if you'd like," he says. "The first day can be kind of a culture shock."

"I can imagine," I say, and step as gracefully as I can into my car seat.

"Good luck telling your parents," Will says, his hand on the car door, leaning over to look at me. "And with packing. Remember bug spray."

"Bug spray. Check." I smile at him. "Thanks for showing me around."

He shrugs. "Anytime, Rainbow Ro. See you Tuesday!"

"Can't wait," I say, and I'm surprised at how much I mean it. I'm in my car and halfway out of the bumpy parking lot before it dawns on me that Will noticed my toenails.

—

4

WEEK 1—MONDAY

Kara sucks down half a strawberry-mango smoothie before turning to us and making the same silly face she's been making since we became friends in fifth grade. It's her best monkey, complete with the puffed-out cheeks, crossed eyes, and ear tugging, and I laugh. I laugh even harder when Meg uses the distraction to steal her smoothie and take a big, noisy gulp.

We're at the mall, as promised, and as promised, there's no Kyle or Lacey in sight. I try not to think about why and keep my bitterness in check, and concentrate on celebrating the last few minutes of summer freedom. Meg starts her first shift at TK's in under an hour—luckily, my first shift wasn't scheduled until tomorrow—and Kara's got to get home and babysit her little sister, but for now we have no responsibilities but sitting here and goofing off.

I haven't yet told them about the Renaissance Faire—or

more importantly, that I'm not going to be spending the summer with them—but I will. As soon as I get the courage.

"So have you heard from *him*?" Meg asks, and I shake my head. "Well, that's fine. That's great, really. You don't need him or his lame apologies. Anyway, I heard that Jenn Houser broke up with Brady Thomas since she's going off to Ithaca. Fed him some crap about how long distance relationships don't work. So . . . Brady's single, and he'll be at Brian's party Saturday. Right, Kara?"

Kara beams at the mention of her boyfriend, Brian. She's been with him nearly a year and a half, which is the record for longest relationship out of the three of us, and they're still going strong. In fact, it was Brian who introduced me to Kyle at one of their lacrosse games.

"Brady's gorgeous, Ro," Kara says, and she looks to me, hoping I'll agree.

Brady Thomas *is* good-looking. He always has been. Even when we were second graders together at Middleton Elementary, he was one of the cutest boys in the class, with his freckles and swoopy, shiny hair.

But he's nowhere near as gorgeous as my knight in shining armor, Christian.

I take the smoothie out of Meg's hands and finish it off, as if that will give me the sustenance to deliver my news.

"I don't think I can come to the party Saturday," I say to them, and I can't miss the look of concern that passes between them. My friends have never exactly been stealthy about that sort of thing.

"Ro, you can't hide in your room forever," Kara says gently. "Yeah, it totally sucks that Kyle's a jerk and cheated on you with that stupid freshman who shall remain nameless, but you've got to get back out there. And a guy like Brady would totally make Kyle jealous."

"It would be so awesome—you hook up with Brady Thomas a week after Kyle's caught cheating. It's like some sort of celebrity story." Meg's eyes get big and distant, like she's imagining it all, and she holds out her hands, pulling them apart like she's setting a headline. "Local senior boy realizes karma's a bitch when ex hooks up with hot guy at a party."

I have to laugh, even if all of this talk is making me even more nervous about spilling my news. They look at me pleadingly, and I decide I have to tell them now, before they get too carried away.

I clear my throat. "I won't be around Saturday. I kind of got a new job."

Meg pouts. "So you won't be working at TK's? Ro . . . what am I going to do without you there? Do you know how boring it'll be with only Julie working with me? Ugh, you know how she goes on about her stupid scrapbooking habit."

I move the smoothie straw up and down and it makes an annoying sound as plastic rubs against plastic. "I won't be around much at all, guys. This new job kind of requires me to live on the campgrounds."

I see Kara's right eyebrow shoot up. "Campgrounds? Oh, Ro, don't tell me you're going to be a camp counselor . . ."

"Hey now," Meg says. "Let's reserve judgment. Maybe it's a Boy Scout camp. Have you seen how hot some of those counselors are? Especially the ones who teach rock climbing." Meg fans herself and then looks at me. "That's it, right, Ro? Hot rock climbers?"

I allow myself a chuckle at Meg's imagination, and then feel awful that I have to crush her dreams. "Not exactly. But there's a hot guy involved. Or I hope he will be."

Kara leans across the table, jabbing at me with her straw. "Spill, Duncan."

I clear my throat. "I'm going to be a face painter at a Renaissance Faire."

"What?" Meg and Kara exclaim in unison, and so I try to explain.

"It's really cool, guys. I found this ad in the paper and it was for an artist, and you know I'm kind of good at that, so I thought I would give it a try. It's this huge place that's out in the middle of nowhere. It's crazy. Just right in the middle of a forest there's this whole village and a jousting arena and these people that talk like they're from another time. Everyone dresses like they're from the Renaissance, too. It really does feel like it's a different world. And, guys, there are actual knights—and I mean full suits of armor, swords, horses, the whole bit—and this one was so hot. The bluest eyes I've ever seen and gorgeous, long black hair, and he's got a body that even Brian would be jealous of, Kara."

Even with my flattery of her boyfriend and the mention of a hot knight, Kara looks unimpressed. I turn to Meg and she's no more enthusiastic, looking at me with a slightly curled lip and her eyebrows scrunching together.

"Come on, guys. Be happy for me," I plead with them. "This is a really cool opportunity. I'll be working on my art all summer and I get free room and board. Plus, you know, hot knights and old English words and pretty dresses."

"But we were supposed to work here and hang out all the time and go to the beach," Meg says, her disappointment like a punch to the gut.

I look to Kara, hoping she'll understand, but she's narrowed her eyes. "I can't believe you're ditching us," she says.

"I'm not ditching you."

"Yes, you are," Kara shoots back. "And this is our last summer together, Ro. Next year we'll be too busy getting ready for college. This is all we've got."

"We'll have time next summer. We won't be that busy," I try to argue.

"Do you know how early New England College starts? If I get in, I'll have to move in July, Ro," Meg says. "That's barely two months we'll have together."

Kara sits back in her chair, arms crossed, her usually alabaster skin pink, eyes locked on mine. "You're running away from Kyle, aren't you?"

"No," I say hastily. "Of course not. I don't care. Lacey can have him. I deserve someone better."

"I totally agree with that," Kara says. "But still, you're running away from him. Or hiding from him, it sounds like."

I grip the smoothie cup so tight that it caves in under my fingers. I shove it across our little plastic table. "I'm not hiding. I want to go work on art and have this totally cool experience in the woods."

"With a bunch of crazy people dressed in costumes who talk funny." Kara leans back in her chair, arms crossed. "And what did your mom and dad think about this?"

My mind flashes back to last night, when I broke the news to my parents. It was an argument, a dignified and polite one, as they always are in my house, but an argument nonetheless. I finally won them over by promising the experience would provide great anecdotes for college essays and interviews.

"They think it's a great opportunity," I say, which is only kind of a lie. "They're happy for me."

"I don't buy it." Kara rolls her eyes, which makes my temper skyrocket into the atmosphere.

But what makes me angriest is that she's right, and she *shouldn't* buy it. Kara and I have been friends since elementary school, and as my oldest friend, she has the ability to see right through me. I suppose it's a good quality for a friend to have, but sometimes I wish she'd just shut up and let me lie.

I'm over Kyle. At least, that's the story I'm sticking to, the only story my pride will let me tell.

I narrow my eyes at her. If she's going to dish it out, I can lob it right back. "What do you care? You're so busy with Brian, you won't even notice I'm gone."

"That's not true."

I'm not listening. "And why you'd want to stay with him when his best friend is a cheating scumbag is beyond me."

"Ro . . . ," Meg begins. It's a warning, a "please stop before you say something you don't mean" that I ignore completely.

"You like Brian." Kara frowns. "You've always liked Brian. I know you're upset right now, but I'm just saying, if maybe you think about it for a day or two—"

"I need to go, Kara," I say. Her frown deepens.

Kara fixes me a look that's as stern as my mother and twice as accusing. "You don't. You're lying to yourself. Listen to me. I'm your best friend."

"And my best friend should get this, Kara. If you really cared, you would. But I guess you don't." I stand and snatch the smoothie cup off the table in an angry, dramatic gesture. "I have to go quit TK's. Have a nice summer."

I glance at my best friends' faces once before I turn away. They're shocked. Stricken, really, and I walk away quickly so I don't have to see the effects of my outburst anymore. By the time I'm across the mall, speaking to the manager of TK's, I'm in tears. He thinks I'm crying because I'm sad to leave my job at his silly Hawaiian restaurant, and he hugs me before I go. I hug him back, slightly embarrassed that I need so much comforting, and then head home. I leave for the faire tomorrow and I have to pack, but mostly I just want to get back to my room and wallow in the misery of my own making.

I stare at my empty suitcase. I'm not quite sure how to go about packing for a summer away at a Renaissance Faire, nor is it the thing weighing most heavily on my mind.

With a sigh, I pick up my phone and glance at the screen. No one's called; no one's texted. I can't blame Meg or Kara for that. What I said was downright awful. We've fought before, sure. All friends do at some point. Just last week, Meg and I got into a rather heated discussion about whose fries were better: the diner's downtown or the cheesy ones from Steak 'n' Shake. But that was silly, and we knew it was silly, and we certainly didn't feel like we were in any danger of ruining our friendship over it.

This feels different. Really different. Kara was trying to look out for me in her own sometimes irritating way, and I accused her of not caring about me. Which isn't true in the slightest, and she was right about me wanting to run away from Kyle. I'm humiliated at the mere *thought* of running into him with Lacey. I would never even have considered a summer without my two best friends if I wasn't, and Kara knew that.

I toss my phone aside and try to focus on packing,

despite the rising nausea I'm getting with all the guilt and self-loathing. Of course, I've never packed for a Renaissance Faire before, which only adds to my mood.

I open up my closet and stare at its contents, hoping something will scream, "Take me with you!" but no dice. All I see are some incredibly trendy clothes Kara picked out for me from the boutique she works at in the mall, some less trendy but still cute clothes I wear to school, a nice collection of Boston College tees and sweatshirts my dad buys me yearly in support of his alma mater, and the staples I wear when no one's looking: pajamas with cartoons on them and comfy yoga pants for lounging.

With a sigh, I resign myself to being woefully unprepared for a Renaissance Faire, and start to fill my suitcase.

I start with the easy stuff: toiletries, my makeup bag, a sweatshirt for the chilly summer nights, pajamas, and a few pairs of shorts and tank tops. (And if I put in some of my cutest tanks because I want Christian to see me in them, well, who can blame me?) Then, after a brief moment's consideration, I take out my underwear drawer and shake its entire contents into my suitcase, because packing a ton of underwear can't hurt. If there's anything you don't want to run out of in life, it's clean underwear, and I have to assume that doesn't change at a Renaissance Faire.

My mother's voice carries, muffled, through the door. "Rowena?"

I call to her to come in and plaster a smile on my face. She enters with some fluffy towels, all warm and neatly folded. "Fresh out of the dryer," she says, and hands them to me. As I add them to my suitcase, she sits on the bed, studying me. Since it's clear she has no desire to leave any time soon, and I have no desire to make polite conversation, I busy myself with trying to organize the suitcase's contents.

"When you were little, I used to bury you in all the warm towels out of the dryer," Mom says, her voice soft and wistful. "You loved it. You'd wrap yourself up in them and giggle. Sometimes you'd get so warm you'd fall asleep, right in that big pile."

My smile becomes genuine then. I might be seventeen years old, far beyond the neediness of a child, but it's still great to feel loved. Especially when your friends aren't speaking to you.

Mom smoothes a wrinkle in my bedspread, then speaks again. "Your dad and I are very proud of you, Ro."

"Why?" I ask, genuinely puzzled. I haven't done much to be proud of today.

"You went out and got an exciting job, all on your own, and it's so much more beneficial than your job at the mall. That shows initiative and leadership. And think about what an experience you'll have!" My mother's thick eyebrows raise up with excitement. "At first, I have to admit, we thought it sounded strange. We still have our reservations, really. But the more I think about it, the more I think you are on to something. Just think about how you'll stand out in the pack with your college applications! 'How the Renaissance Faire Changed My Life.' Who else is going to have that kind of title for their college essay? You'll get into Boston College for sure with this."

"Boston," I say. "Right."

My mom stands and kisses me on the forehead. Her big hair tickles my cheek. "So proud of you. I'll be downstairs if you need anything."

When she's gone, I sink down onto my bed, heavy and sick with guilt. My parents think I'm going away for the summer to make myself a more well-rounded person so that I can get into a good school, but Kara's voice keeps ringing in my ear.

I'm running away from Kyle. It's true. It's not about being well-rounded, or the adventure, or even about my art.

But it could be.

With new determination, I turn and gather up all the art supplies I can fit into the space I have left in my suitcase: my box of oil paints and watercolors, my tube of brushes, my sketchpad, and my mixing palette.

This summer doesn't all have to be a lie. Maybe I can have my adventure, become more well-rounded, and devote time to art, all the while staying someplace far away from my jerk of an ex-boyfriend. Maybe I can write that essay my mom proposed.

Going away might be about Kyle now, but if I'm lucky, by the end of the summer it'll be about much more.

5

WEEK 1—TUESDAY

I pull into the parking lot of King Geoffrey's Faire, stricken so badly with nerves and jitters that I can't make even a simple decision, like where I should park my car. It's early, eight a.m. to be exact, and there's not a soul or a car in the parking lot, which means there's no Will to tell me where I should go.

I blow out a breath and order myself to just drive. My car bumps and rattles across the field until I get to where a line of trees meets up with the tall fence that encircles the fairground, and park there. I hoist my gigantic suitcase out of the back and drag it along the ground on its wheels, too nervous and unsure to care about the bottom getting dirty.

When I reach the Tower of London front gates, a small bar in the main door opens to reveal a pair of familiar eyes.

"Password?" a voice calls out, muffled by the thick wood door.

I blink in confusion. "Um. I'm Rowena Duncan, the new face painter. I interviewed with Jeff—erm, King Geoffrey—two days ago."

The eyes blink back, and I could swear there's a smile in them now. "Password?" the voice demands again.

"Um, I don't have one." I lower my gaze to my rainbow toes and wish Will would come by to vouch for me.

"That's a pity. We sure could use a face painter." The bar starts to slide back across the door, covering up one eye. Then, before I can protest, it opens back up. "But of course, you could always guess . . ."

That voice. It's so familiar, and so are the eyes. I recognize the tremor of laughter when he speaks, the hint of mischief in his irises . . .

I smile and look directly through the slit in the door. "How about . . . Will Fuller should be king because he's the most awesome person at the faire?"

There's an outburst of muffled laughter, then the door opens. Will's standing there, dressed like a Renaissance peasant, a grin wide on his face. "Knew you'd guess it on the first try."

"I had a feeling the gatekeeper might have a bit of an ego, is all."

"If I was an egomaniac I'd have asked you to go on." Will shuts the door behind me as I step inside the faire. He's still grinning when he asks, "How are you?"

"Tired," I tell Will, even though I'm sure he was only

talking pleasantries. I've been up since about five, worrying and unpacking, then packing again. Before then I'd slept only fitfully, upset about how things went down with Kara and Meg. The nerves and the fatigue all add up to me being on edge.

"Well, we can fix that." Will holds up what looks to be a canteen made out of leather. "Ramón makes some strong Highlander Grog. All the energy, none of the jitters. I could use a refill, so how about you check in with Lindy and get your clothes and then I'll take you for a coffee fix?"

I say yes to that and his mouth parts into a goofy smile. He looks like he hasn't shaved since I saw him last. The scruff on his jaw is fitting, and it makes him look a little older.

"Great," he says. "We'll have to get a sticky bun, too. Trust me."

Will picks up my suitcase easily, as if all my clothes and art supplies are made of helium.

"Oh. I can—"

"I'll get it," Will says, and he starts off through the village. I follow. "You need to go to Lindy right away. If Jeff catches you in street clothes . . ." Will slides his finger left to right across his throat and makes a choking noise. I get the picture. "And believe me. He sees everything."

That kind of creeps me out, so I walk closer to Will, as if he could protect me from Jeff's all-seeing eye. But soon enough we're on a path that I recall from the tour of the faire, and Will points to the left.

"Lindy's shop is that way. Think you can find it?"

A ripple of panic shoots through me. I don't know what I expected. Perhaps that Will might be with me all day long? Or at least that someone I knew would always be within a comforting distance.

"But where are you going?"

Will must sense my apprehension because he looks at me the way one might look at a crying child. "I'm off to put your things in your tent. I'll meet you at Lindy's, okay?"

No. "Sure."

Will does an about-face and leaves me in the street. My insides sink as he gets farther and farther away, whistling as he disappears into the forest with all of my art supplies and underwear. I screw up some courage and set off toward Lindy's, which is even easier to find than I imagined. Her particular cottage is a lovely shade of pink, and the windows are filled with beautiful, hand-crafted dolls, some of them with wings, magic wands, and crowns of flowers.

I open the screen door and find Lindy bent over an antique sewing machine, the kind that requires you to push on a pedal to make the motor run. She guides a strip of violet fabric through, and when it's sewn all the way up to the end, she finally sees me standing there.

"It'll be a corset fit for Queen Elizabeth herself, not that the good queen has need for something so saucy." Lindy pushes her glasses up to the top of her head and beams at me. "Or it could be yours. They're fun to wear on an evening out, you know, as a top, if you want to catch someone's eye."

Of course I can't help but think of Christian, even though the thought of him seeing me in something as revealing as a corset is enough to make me break out in red splotches all over.

Lindy notices and chuckles as she pushes herself up from her seat and crosses to a rack of clothes on the front wall. "I suspected so. Well, they're not purple corsets, but these will do just fine, I suppose."

She takes three dresses off the rack and holds them out to me, spread over her arms. They all have the same look—plain, with a laced-up bodice that will hug me from waist to armpit, and a flaring skirt. All have a flowing peasant-looking top underneath them. The colors aren't meant for royalty, but they're still pretty. One is the color of red wine, one is a rich russet, and the last is a dark forest green. It looks like she's holding autumn in her arms.

"Hard to believe these fit my Susannah only last year." Lindy shakes her head. "Shot up like a weed over the winter. I suppose she takes after her father's side. Oh, but these colors will look lovely on you, Ro, with your dark eyes and hair."

Lindy has me try on one of the dresses, the red one, and teaches me how to lace up the front properly. In the end, I transform into a proper Renaissance maiden. The dress looks like it was made for me, fitting snugly in all the right places and falling elegantly from my waist to the floor.

Lindy stands behind me, a satisfied smile on her face. "Just as I thought. Perfect for your skin tone. Unfortunately, your feet look much too small for Susannah's shoes. She wears a nine."

"I guess my flip-flops will have to do," I say, frowning as I think of Jeff. "I wear a seven."

"Just don't pick up your skirts. You'll be fine." Lindy smoothes a wrinkle on my shoulder. "But you'll need to go to The Bone Needle and pick up some sandals eventually. Davis will fix you right up."

"Thank you so much, Lindy."

"Don't mention it," she says. She casts a glance out the window and her smile broadens before she takes my other two dresses and hangs them back up. "You can come by for these later, dear. I suspect you have plans right now."

Just then the bell over her door jingles and Will enters, taking off his hat and shaking his hair out. His gaze falls on me and he says, "Wow, Ro. You look great."

I blush while Lindy agrees with him. "Like she was born to be a Renaissance maiden, right?"

"Truly." Will looks at me a while longer, then suddenly rocks back on his heels. "Well, I think we'd better get some of Ramón's sticky buns before the crowd gets here."

"They go in minutes!" Lindy says. "Go on. I'll keep these other dresses until later. Just come by whenever you have a moment."

I thank Lindy again, and follow Will out of the shop and into the street. It's so quiet compared to how I saw it the other day that it's almost spooky.

"What time do the gates open?" I ask.

"Ten, and they don't close until seven."

"That's a long day."

Will laughs. "Aye, but it goes quickly. Especially if you've got two jobs. By the way, Jeff radioed that you'd be starting in the tavern today, so we'll head over after breakfast. Ooh, I can smell them now . . ."

Will practically jogs off down the street and I take off after him. That lovely sweet smell I'd noticed the other day is there, but not yet any of the grilling meat or potatoes smells. Will heads up the front stairs of a one-level store, its windows a diamond pattern of glass and what look to be bona fide lead joints, although I'm sure it's merely a careful reproduction. Over the doorway hangs a wooden sign with one simple word on it: BAKERY.

I follow him up the steps of the bakery and inside, where the heavenly scent of cinnamon and bread greets me, far more powerful than it was outside. There's a plump woman behind the counter whom Will waves to, and she smiles before disappearing into the back, where I hear some rummaging around.

When she comes back, she's got a yellow box in her hand. She sets it on the counter and takes out some twine to tie it up, but Will waves her away. "No need, Magda. We're going to dig right in. This is Ro. She's going to be our new face painter. I thought I'd introduce her to Ramón's best work first."

Magda smiles, revealing a large gap between her two front

teeth. "Eh, better than his mystery stew, that's for sure."

Will pulls a face that makes me certain I will never touch Ramón's "mystery stew."

"Seriously. See ya tonight!"

She waves, but since Will is already turned around and halfway out of the shop, I wave back in his stead. Magda's grin widens, the gap in her teeth large enough to be the perfect spot for a soda straw.

Will's waiting for me, box open, by the steps. He has a sticky bun in his hand and a large hunk of it in his mouth, which he chews with gusto. He thrusts the box toward me.

"Mnnnhhf fhhhhmm fmmhh." Will swallows and then grins sheepishly. "Sorry. What I meant to say is that these are the best things Ramón makes. Honestly. He's a decent cook, but he is a *magical* baker."

I select a sticky bun that is just dripping with sugary goo, pecans glistening on the top. To my delight, it's warm. I take a bite.

"Ramón's the head cook. Organizes all the food stands and tents around here, does the staff cooking, et cetera, et cetera. Magda's his backup. She's decent enough with pies and cookies, but she's got nothing on Ramón with these. These are just—"

I let loose a sound that is half pleasure, half surprise, and completely primal.

"Agreed," Will says, laughing.

I barely hear him. The sticky bun in my mouth has rendered

me useless. It's just a ball of warm dough, cinnamon, butter, and sugar. It's a heck of a lot better than anything at TK's. It might be better than anything I've had in town. Or any-where.

We take a while, savoring each glorious bite in silence. The village around us is starting to come to life. Shopkeepers are opening up windows and doors, straightening displays, and chatting with one another before the day begins. It's a strange thing to behold, because as modern as the people seemed at the start, by the time I've finished my sticky bun, they're speaking in Elizabethan English, and I could swear I've stepped into another world.

"It's a little like Brigadoon, isn't it?" I ask Will.

"It is, but easier to find. It's in most of the tourist guides." Will snorts at himself. He licks sugary goo from his index fin-ger and then stands, glancing up the street. "I should prob-ably get back to the parking lot. People come early and wait at the gates. The tavern is on the other side, almost exactly. Think you can find it?"

I stand and look around, coming up blank. "The other side of what?" I ask him.

"Fair question." Will removes something from the inside of his vest, and I realize it's a King Geoffrey's Faire brochure. He unfolds the trifold and points at the map printed there. "The whole faire makes a big loop. We're here, in the main village. This is where the more touristy shops are. Lindy's, Robbie's art shop that we call the Michelangelo Gallery—you really should check that out sometime—The Bone Needle for leatherwork, and tons of craft places that sell everything from soaps and incense to dragon tapestries. If you go off that way . . ."—Will points over to our left, where it's woodsy and there's a small bridge crossing a stream—"you'll see the kid's section. That's where your face painting tent is, and the jousting ring is on the other side. Keep walking on that loop, past all the toy shops and the petting zoo, and that's the grittier part of the faire. The tavern, the jouster's pub, the smaller acts like Patsy and Quagmire's mud show and the acrobats, and a big chapel where our king holds ceremonies and public announcements. Farther down is Craftsman's Row, with the blacksmith, silversmith, and carpenter." Will's finger follows the loop around. "Then you're back to the gates and the village."

"So basically just follow this loop around?"

Will nods. "If this were a clock, we're at six, and you need to be at twelve."

"I think I can handle that."

Will hands me the brochure, which I tuck into one of the convenient pockets of my dress. "All right, good luck serving. I'll see you tonight!"

I don't know why or how I'll see him tonight, but it's reassuring that he thinks so, so I set off toward the woodsy part of the road with the bridge. I'm halfway across the sturdy structure when I realize that, instead of plain boards holding up the handrails on both sides, fat trolls like the one I spotted at the entrance are doing the work. I smile at them as if they can see me, and walk on.

After coming out of the woods, I no longer feel nervous about finding my way. Just as Will said, the kid's section and petting zoo is easily spotted, and the jousting field takes up a whole corner to the right. I know that if I walked across it right now and through the woods, I might be able to find Jeff's trailer again. But more than that, I can *smell* the tavern, and I smell it long before I spot it.

The road opens up and the businesses here are much more sprawling and farther apart. In the middle of the square, a large Tudor-style building emits steady, mouthwatering scents of roasting meats and frying grease from several large chimneys. On one side of the building, there's a patio that's nearly as big as the building itself, and it houses probably twenty tables. The tables, and the patrons if there were any sitting there, are beautifully shielded from the harsh glare of the summer sun by a canopy of crisscrossing wood and waxy, leafy vines growing overhead.

Suddenly the phrase "beer garden" makes sense.

A blond girl who looks just a bit older than me bursts out of the front door with a laugh. She's holding a pewter mug that's spilling over with something frothy. On second glance, I decide that everything about her seems to be spilling over: her low, breathless laughter, the loose tendrils falling from her braids; even her ample bosom can hardly be contained in her bodice.

"Quit your bellyaching, Ramón. I'll get to the silverware soon, I promise," she calls into the building before she sees me, and when she catches sight of me, everything about her becomes even more radiant. I know right away it must be Susannah—I catch the similarities to Lindy in her eyes and the curve of her mouth, but mostly in the warmth she exudes. She cocks her head at me. "You're wearing my dress, so you must be Ro."

Before I can answer, a tall, skinny man marches outside. His glossy black hair is flattened by a hair net, and his golden brown skin has stripes of flour all over it. He's dressed in what appears to be a nearly full-body leather apron over a tunic, replete with a scowl. When he speaks it's with a slight Spanish accent, and he keeps his sentences brusque and percussive. It's like he hates talking, so he does it as little as possible. "Suze, silverware and napkins. Now."

"Cool your jets, Ramón. The new girl's here. Don't scare her." She turns back to me, chin raised high. "I'm Susannah. Everyone calls me Suze. And this poor guy is Ramón." Suze turns back to Ramón and sticks her tongue out at him. "We have a new tavern wench to train, so do be on your best behavior."

Ramón doesn't answer, but he looks me up and down, nodding once. "You're just as Will said." He doesn't elaborate on that, which makes me wonder what, exactly, Will might have said. "Suze will train you right. Listen to her. She's my best wench."

"Ah, Ramón, quit. You'll make me sniffle with all that sappiness," Suze says, and rolls her eyes heavenward. She steps down from the tavern's porch and grabs my hand, pulling me inside. "Wench bootcamp. Come on. We open in an hour."

The inside of the tavern couldn't be more rustic, which is exactly what I was imagining. Long tables span the length of the place, with a few smaller tables off the side, closer to the bar. There are two sets of swinging wooden doors in the back, where I have to assume the kitchen is, and in between is one wide fireplace. Nothing's burning in it right now, seeing as how it's the dead of summer, but I can guess that on the chilly nights here in the woods, it's a great draw to faire patrons and workers alike. Above my head there are wooden beams that cross the high, cathedral-like ceiling. They're roughly cut and barely varnished, as if someone hauled them straight out of the forest and propped them there, and between those beams hang iron chandeliers that have fake candles flickering in each holder.

I decide that it's pretty in an untamed, uncivilized kind of way.

Suze takes her time explaining the ebb and flow of the usual crowds on weekdays and weekends, the general areas for different servers, what we're supposed to do in our downtime (unpacking boxes of sporks and condiments), and filling me in on Ramón's managing style. "He may not look like much, but if you serve a turkey leg that's too cold or an ale that's too flat, he morphs into the Hulk. I'm telling ya . . . ,"

Suze says. But then she gets down to wench bootcamp, and she wasn't kidding about it.

First, we merely practice holding three or four steins of water in each hand and carrying them from the bar to the table in the farthest corner. It seems easy at first, but after three trips, my arm muscles are crying uncle and shaking from exhaustion. As if that wasn't bad enough, Suze gives me a tray stacked with steins and a normal food order. The weight of it makes me feel like I could crumple to the floor, and raising it any higher than my elbow is impossible.

"How on earth do you do this?"

Suze flexes her arms like a weight lifter, showing off some impressive muscles. "This is my third summer serving. I can win nearly every arm wrestling competition in the world at this point."

Suze shows me her trick for picking up large trays of food. She has me set the tray on a table, bend at the knees, place my shoulder under one side of it, and then slowly stand so that I'm supporting the whole thing. Still, even with this method, I feel exhausted after just a few practice runs in and out of the kitchen, and all I want to do is sit down and rest.

But before Suze lets me have a break, she also lets me in on the wench's number one moneymaking secret: flirting.

"Toss your hair, bat your eyelashes, laugh loudly at their jokes," she instructs, and then leans in so she can whisper conspiratorially. "And don't be afraid to show a little skin. I used to get only a handful of singles at the end of my shift.

After I started wearing this corset? Some men just flat out hand me a ten."

I feel myself blush. The thought is as horrifying as it is intriguing, and as soon as the doors open for lunch, I see it in action.

"Watch and learn," Suze instructs, and that's what I do. I shadow Suze for the first hour, learning the routine. She winks at her customers, leans over the table close to talk to them, plays with her hair, and her speech is filled with flirtatious barbs and innuendos.

By the end of my shadowing time, I'm amazed at her. Not because she's collected so much cash in tips, but because of how at ease she is with it all. Everything comes so naturally— the flirting, the language, the whole Renaissance act—that I almost forget there's a whole modern world outside. And Suze is just resplendent, dazzling everyone she comes across, including me. She's pretty in an old-fashioned kind of way, with a strong chin and wide-set eyes and high cheekbones, like she walked straight off an old black-and-white film reel, but her looks are only a small part of her beauty; the rest is all attitude.

I try to mimic her when I'm set free and have a few tables on my own. The heaviness of the food and ale, doled out in Viking-size portions and served in pewter steins, fatigues me even faster than I thought it would. Although I manage to keep it all upright, it's so tiring that there's not much room for small talk with the customers, let alone a good round of flirting. Plus, I am really not used to serving in a long skirt and tight bodice. I feel like I might trip, or that at any point the lacing on my dress could snap and my dress could fall off.

It's *busy*, too. Suze claimed the lunch rush wouldn't seem that long, but it feels like a decade. I look over at Suze while I'm dashing to and from the kitchen, and she's barely broken a sweat, whereas I'm drenched, I have ale all over my billowy sleeves, and I'm almost positive that the white stuff in my hair is mashed potatoes. She also has a wad of bills in her hands from tips, and I've got a measly fifteen dollars.

As soon as we have some time to breathe, I tell her I'm in awe of her. She laughs and waves me away. "It's all in the tight bodice."

"It's not. At least I hope not." I look woefully down at my own chest. "No matter how tight you pull the strings, I don't think I have a prayer."

Suze laughs again. "We can't all be blessed with the inability to see our own feet, I guess. But you've got that hair. I'm totally jealous of your hair. It's perfect."

I pull a few tendrils out in front of my face to inspect. My hair has always been the bane of my existence. Dark and curly, with a coarseness to it that makes me feel completely unsexy whenever anyone touches it, it's also thick to the point of being ridiculous. It falls around my head like a lion's mane, and no matter what I do to tame it, it always disobeys me and goes wild.

"My hair is awful," I tell Suze. "It's too big and I think it got in someone's beer. And worse, their mashed potatoes."

Suze inspects me with an amused smile. "You really are a mess. Come here. Let me try something."

She leads me back into the kitchen, which is a flurry of cooks preparing food for hundreds of faire patrons. There's a small mountain of potatoes on one counter, and deep pans of raw, pink and fatty turkey legs. It seems like everything inside the kitchen is coated with a fine layer of grease. Some of the cooks give us a curious glance, but mostly they're too busy to bother even looking as Suze leads me to a stool and starts to work some sort of voodoo on my hair. She rolls the sides of it back and then tucks it underneath itself, making it look not only Renaissance-esque, but neat and tidy as well. The best thing? No chance of getting it in mashed potatoes this way.

"Thanks," I tell her, and she shrugs like it's no big deal.

"Get out!"

I turn, startled. Ramón is brandishing a potato peeler at us, nostrils flaring, but Suze merely chuckles at him. "We had a hair emergency, Ramón. We'll go back out in a second."

"You'll get hair in the food," Ramón complains. He crosses his arms over his scrawny chest and gives us a stare that's meant to be threatening. My ears burn at the scolding and I worry about the impression I'm making. He's not Jeff, but he's definitely a boss in a way.

Suze doesn't seem at all fussed, waving him away. "We're going, we're going . . ."

"Yes, now. Before—"

"Before you get angry, I know," Suze says, and as we walk through the swinging doors and back into the main part of the tavern, she looks back and blows him a kiss. Ramón's face screws itself up, and I can't tell if he's annoyed or completely uncomfortable or both.

"Don't worry too much about him. Mostly empty threats. And, Ro, I should have mentioned . . . don't forget the children," Suze says. We pause to look out over the tavern's patrons who are, blissfully, all fed and happy at the moment. "Even if you don't have the flirting down, children and parents are big tippers too. Tell them their baby's the cutest, don't make a fuss when the kids make a mess, and be playful with them. Parents love it."

I smile at her, grateful for more advice. There's something about Suze that reminds me of Kara. Something in the way she's really caring without making a big deal about it, like it comes so naturally to her that she doesn't even realize she's doing it.

It's the first time I've thought of Kara since this morning, and regret and guilt seep deep into me, fitting alongside my tired muscles.

I finish my shift, exhausted, and although I'm getting the hang of it, I have a long way to go. Especially with the flirting. I probably should start lifting weights so I'm more comfortable with the heavy trays, and maybe do some cardio so I'm used to running around the tavern in long laps, but the flirting is where I need the most work. With Kyle, flirting was always easy. But this fake variety while balancing turkey legs and mugs? Not so much.

"Wenches have to be good flirts, Ro. It's part of the atmosphere," Suze says as she walks me to my next shift: face painting. Suze is trying to be gentle, but as my wench mentor, it's her duty to dish out some criticism. She hesitates before saying, "I'd give you a rating of Fine in serving, but a Fail in flirting."

"I'm no good at it in real life, either, so that's no surprise," I say, and sigh at my ineptitude.

Suze giggles at me and squeezes my arm. "You're going to be fine, Ro," she tells me. Then she leaves me outside the face painting tent. I watch her walk away, missing her reassuring presence already.

She thinks I'm going to be fine. I have no idea if she was talking about the flirting or the Renaissance Faire in general. All I can do is hope she's right.

6

The face painting tent, I decide, looks happy. It sits back on a small hill in the kids' section of King Geoffrey's Faire. A winding path climbs up the hill to the opening in the front of the tent, and when the kids are done here, there are games, toy shops, and a petting zoo to explore just down the way. I make a vow to go down to the petting zoo soon and make a few furry friends, but for now, this tent is going to be my workplace, and just looking at it makes me smile. Unlike the more adult sections of the faire, everything in this section is brightly colored, and our tent is striped in purple, orange, and yellow, making it look more like something out of a carnival than the 1400s.

The sign over the opening says FACE PAINTING in calligraphy, and a face painted with stars is displayed right next to the G. I duck inside and a girl is sitting there on a wooden chair, looking bored.

"I'm Ro," I say to her. "I'm the new face painter and server. I guess you and I are going to be trading shifts between here and the tavern?"

She looks at me blankly before reaching into the pocket of her long skirt and withdrawing a tube of lip balm. She applies it generously to her full lips, which seem to be her best feature. Although she's cute, she's definitely not up there with Suze looks-wise. And Suze slays her on warmth and friendliness as well. She takes her time, all the while looking me over. As she inspects me, I take note of the brand name on the lip balm tube. It's good stuff from a great place in the mall; it would have cost me a day's tips at TK's.

I wonder if her parents are rich or if she just manages that much in tips from the tavern.

"Cassie," she says by way of introduction, but doesn't offer me her hand to shake. Instead she turns, removes what looks to be a photo album from a small wooden stand by the entrance of the tent, and holds it out to me. I take the heavy book in my arms.

"The face painter's bible," she says when I look at her in question.

"It's huge."

"Uh-huh. Stick to it and you can't go wrong."

I glance down again at the big-ass book and decide the name has a certain ring to it. The B.A.B., we can call it, and have a good laugh. I'm about to say so to Cassie, but then I realize she's already seated herself back at the table and is doing a great job of pretending I'm not there.

I sit down in the unoccupied chair on the other side of a desk that is covered, literally covered, in paints. There are probably more than thirty small, round metal tins of face paints, in colors ranging from neutrals and browns to neons of pink and green. The spaces between have drips of paint, water, or stained cloths where brushes have been wiped. At the end of the table there are jars upon jars of brushes in all sizes and shapes for all of their different purposes. There are jugs of water, too, each painted with a pretty design of flowers or ivy. I briefly wonder if my predecessor had the talent to make the leaves and petals as realistic as they are, or if it's my current tent partner who painted them.

I glance over at Cassie, who is again slathering her lips in expensive lip balm, and take a wild guess that it was my predecessor.

I sit down at the set of chairs on the other side of the table and begin to look through the B.A.B., but it all seems really basic. Daisies, cat whiskers, hearts, music notes. Even the full face masks are all variants of the same theme: zombie, ghost, ninja.

I close the book and set it aside with a bored sigh. Cassie glances at me, pursing her glossy lips in disapproval, then busies herself with cleaning a brush on a cloth.

I'm about to start taking a mental inventory of the brushes

when a little boy who can't be more than seven rushes in, his mother lagging behind, winded. The boy sits in the empty chair at my station and stares at me.

"Badger," he proclaims.

"Say please, Aedan. Please, may I have a badger?" his mother intones, and the boy ignores her and says once more to me, "Badger."

I look over at Cassie, who has taken a decided interest in her fingernails, the hint of a nasty smile on her mouth. She's clearly going to be no help.

"Okay," I say to the little boy. "Do you want to look like a badger or do you want a badger on your cheek?"

"Badger."

Aedan is clearly not going to be any help either.

I look askance at his mother, who only shrugs. "Just make him look like one, I guess."

All right. Make the kid look like a badger. Which seems easy enough. Only I have no clue what a badger looks like. Aren't they sort of like raccoons? Or are they more like meerkats?

I give the mother a bright smile and grab the B.A.B., flipping through with frantic hope. Again, all I see are butterflies and whiskers and superhero masks. Nothing at all that looks like what a badger might look like, not that I have any clue.

Desperate, I look once again to Cassie for help, but she's put her feet up on the empty chair at her station and is doodling in a leather journal. (It's just doodles, made with a ball-

point pen, but even at a glance I can tell she's decent, and she
might have been the one who painted those flowers on the
jars. Darn it.)

"Um, give me just a moment. I think I'll need some fresh
water for this," I tell the boy and his mother, and then duck
out the back of the tent and make sure the flap is tied so they
can't see me pull out my phone. I hold it up like it's baby
Simba in the *Lion King*, hoping to catch some signal, however faint.

"Staff members are not permitted to use cell phones, Lady
Rowena."

I gasp and whirl around at the booming voice, only to be
confronted not with my boss, but with Will. "Don't scare me
like that. Geez. I thought you were Jeff."

Will chuckles. "Clearly I'm not, and thank goodness for
that, but he is on his way. I just saw him leave the tavern
with his royal entourage, and he's making his way around the
loop." Will taps on my phone. "This is one of Jeff's biggest pet
peeves. Instant strike on your record, and just like baseball,
you only get three before you're out of here. Why are you
using it, anyway?"

"This kid asked for a badger and I don't know what a badger looks like." I tuck my phone back into my pocket, feeling
defeated. "Have any clue?"

Will is hopelessly amused by my plight. "Did you actually
look at the brochure I gave you today?"

"Not yet. Why?"

Will pulls another one out of his vest pocket and holds it up. There, in the King Geoffrey's Faire crest, is a wolf, a lion, a dragon, and something that looks like a skunk, though more weaselly.

"Oh," I say. "That's what was on Grant's horse quilt. I see."

"Yep. Each of the knights has a symbol of the kingdom on their horse." Will tucks the brochure back inside his vest. He leans close, whispering in my ear. "Leave the phone in your tent tomorrow. Even having one on your person could send Jeff into a conniption."

I laugh, and when Will leans back to look at me, he adds, "And read the brochure. Jeff's been known to quiz us on its contents."

"You're not kidding, are you?"

Will squeezes his eyes shut. "You have no idea how bad I wish I was. I've got to get back to the parking lot. I'll see you . . ."

I watch him walk away. I have no idea why he was over in this part of the faire when I needed him, but thank goodness he was. I pull the brochure out of my pocket and study the badger. Educated, I slip back inside the tent. The little boy is still there, waiting only somewhat patiently for me. I take a seat across from him, and although I can feel Cassie's curious eyes on me, I don't look over at her.

"Okay, a full badger mask coming right up," I assure the boy, and he grins. His two front teeth are missing.

The face paints are thick like clay, and it takes longer than

I would have expected to soften them with my watery brush. But once the paint is on my brush, it's like the oil paints I'm used to. I start by giving the boy a black nose, filling it all in like a triangle. It's strange painting on skin. It doesn't immediately accept color, and I have to paint several strokes to make the color as vibrant as I would with just one stroke on one of my canvases. Added to that, his face is not flat. I don't have to work to create depth, I only have to work with the depth that's already there.

I draw stripes up his face, leading from his nose over his eyes, up to the beginning of his hairline. I give him a nice little beard of stripes on his chin, and then I fill the rest in with bright white. When I hold up the mirror in front of his face, he yelps in delight. There's no thank you, despite his mother's instructions, but she tells me to keep the change out of a twenty, which means that just from one job I've almost earned more tips face painting than waiting tables today.

Before he leaves, I take a picture of him grinning his toothless badger smile with a Polaroid camera that I find on the worktable. It's wrapped in velvet and reads DA VINCI'S WONDER on the side. I pin the Polaroid up on the tent wall next to my station. When I turn around, Cassie is watching, arms crossed.

"Stick to the book. That way you won't have to bother other workers for help." Proud of herself, Cassie plops back down in her chair, reapplies her lip gloss, and begins to doodle again.

In spite of myself, I'm embarrassed. She probably heard

the whole conversation with Will. Effectively chastised for the second time that day, I sit back down in my chair, take out the B.A.B., and begin to study.

I'm so absorbed in the B.A.B. that when Cassie pulls back the flaps of the tent so that even more sunshine comes in, I'm startled by the sudden brightness.

I lift a hand in front of my face to shield my eyes from the glare. "Where are you going?"

She smiles at me. It's not exactly a friendly smile, but it's a smile that means she's up to no good, and the fact that she's shared it with me makes me feel like I'm on the inside of something. "The final joust is starting soon."

"Are we allowed to go?"

Cassie shrugs and that naughty smile deepens. "Business hasn't exactly been booming."

That isn't untrue. Cassie took a customer after my badger left, a teenager who wanted stars on her face, but since then we hadn't even had a whiff of interest.

"Have you seen the joust?"

"No, but Will explained it a little bit."

"Ah, Will." Cassie says his name the way a lot of people say the word "syphilis." "Well, it's the final one of the day. The championship."

"I wonder who made it to this round," I say, making my voice as neutral and calm as I can manage, even if my heart is beating a shaky rhythm in my chest that sounds a lot like, "Chris-tian, Chris-tian, Chris-tian."

"Let's go," Cassie says, and flips our OPEN sign to CLOSED. I follow behind her, unsure of where the jousting field is in relation to the face painting tent. It's a relief, too, to be doing something with her. I've worked with people before who I didn't become friends with, but I can't stand the thought of anyone disliking me. Especially since I haven't given her a reason.

We head down the hill and cross over the main road. The crowd is gathering fast, all headed in the same direction, and I have to concentrate on Cassie's stick-straight blond hair so I won't lose her. Even though I saw the field this morning, it was empty, and that memory doesn't prepare me at all for what we find.

The field is a huge oval of uneven dirt and mud, guarded all around the edge by a simple wooden fence. The two longest sides both have bleachers, although one side is plain wooden bleachers and the other looks like a giant luxury box, with sides and a roof to provide shade, and King Geoffrey's crest painted in a pattern all over it. In the middle of that is a smaller box where the king himself is sitting. If this were a lacrosse game, the box side would be for the home team, the plain wooden bleachers for the visiting team.

Unfortunately, we're too late to sit on the pretty side, so we have to take a seat in the last row of the wooden bleachers. Fortunately, from this height I can see everything, and I catch a glimpse of royal blue and silver at the right side of the field.

Jeff—erm, um, *King Geoffrey*—stands and gestures grandly

from his throne in the box. He calls out a greeting in a voice magnified by a hidden microphone, and the crowd quiets. Then, with great showmanship, he tells us the plot of today's joust.

"Lords and ladies of the realm! This morning, our honorable Sir Richard, the king's champion, was unseated by a mysterious knight in black from a far-off kingdom!"

The crowd boos and I have to chuckle. We don't take kindly to mysterious knights who unseat our champions in King Geoffrey's realm. No, sir.

Jeff continues his tale in an exaggerated accent. "Sage, the kingdom's only lady knight, challenged the knight in black for the sake of the realm's honor, but sadly was also defeated by the knight in black."

The crowd makes a collective noise again, this time an "Aww" of pity, and I see Sage hang her head in shame.

"The realm's last hope, then, is Sir Christian, newly knighted and ready to prove his loyalty to the king!"

A pleasant shiver ripples through me at the sound of his name over the loudspeakers, and Christian rides through the center of the ring, his horse trotting proudly as he waves and the crowd goes nuts.

Cassie and I are on our feet too, cheering and whistling for him. I know that Will explained how the stunts work, and that everything is scripted, but it's exciting anyway. It's clear they work hard to put on a good show that grips the imagination and won't let go. I'm caught up in it, just like the oblivious crowd. I want to see that mean old knight in black get knocked off his horse, too.

Honestly, it kind of reminds me of sports matches back at home, with us cheering on the lacrosse players and wanting to see them knock the hell out of each other. And just like the lacrosse players at home, it seems like everyone wants a piece of the knights.

Just as I'm thinking it, I see Christian ride up to the fence that keeps the crowd from stepping on the jousting field and bend down to take a daisy from a girl's offering hand. She's young, maybe ten years old, and she's wearing a crown of flowers and a Renaissance dress she must have bought from Lindy's shop. Christian bends lower, points to his cheek, and the little girl gives him a bashful kiss.

The crowd goes absolutely wild for that, and while I clap, I have to admit: I'm jealous of a little girl. So far, she's gotten much closer to him than I have.

Cassie's laughing next to me, and she leans in to whisper, "He's such a flirt. That poor little girl doesn't even know what hit her."

Neither do I, I think.

King Geoffrey goes over the rules with the two knights and they bow to signify that they will honor them. The knight in black, who I now realize is Grant, the badger, goes off to the left, Christian goes to the right, and squires run onto the field to fit on the rest of their armor and give them lances. Then, at a signal I neither hear nor see, they turn on their horses, the squires scatter, and the two knights ride hard at each other.

There's a harsh thud and then a crack as Christian's wooden lance breaks in half. I scream. Luckily, I'm not the only ninny who's horrified. Several women around me also screamed, and Cassie gasped so loudly that she almost drowned me out. I look at her, and she's covering her mouth as if she could retroactively quiet herself down.

She turns to me, sheepish. "I know they don't get hurt, but it's hard to watch sometimes."

"No joke."

The next round, Christian is the victor, sending Grant's lance flying several feet from his horse. Cassie turns away so violently that her hair whips me in the face. She laughs at herself, saying, "I know, I know. I'm a wimp."

The third round is winner take all, since they're tied. Christian, of course, knocks Grant clean off his horse with a showy strike of his lance. He circles the felled man, then jumps off his horse, making a spectacle of withdrawing his sword and lowering it until it's at the tip of Grant's nose. Grant holds up his hands in the universal sign of surrender, and everyone in the crowd loses their minds. Satisfied, Christian sheaths his sword and climbs back on his horse, doing a victory lap while the crowd chants his name. King Geoffrey's kingdom has the honor of a champion once again.

The crowd starts to filter out and for a while it's chaos as people push in different directions. Cassie and I stay seated, content to watch the knights in the ring as they shake hands with one another and joke around. Christian dismounts, picks up some of the flowers that have been thrown to him, and pulls off his helmet. He shakes out his dark hair and then presents a flower to Sage, bowing deeply. Sage accepts the flower and hugs Christian, their armor clanging together. It's cute and familiar and it makes my chest hurt with jealousy.

"Ro! Thought I'd find you here."

Cassie and I turn at the sound of the voice, and Suze is walking toward us, somehow graceful even though the ground is nothing but mud. When Suze reaches us, she cocks her head to the side, looking at Cassie.

"Mind taking the face painting tent alone the rest of the day? Ro's rooming with me, and I'd like to get her settled in."

Relief spreads through me that Suze, so far the coolest person I've met here at the faire, is going to be my roomie. Cassie seems decent enough now, but she isn't nearly as fun, and everyone else is a complete stranger.

Cassie hesitates; for a moment I think she's going to tell Suze no, but then her shoulders drop and she nods. "Sure. I guess."

"Best get along then," Suze says pointedly. "There's always a rush after the joust."

Cassie slides off the bleachers and starts back to the tent, not even bothering to say good-bye.

I grin at Suze. "Everyone pretty much does what you tell them to do around here, don't they?"

"If not, I make them," Suze says with a wink. She holds up

a keychain full of shiny, brassy keys between us. "Come on. The fairy dollmother gave me the keys to her car. You need an air mattress. Trust me, those cots Jeff provides? Infested with spiders. Or worse."

I don't want to imagine what could be worse than a spider infestation, nor do I want to find out.

Air mattress it is.

7

The accommodations at King Geoffrey's Faire are somewhat lacking. Everyone lives in tents, and not the high-tech kind that campers use. These look like standard issue military tents. They're green canvas, have a pole in the front and the back to keep them upright, and the doors are flaps that can be tied together for privacy, if you consider three lousy strings tying canvas together privacy. The whole thing is set up on a wooden platform, so at least you're not sleeping on the ground, but still, it's kind of the pits. Added to that, the nearest bathroom—erm, latrine—is on the other side of the campground, meaning to get to it you have to go over the river and through the woods, dodging tree roots and mud puddles, keeping an eye out for lions and tigers and bears.

Oh my.

As we get settled in, I keep repeating to myself that I

wanted remote. In other words, I asked for this. Still, this lifestyle is going to take some getting used to. It's a far cry from Kara's beach house, that's for sure.

Somehow, Suze and I manage to arrange the tent so that my air mattress and all my stuff can fit next to hers. It defies the laws of physics, since the mattresses alone take up nearly the whole floor, but all our meager summer possessions are piled at the foot of our new beds, and there's still room for a very small walkway between them.

"So this cheating boyfriend of yours . . . ," Suze says, continuing our conversation from earlier in the car, when she asked what had possessed me to apply for a body art specialist job. "Should we go egg his house or something?"

I laugh at that, and I'm grateful for the sentiment. It's exactly the kind of thing Kara and Meg said to me after I found out about Lacey, and it tugs a little at my heart. I hadn't told Suze about the fight with my friends; I hadn't felt the need to burden her with all the drama in my life in one fell swoop.

"Nah. Just help me find a hot guy so I can drown my sorrows in sexiness all summer," I tell her, and it has all the sass I'd been aiming for during my lunchtime shift.

Suze grins at me—a mischievous, I-know-something-you-don't-know grin. "Maybe you can find someone tonight."

"Tonight? Why? What's going on tonight?"

The grin gets even more impish. "Put on something cute. We have plans."

I decide to trust Suze. I choose jeans and a turquoise, one-shouldered top that Kara bought me, which earns me a thumbs-up from Suze. She's in jeans herself, and a peasant top that looks homemade, like she's still half in the Renaissance world. Regardless, she looks stunning, and if she's looking for someone tonight too, she's definitely going to hook him.

Suze pulls me out of the tent and in the opposite direction of the main part of the faire, back toward the parking lot, where the woods grow thicker and darker. The sun has started to set, and the light is a weak, purplish gold. The trees over our heads are so thick with leaves, however, that after only a minute of walking, it seems like we've entered the dead of night.

I want to ask her where the heck we're going and why, but I don't. I'm enjoying the suspense, which is something I'm not used to liking, but tonight it's exactly what I need. There's something about the woods, and maybe the faire itself, like everything's a little magical if you just trust in it. I let Suze lead me farther and farther away from the light, hoping that fortune favors the bold.

The music is the first thing I hear. The same flutes and drums I heard my first day at the faire and all day long today are calling out into the woods, getting louder with each step. It takes me a moment, but I recognize the song and start to laugh. It's Katy Perry. In the style of a Renaissance band.

Suze laughs with me, turning her head back to look at me.

"We know how to party out here. Just wait . . ."

As the forest opens up into a clearing, I can see that she's right. There's a bonfire raging in the center of the clearing, its flames reaching up to lick at the purple sky over our heads, the dark smoke billowing into the heavens. It looks as if everyone who works at the faire is here, all gathered in the small clearing. Some people are sitting on felled trees. Some are standing, gathered in groups, chatting and laughing and clanking leather and wooden mugs together. Some are standing farther away, where the light doesn't quite reach, paired off already for a romantic evening. For a moment I am hit with a rush of homesickness—this is so much like our beach parties, and if I wasn't here, I'd be at home on the beach with Kara and Meg. But Kyle would also be there, which is a point in the King Geoffrey's Faire column.

When Suze and I stumble into the center and park ourselves next to the fire, everyone stops what they're doing to look at us. Even the flutists and drummers stop. Suze seizes the moment and hops up onto a bench made of logs, pulling me up next to her. As I clumsily try to get my balance, Suze hoists our joined hands up to the sky and shouts, "King Geoffrey's Faire, this is your new face painter, Ro Duncan. Let's teach her how to have a good time, Renaissance style!"

About thirty mugs are raised in the air and a boisterous, jubilant shout rises up over the crackling sounds of the flames: "Huzzah!"

After the toast, there's laughter, more chatter, and a few

cat calls. Suze laughs them off, turning to me again. "Welcome to your summer home, Ro. It's paradise, I promise."

I look over Suze's shoulder to the fire and the people gathered around it, all smiling and laughing, and I'm inclined to agree with her. Honestly, it's already better than the nights I'd spend at the mall at home. It's far more interesting, anyway.

"So this is an official Renaissance Faire party?" I ask her, my voice tight with excitement, and Suze wrinkles her nose.

"Well, not really. We usually have a bonfire that's officially sanctioned on Sunday nights, since we have Mondays off." Suze winks. "But this is clearly a special occasion."

I give Suze a wry look. "I can't possibly be the special occasion. So what's going on? Spill."

Suze's grin is made of pure mischief. "The special occasion is that Jeff is conveniently predisposed at the moment. A meeting with the tourism board or something. We didn't ask too many questions. All we know is that he's not here, and you know what they say. . . . When the king's away, the peasants have their day!"

With a laugh, Suze grabs my hand and takes me around, introducing me to everyone there. In a matter of minutes, I feel like I've known most of them my whole life. I'm overwhelmed by how welcoming they are and how excited they are to meet me. At some point, a mug is thrust into my hands, and even though I have no idea who put it there or what's inside, I take a sip. My eyes widen and I hum with delight.

"Mead," someone whispers in my ear, and I realize it's

Will. I turn to him, thankful for a familiar face, as I've lost sight of Suze, and the names of all the people I've met are blurring together in my head into one indecipherable blob.

"It's good," I say, and I can hear the surprise in my tone.

"We make it here. In the Jouster's Pub. Someone, I won't say who, broke into the stash tonight." I narrow my eyes at him and he gives a startled laugh. "Not me, I swear! But I took a vow of silence, and you can't break me, Ro."

I giggle at him and take another sip. "It tastes like honey."

He nods. "Just wait until you have it warm. When it's rainy and chilly, heat some of this up and you'll feel like you've got some of the campfire inside you. Just be careful. It tastes so good that you forget how strong it is. Trust me. Made that mistake many times my first summer . . ."

He winks again, and then he's gone, off to join a group of guys on the opposite side of the fire. One of them, a boy about my age, is clearly doing an impression of Jeff, sticking his lower lip out comedically, his eyes narrowed to slits, barking orders at the other guys about the proper way to lace your boots and memorizing the brochure. He can't keep up the impression for long and soon devolves into laughter, his white teeth flashing brightly against his dark skin. I chuckle with him and turn away, looking for someone else to talk to.

On the edge of the bonfire light sits another group, this one serious and muted. Even in the dark, Christian's eyes stand out: two pale sapphires shining in the dusk. I take a long pull from the mead in my mug and make my way toward him, hoping the alcohol might give me some courage that I'm not feeling yet.

Christian's gaze slides to me and the corners of his mouth curve, subtly, but enough for me to see it as a welcoming sign. He shifts a little, making room for me on the log next to him.

Everyone in his group is hunched, leaning forward over a makeshift table in the middle. There's a deck of cards, divvied out to everyone in small stacks, and a shot glass next to every player's hand.

"Cheers, Your Majesty," Christian whispers to me. When he does, he leans close so that his thigh touches mine. It's thick and warm, and even with the slight contact I can feel the tension and strength of his muscles. I lean closer, making the connection solid, and his mouth curls into a more obvious smile.

"You don't have to address me as your majesty," I whisper back, doing my best to keep it light, teasing.

Christian turns his face toward me. He licks his bottom lip slowly, then returns to his sly smile. "It's a drinking game. Numbers. Requires a lot of concentration."

As he speaks, I can't help but notice how perfect his mouth is—full and luscious and completely kissable. I wouldn't mind nibbling a little on that bottom lip, either, if the opportunity arises. And I hope it will.

One of the players in the circle puts a five of diamonds down on top of Christian's shot glass, and Christian groans. I look at him, confused.

"Now I have to pull an ace if I want to drink again," he explains, but I don't understand why. He looks at his hand, fanning the cards out so I can see them. He points to the queen of spades next to his thumb. "Let's get them all back."

Christian throws out the queen into the middle pile, sending a challenging, mocking look all around the circle. They all lean forward to look at the card he's laid and laugh.

"I knew he'd do that. I blame you, Grant. You know Christian always takes the bait."

I know the voice and look up at the source, surprised I didn't notice her before. It's Sage, and she's grinning ear to ear, gazing at Christian affectionately. It's then I realize I've placed myself in the knights' circle (their round table? Ha!). It's not just Sage and Christian, but the others I've seen jousting as well, like Grant and a handful of the squires. I'm taken aback by the fact that Christian easily let me into their group, which has already given me the impression that they're tightly knit and very protective of one another.

I sit up a little straighter and remind myself that I sit at the most desirable table in the cafeteria at school. There's no reason to feel intimidated.

With the queen lying face up on the table, Grant stands, a bottle of amber liquid materializing somehow from nowhere. "Drink up, lads," he says as he pours a healthy shot into all the open glasses, skipping Christian's, which is guarded by the five of diamonds. The knights and squires raise their glasses, yell out a hearty, "Cheers, Your Majesty!" and knock back the shots.

Sage makes an awful face and sticks out her tongue. "Ugh. Why did we agree on whiskey?"

"Because Grant can't handle rum. Remember last time?" Christian says. I notice his beautiful eyes are sparkling with humor. "We can't have him waking up in the stables again."

Grant mumbles something darkly and gives Christian a good shove, which, thankfully, makes Christian move even closer to me.

"Yeah, well . . ." Sage tosses her hand on the table and looks around at each of the men. "At this rate I'll be puking my guts out on the field tomorrow. Want to take over for me, Ro?"

I'm equally startled and flattered by the invite, and I look at Christian when I answer. "I don't know how to play."

"That's the best kind of player," Christian says. His voice is low. A little dangerous. I think once again about how this place favors the bold, and I can only hope I'm ready for what's in store.

"Christian will help," Grant says. I study him. He's nowhere near as good-looking as Christian, though he's not ugly. He has a meathead kind of look to him, as if he were a wrestler in high school and helps himself to a few protein shakes a day. His neck is thick and his ears stick out a little, but he's got a great smile and deep brown eyes that shine with warmth in the golden firelight.

"I'm a really good teacher," Christian says, and I turn my gaze back to him. His pretty eyes are staring into mine, his thigh is still flush against me, and I'm definitely feeling fire inside me, though I'm not sure if it's the fault of the mead.

I nod and take up Sage's hand, and Grant passes her shot glass over to me. It's Grant's turn and he throws down a jack, then a squire throws an ace, and before I know it, we're taking two shots in a row.

I'm not exactly a stranger to shots. After prom we broke into Kyle's mother's stash of cherry schnapps and had a fun night playing Never Have I Ever. But this is the first time I've ever had whiskey. It burns—my tongue, the back of my throat, my esophagus, my chest. Worse yet, stinging fumes come back at me after I've swallowed it down, as if the burning wasn't evil enough, and it makes my eyes water and makes me want to sneeze. I cough, sputtering, and Christian puts his hand on my back.

"It's a bit stronger than mead," he chides me. I nod to him, his face all hazy from the tears in my eyes, and blink them away the best I can. "Your turn. What've you got?"

I show him my hand and he points to a queen. We share a conspiring wink, even though I have no idea why throwing the queen warrants one.

When she lands face up on the pile of discards, the knights and squires groan, and Grant gets up to refill our glasses. I turn to Christian, eyes wide. "I have to drink again?"

"Isn't that the point?" he says, trying an innocent act, but the humor and mischief in his eyes gives him away.

I bump my knee into his and do my best to glare. "Are you trying to get me drunk, Sir Christian?"

"Now, why would you think that?" he says, biting his bottom lip. It should be off-putting, but all it succeeds in doing is reminding me how much I want to feel his lips against mine. "I'm insulted."

"Just trying to protect my honor," I say to him. I'm a little surprised at myself. I know I'm not good at flirting, partially because I've never been a forward kind of girl. But tonight I'm keeping up a conversation with the hottest boy I've ever seen, an electrically charged conversation at that, and right now I'm leaning so close to him that I'm practically in his lap.

"Your honor's no good around Christian," Grant says, and I blink, surprised there are still people around us and that they've heard this conversation clearly.

Christian only laughs. He makes no attempt to deny Grant's words; instead, he turns to me with my glass in one hand and his in the other and says, "Cheers, Your Majesty."

We drink.

Then Christian leans close, his mouth only centimeters from my own, and whispers, "Grant's right. You shouldn't trust me. I'm a rogue, a miscreant. You're a nice girl. You don't want anything to do with me."

"Oh, really?" I ask in a whisper, moving closer. I can practically taste his mouth, the air he's breathing, tinged with whiskey; I can smell a hint of campfire and aftershave, woodsy and clean. It's ten times as intoxicating as the alcohol. "I think you've misjudged me. I'm the best wench here, besides Suze."

One of Christian's dark brows raises to a high arch. "I'm not sure I believe that. You seem much more the innocent, schoolgirl type."

"Not. Innocent." I meet his eyes with the most flirtatious look I can muster, and his burn into me, straight down to my toes. "Maybe I'm looking for a rogue."

"That's good, because I'm not the kind of guy you want to bring home to your mother."

I almost laugh at his choice of words. "Not looking for that. Just want to have fun," I claim, and it's not untrue. I have no interest in a boyfriend again. Not right now. Boyfriends are a lot of work, and for what? All they do is end up kissing freshmen girls behind your back.

Christian says nothing to me in return, but his eyes have changed. Instead of the twinkle of mischief in them, they're now intent. Serious. Purposeful. He looks away, takes a card out of his hand, and throws it down. It's an ace. With a flick of his fingers, the five of diamonds on top of his shot glass goes flying, and Grant fills his glass to the brim. Christian downs this shot without grimace or complaint, then nods at his fellow knights.

"Well played," he says and stands. The rest of the knights throw down their hands. I'm not sure if Christian ended the game with that ace, or if it's ending simply because he's done playing. He smiles down at me and offers his hand, which I take. "I'm going for a walk. I'll see you losers in the morning."

There's a round of groans, name-calling, and catcalling. Christian waves them away and swipes the bottle of whiskey from Grant's hands. We move away from the group, farther from the light of the fire, so that it's just a soft, flickering glow at our backs. I'm warm, despite the coolness of the evening. There's a pleasant humming in my head, too, that's not caused by the low murmur of the bonfire or the sweet, high melodies of the flutes. Maybe it's because I've had a glass of mead and a lot of whiskey in a short amount of time, but I have a sneaking suspicion it has more to do with the strong hand wrapped around mine. When Christian pulls me back, though, causing me to stumble, I have to admit that maybe it's more the whiskey's fault than I thought.

He laughs as I smack into his chest, very undignified, and pulls me close to him.

It's just as I imagined days ago, when I first came across him in his armor. His chest is broad and strong, and I press my face into him, partially because I'm having trouble regaining my balance, partially because it's all I want to do in the world right now. He's wearing a thin T-shirt, and I can feel his heart thumping against my cheek. I can feel the pleasant softness of skin over the hard stretch of muscle—such a wonderful contrast.

Christian pulls back, using his hand in mine to keep me steady. With his other, he takes a deep swallow from the whiskey and then holds the bottle out to me.

I drink, despite the fact that I'm having trouble controlling my limbs already. He looks at me with something resembling pride. "Impressive. Not many people can keep up with us knights."

I smile at him. I feel like I'm half asleep, then my vision goes all slanted and I sway dangerously, falling into his chest again. The rumble of his low laughter fills my ears, muffled by the muscles in his pecs.

"Wow, I'm sorry. I think the whiskey hit me all at once."

I look up at him. He's got that intent look in his eyes again, and the earnestness of it takes my breath away. I can't remember Kyle ever looking at me that intensely, even before our first kiss. It's flattering, and it sends a shockwave of heat throughout my body. That look, this look that says that beyond a doubt, Christian wants me, is all mine.

Then Christian leans down, his lips hovering a whisper away. I can smell his clean scent again; I can see each eyelash resting on his cheek; I can almost taste the whiskey wetting his lips, and it hits me: Sir Christian, Prince Charming of King Geoffrey's Realm, is going to kiss me.

I close my eyes and prepare myself. There's a loud ringing in my ears, as if we're causing a six-alarm fire.

"Hello?"

I open my eyes. Christian has pulled out a cell phone— hence the fire alarm—and is a couple of paces away from me, talking into it with one finger in his other ear. I'm still standing there like an idiot, leaning into the air where he once stood, waiting for a kiss. He shoots me an apologetic look and so I stare down at my rainbow toes, embarrassed.

"Ro," Christian whispers, and I muster enough bruised pride to look at him again. His face is soft, disappointed, and I can tell he didn't want to take the call. I can only hope it's because he'd rather be kissing me, not because he doesn't like the caller.

He rolls his eyes and points to the phone, so maybe it's a combination of both. "I'm sorry, I have to take this. Can you find your way back to the fire?"

I swivel my head in the direction of the light. The golden glow isn't that far away, but it looks like a major obstacle course of tree roots and shrubbery to get there, and I'm more than slightly impeded by three shots and a glass of mead. But what other choice do I have? I can't stay out here and listen to Christian's phone conversation and wait for a kiss. That would be pathetic. And needy.

So I nod. "See you back at the fire," I whisper back.

It takes me twice the amount of time to get back to the fire as it did to leave it, and I trip on a fallen tree branch once, falling headfirst into a pile of leaves. I'm picking twigs and other miscellaneous forest items from my hair as I step into the clearing.

Suze is right by the fire, cuddled up to the knight I recognize as Grant. When she sees me, she untangles herself from his arms and comes over.

"Get lost?" she asks, smirking.

"Yeah, a handsome knight led me into the woods and then abandoned me for a phone call."

"A knight, huh? Who? Richard?"

"Christian," I say, and Suze's eyes widen.

"Seriously? You hooked up with Christian?"

"Almost hooked up with," I clarify. "I think."

"Girl," Suze says, impressed. "*Girl.* I bow to you. Your first night here and already hooking up with Christian. He's a Grade A, certified USDA hottie."

I look over at Grant, who is watching us with irritation. I guess this little girl talk has put a cramp in his evening. I can't help but notice again that, although he's not unattractive, he's not the best-looking boy here by far. In fact, Will (who is currently watching one of his friends try to light his farts on fire with a lighter) might be better looking.

The whole thing makes me curious. "Why didn't you go for Christian, if you think he's so incredible?" I ask bluntly.

Suze doesn't seem to be bothered by my rudeness. She shrugs, looking at Grant warmly across the way. "Christian's out of my league."

I look at Suze, with her generous figure and bright eyes, and I'm flattered down to my bones that the boy she thinks is out of her league was close to kissing me tonight.

I laugh it off. "Hardly. Grant seems like a nice guy. I played a drinking game with him earlier."

"Oh, he's nice," Suze says. She wiggles her eyebrows, her voice dropping down, low and naughty. "And talented in more than just jousting, if you catch my drift."

Drift thoroughly caught, I nod with her. Someone stumbles

by us, a fellow I noticed in the kitchen earlier today whose name escapes me, and he hands off a mug of mead to each of us.

Suze, who doesn't know I've already had three shots, taps her mug against mine. "To Ro, my best wench-in-training!"

I drink to that, even though I'm her *only* wench-in-training. I take the mead in big gulps, hoping to just get it over with. Bad idea. It wants to come back up immediately.

I clamp a hand over my mouth and Suze recognizes my distress right away, probably from dealing with drunken pub patrons most of her life. She grabs my hand and pulls me back into the dark forest, and is quick to gather my hair behind my head as I lean over and let nature take its course.

I was not impressed with the turkey legs earlier today. They were gross-looking, tasted strangely like ham, and made me seriously consider vegetarianism. I am even less impressed with the turkey leg in this second round, and the whiskey burns worse on its way back up.

Suze holds my hair and rubs my back, cooing words meant to comfort me as my body exorcises everything it finds offensive.

When it's over, Suze looks at me with a mixture of amusement and pity. "I puked at my first bonfire, too."

"I guess maybe I won't mix whiskey and mead anymore. Lesson learned."

"A drink of mead and none of rum or something wicked this way comes," Suze says, singsong, and even though my stomach hurts, my throat is burning, and I think I'm already hung over, I laugh. If I had to puke my guts out in the woods, at least it's with someone like Suze. And thankfully, Christian is nowhere in sight and didn't witness my spectacular vomiting.

Suze hugs me, and I lean into her drunkenly, grateful that she somehow ended up as my roommate. Then we both jump as someone crashes through the woods and runs by us.

"Davis!" Suze calls out to the retreating back. "Can you bring us some water?"

"NO TIME GOTTA PEE!" the boy named Davis answers, and keeps going at a dead sprint. I recognize him as the boy who was hanging out with Will, lighting his farts on fire and doing impressions of Jeff.

Suze turns to me, face full of apology. "Well, welcome to your summer home, Ro. In one day you've puked at a bonfire and almost kissed Christian. I'd say you broke even."

Somewhere in the distance, we hear Davis let out a satisfied groan and the unmistakeable sounds of him relieving himself on a tree, and over that, I tell Suze, "I think I'm going to like it here."

WEEK 1—WEDNESDAY

I wake up alone, with the hammering in my head like the blacksmith in Craftsman's Row. Suze's bed looks slept in, so she must have come home with me instead of Grant, as I imagined she would, probably to make sure I didn't puke my guts out again.

With a groan, I force myself to stand and put on the russet dress Lindy hemmed for me. My head feels like it wants to roll right off my shoulders, it's so heavy and throbbing. I need coffee. And toast. And a bottle of aspirin.

The tents at King Geoffrey's Faire are far away from the tourist routes so unwitting patrons don't stumble upon the staff and ruin the illusion that we're all from five hundred years ago. The paths to the tents make three loops like a large clover in the forest, and mine happens to be in the first loop, which is closest to the faire itself but farthest from the showers and the eating area. Although I can see the picnic area from my tent, it looks (and feels) miles away this morning. With another groan, I tie back my crazy hair and get moving.

The picnic area has a shelter house with a few long tables. At one of them, Ramón is stationed with giant cauldron-looking pots and deep pans of sausage and bacon.

Ramón, God bless him, seems to read my mind. He hands me a plate of toast and bacon and a whole thermos of coffee, and I mumble incoherent praises to him before turning to find somewhere to sit.

Suze is here, though she's hardly noticed my arrival. She's busy feeding Grant a strip of bacon, and the way they're cuddled together on one side of a table tells me they're not open to another breakfast partner. Christian isn't here, which is disappointing, but at the same time I'm thankful he can't see me in this hungover state. I know some other people there but only by name, and I'm not keen on trying to sit with them and make conversation, not with this pounding in my brain. My only option is Will's table, where Ramón has parked himself after feeding me, and so has Davis and a few more familiar faces. Will's wearing glasses, which is new. I have to assume he's probably too tired this morning to bother with contacts, though I'm not sure about the look. The dark frames kind of overshadow his face, although he gets points for looking more hipster than nerd.

I drop down next to Will and flash what I hope is a bright smile at everyone.

Davis turns to me, mouth full of bacon and egg, and shouts, "HEY, HOW ARE YOU FEELING?"

As I clutch at my head in pain, the table roars with laughter. Will puts a hand on my back, one solid whack and then an apologetic, soft circle.

"I'm so sorry. I have no excuses for Davis." Will resumes eating his breakfast. "But I did warn you about the mead."

"Yes, but I don't know how to play Cheers, Your Majesty. That was the bigger problem," I say to him, still wincing. I lift a piece of toast and inspect it. Ramón frowns at me from across the table, so I take a bite and chew, giving him the thumbs-up.

"Oy, that game got me last year. Remember, Patsy?" a man on the other side of Will says. I vaguely remember meeting him and Patsy last night. They have some sort of comedic mud-wrestling act on one of the side stages. I thought his name was funny: Quagmire. I'm pretty sure it's only a stage name, but no one, including him, has bothered to tell me his real one. I'm also pretty sure they're married, though no one has bothered to tell me that either. But they sure do fight like it.

Patsy, a woman with unruly brown hair and a large nose, snorts at him. "Aye. You lay in bed like an invalid all day, clutching your head and moaning about your bellyache like a baby."

"Ramón's coffee works wonders, and so does the sausage," Will says, and takes a huge bite of a sausage patty he's speared with his fork as if to prove it. He chews noisily, mouth open.

Watching him makes my stomach roll, so I turn back to my toast and try my best not to draw attention to myself. I listen to them talk, gossiping about the events at the party last night, chatting about all they have to do that day, Patsy and Quagmire peppering their jokes throughout the conversation.

As they talk, Will leans close and whispers to me, pointing out various groups at the tables in the shelter house. "So this is the fun table. Believe me, you want to sit here, not with the knights. It's way too much ego to stomach on top of food. The vendors talk shop the whole time. Very boring. Over there are the dramatic performers. They never break character. It's irritating, to say the least. And the table way over there? Troubadours. The snobbiest bunch you'll ever meet. If you can't sing or discuss the merits of the Italian madrigal in depth, forget about sitting with them."

"So this is the fun table, huh?" I ask, eyeing Ramón's scowl with doubt.

Will follows my gaze. "You want to be friends with the cook, trust me about that."

That might be true, but Ramón looks about as friendly as the pointy end of a jousting lance, and twice as prickly. He catches me staring at him and his scowl deepens.

I finish two slices of toast and drink a healthy portion of my thermos of coffee, which seems to dull the ache in my head. I even find the steady rhythm of the table's conversation soothing, as they oscillate between jokes and the day's plans. But when Patsy challenges Quagmire to a contest of who can eat the most Scotch eggs, my upset stomach can't take it.

Thoroughly nauseous, I take my coffee, thanking Ramón again profusely, and stand to go. As I gather my trash, Sage walks in and slaps me on the back. "Nice party last night, Ro, although I'm going to have to teach you how to play cards. How's it going, Indy?"

Will lifts his cup toward her to acknowledge that he heard her, but his attention is on Quagmire, who might have more than four Scotch eggs in his mouth. It's the second time she's called Will that, and I'm about to ask him if he's from Indiana or something when Quagmire launches a Scotch egg from his mouth that goes whizzing right between me and Sage.

"Charming, aren't they?" Sage asks me, and winks. The table behind us erupts with whoops and hollering and congratulating Quagmire on his distance.

"Disgusting," I reply and take one last look at the buffoons I've shared breakfast with. Quagmire and Patsy are going for round two, and Ramón is looking down at his plate as if he's going to be sick.

Smiling at the thought of anything making tough old Ramón squeamish, I set off for the face painting tent.

The morning and afternoon go so slowly that it's all I can do not to fall asleep. My head is still pounding but, thank goodness, I don't have waitressing duties today. Cassie's on lunch duty, which means not only do I get to avoid the busy, demanding tavern job, but I have the face painting tent to myself. A couple of kids stop by, kids who behave well and don't complain, whose parents tip decently, but other than that, I'm all alone. I repin my Polaroids on the tent wall, secure them tightly, clean all the brushes and organize the paints, and study the B.A.B., but all of that takes an hour, tops. The B.A.B. isn't that thorough or detailed, and I'm sure I can master these designs in minutes.

With resignation, I turn the pages of the B.A.B. again and find something that looks at least a little challenging, but before I can try to practice it, Suze steps into my tent with a big mug in her hands.

"If that's mead, I'll kill you."

She grins at me and lowers the mug in front of my face. It's steaming, and the white string and tab of a tea bag dangles over one side. "Chamomile. It'll settle your stomach. Sorry I missed you at breakfast. I was, um, busy."

"You looked it," I say, taking the proffered mug. The tea isn't too hot to drink, thankfully, and I take several soothing sips before speaking again. "You and Grant seemed rather . . . involved."

Suze takes Cassie's empty chair, waving me away. "Yeah, well, I guess we got along well enough last night. Perhaps if I hadn't been so busy taking care of a certain Pukey McPukerson, I would have gone back to his tent with him."

I wince. "I'm so sorry. Thank you. I'm surprised I'm not sicker, honestly."

Suze nods. "Eat more next time. And don't play card games with the knights. No good can come of that." She grins. "Besides, no worries. I have plenty of time to lock it down with Grant."

"Lock it down?" I ask, interest piqued.

"Yeah. You know, for the season. We workers tend to pair up." Suze leans back into the chair, smiling, a distant look in her eye. "Fairemances. Hook up with someone for a season, have fun for a few weeks, and it's over when we strike the faire. No worries, no big commitments, no stress. Just fun and sexy times."

I giggle like a ten-year-old at that. Normally, the idea of a summer hookup wouldn't appeal to me, but with the wounds from Kyle still healing and a possible tryst with Prince Charming on the horizon, it sounds like exactly what I need. I say so to Suze, who agrees wholeheartedly.

"Perfect remedy for a broken heart," she concludes. "Lord knows, Christian would make me forget about any other boy. Hell, he might make me forget my own name."

"He's already done that to me," I confess. We laugh, but I sober almost immediately. "So basically I need to lock it down before someone else hooks up with him for the summer?"

"Exactly, my friend," Suze says. "Lock it down and fast. You don't want to be dateless for the Revel."

"The Revel?"

"The Fairie Queen's Revel!" Suze says excitedly. "It's a ball at the end of the season. A whole bunch of people come and we dress up as animals. But not, like, costumes. Just cool masks and stuff, to give impressions of the animal. We're not freaks. Or at least, we're not that kind of freak." Before Suze can say more, a stunning figure walks by the opening of the tent, and Suze calls out to him. "Hey, Christian! Looking for Ro?"

I shoot Suze a near-lethal look as she waves him in. She widens her eyes at me and scoffs, "I'm just helping!"

Christian ducks in the tent, his mouth widening into a smile when he sees me. "Hey, Ro. How do you feel?"

"Um, I've been better. I don't think I'll be playing drinking games with you and your friends again anytime soon," I joke.

"It's so sweet of you to check on her," Suze coos.

"Oh, yeah. Well, you know." He shrugs. "I was on my way to the stables so . . ."

"Ro was just mentioning how much she wanted to see the stables," Suze says, and I'm about to ask her what the hell she thinks she's doing when I catch on: She's "helping" me again.

"Oh. The stables. Yeah," I agree with Suze and smile at Christian, trying to appear intrigued and interested.

Christian gives me an appraising look, and the corners of his mouth turn up, stopping just short of a smile. "Come by after the joust. I can show you around. Just the two of us."

"Okay. Thanks," I say to him. My voice, annoyingly, sounds

like I've just run two laps around the entire faire grounds. He gives me a small wave and then he's gone, the tent flaps falling airily behind him.

"Lord. Those are your flirting skills, woman? No wonder your tips were so bad yesterday."

I set my tea on the supply table and run a hand through my hair, pulling slightly in frustration. "I know. I'm a disaster. It's a wonder Kyle even wanted to date me."

"Relax. I didn't mean to make you feel more nervous. You'll get better, I promise. You can't spend whole summer with me and not." Suze reaches over and pats my hand. "And he's going to show you around the stables. *Alone*. How sexy is that? I certainly wouldn't mind a roll in the hay with that one."

"Suze!"

She cracks up. "I'm sorry, I'm sorry. I'll stop fantasizing about your man."

"You have a good one of your own, from what you've said," I say, and stick my tongue out at her.

"Grant, yeah," Suze says, and her gaze goes all fuzzy again, most likely thinking of Grant and their own roll in the hay. I wave in front of her face, snapping her back to reality. "Sorry. Yeah. We both need to lock it down."

"Totally."

"Just remember, fairemances only last for the season," Suze says. I give her a puzzled look, unsure of what she's getting at. "I'm just saying, don't fall for him. This kind of thing isn't meant to last."

"Gotcha," I say, and reassure her. "That's exactly what I want. A fun fling to help me get over Kyle. Nothing serious."

"Christian's got the cure for what ails you, I'm sure," Suze says. She picks up my mug of tea and hands it to me. "Except for not knowing how to play Cheers, Your Majesty. Drink up, McPukerson. Drink."

The joust today does not go in Christian's favor. Sir Richard knocks him off his horse twice, to the delight of the crowd, and when it's over and we disperse, the losing knights and squires are left to clean up the field.

Because I don't want to hang around the field like a desperate idiot, I walk back toward the stables alone. Cassie is covering the face painting tent until close tonight, which means I have at least until dinner to hang out, alone, with Christian.

I wring my hands together and try not to notice they're damp. All afternoon I've done nothing but work myself into a messy pile of nerves, which was great for hangover relief but terrible for business. One poor child, who had wanted to look like a tiger, got zigzagging stripes because I just couldn't stop my hand from shaking. Good thing he liked it and said it made him look like he was in a heavy metal band.

The stables are back behind the petting zoo, tucked nicely away from the traffic and tourists. They're bigger than what I would have imagined, since I've only seen four horses around the faire. But as I enter, I realize they're not just for horses.

There are a few goats in a small pen right inside the wide double doors, and a handful of cows and sheep as well. Even better, far down on the other end, in a pen all by itself, is a camel with two humps. I've never seen a camel before, but I always imagined they'd be the size of a horse, maybe a little bigger. This one might as well be the size of a giraffe. Its neck is so long it can scratch its head on the beams crisscrossing the ceiling, and as it scratches itself it does a funny, fluid dance, like a belly dancer.

Giggling, I walk through the stables and right to its pen so I can get a better look.

"Ah, Eli. Stop showing off for the pretty girl."

I turn and Christian's standing there in the doorway, his horse behind him, laughter in his eyes.

"Eli?"

"Elijah, the camel. You haven't seen him yet? He's our biggest moneymaker down at the menagerie."

"Are you kidding? If I'd known there was a camel, I'd be down there all the time. Can you ride him?"

Christian nods and comes closer. He's braver than I am, or at the very least he knows the animal decently, because he sticks his arm through the wooden planks and pets Eli's massive chest. "Yep. It'll only cost you five dollars. Of course, it's a bumpy ride. Eli doesn't have the grace of Blaze, here."

As if responding to his name, Christian's horse lets out a snort that blasts hot air across my face. I turn my attention to Blaze, intrigued. The first time I saw the horse up close, I'd been much too interested in his rider to notice that his white coat and mane were beautiful, and the accents of gray around his hooves and muzzle gave him an air of sophistication.

I reach my hand out, stopping just short of Blaze's snout, and look to Christian for permission. "May I?"

"Yeah. Blaze loves attention almost as much as I do."

I giggle at that and then cautiously brush my fingers down the horse's snout, from his wide-set eyes all the way to his nostrils. He raises his massive head and licks my hand.

"He's got good taste," Christian says as I study the drool on my fingers.

"He's certainly a charmer."

"Well, what he meant to say is that he's glad you came to visit." Christian takes my slobbery hand and pulls a handkerchief from out of his armor sleeve, wiping my hand off gingerly. I can't help but notice that the handkerchief is lavender, with white flowers embroidered in the corners. Christian catches me looking. "From a fair maiden at the joust today. She looked like she might be seven years old, and I'd put money on this handkerchief being her mother's. Probably should have given it back."

"But it's coming in so handy," I say as he wipes away the last traces of Blaze's adoration of me. "I'm sorry you lost today."

Christian shrugs, tucking the damp handkerchief into his sleeve again. "I drew the short straw. It happens."

"That's how you decide?"

"Either that or Rock, Paper, Scissors," Christian says,

grinning. "Sage always beats me at that. And she loves to gloat when she wins. She does an extra victory lap and makes a big show of collecting all the flowers. Plus, sometimes she doesn't move her lance fast enough and actually nicks you as you go by."

I shake my head slowly, unable to comprehend why any of them would put themselves through it. "It looks so painful."

"Are you worried about me, Ro?"

I flush and try to look away, but he takes my chin in his hands and turns me back to him. He's smiling at me, amused and so amazingly confident, and I feel small, nervous, and hopeless next to him. "Don't get a big head about it," I tease, hoping I sound flirty enough.

"Me? A big head?" Christian laughs, then he reaches down and takes my hand in his, smartly taking the one that Blaze didn't assault with slobber. He raises it to his lips and gives me a small, feather-light kiss on my middle knuckle. The touch of his lips on my skin seems to send my nervous system into overdrive, nerves sizzling all the way up my arm, igniting goose bumps all along its path. He lowers my hand slowly, keeping it folded into his, and the joints of his armor groan as he moves. He looks down at himself, as if he just realized what he's wearing. "Want to help me out of this?"

I gulp, like one of those ridiculous cartoons where a character realizes he's in big trouble, about to fall off a cliff or get a safe dropped on his head. It's just as scary, honestly. *Christian wants me to help him undress.*

"Um, sure. What do I have to do? Use a wrench?"

Christian shakes his head like I'm hopeless, laughing a little. "Nothing that complicated. There are leather ties . . ."

He turns around and I see what he's talking about. The joints of the armor are tied together like shoelaces. There are three knots in the back, and two on each side of his waist. I'm thankful he's turned away from me because when I lift my hands to untie him, they're shaking in the most unattractive way. As I work, he takes off his gloves. He may not be doing it specifically to tease me, but he does a fantastic job of doing it anyway. He pulls at each finger with deft, practiced moves, much like I've seen suave gentlemen in old movies do, never mind that the gloves are thick and plated with metal. The gloves come off with ease, revealing his long, slender fingers. I'd never thought about it until just then, but fingers and hands can be sexy. At least hands like his, that seem elegant and muscular, not stubby and useless.

My own fingers seem to be the latter, rough with callouses at the tips where I balance my paintbrushes, but I manage to untie his chest piece. When Christian feels it fall open, he shrugs out of it and folds it together, setting it aside with his gloves and arm pieces. He turns his right side toward me, catching my gaze with his own, and gives me a naughty smirk.

"I could untie that myself, but I think I'd rather you do it." He glances pointedly downward, to where the ties rest temptingly at his hips, issuing a challenge.

"I don't untie leg armor on the first date," I quip, and Christian laughs.

"That's a pity. Is untying leg armor a third date or a fourth date thing?"

"Fourth. But I suppose this once wouldn't hurt." I give him my cheekiest smile. "Just don't tell the other boys."

"It'll be our secret."

I nearly sigh at that, then set to work untying the laces at his hip, then his other, and then the ones around his knees and ankles. He steps out of the metal, adding it to the pile from his chest, and tries in vain to right his clothing. He's wearing a deep blue tunic over black riding pants, with sturdy boots on his feet. The tunic is the only shirt he's wearing, and the front leather ties are mercifully undone, revealing the smooth skin of his chest. I remember how it felt to press my face into that part of him last night, the smell of him in my nose, the sound of his heart in my ear. For a moment he simply looks at me, watching me as I'm watching him, looking entirely too pleased with himself.

And for good reason.

I finally rip my eyes away as he reaches for Blaze's reins, and it hits me that the horse has stood there obediently this entire time. I'd forgotten he was even here.

"So these are the stables," Christian says in a tone that's overly showy, like I'm one of the patrons coming in for a tour. It breaks the tension and I smile. "This is where we knights keep the horses, and of course the cloven-hoofed animals from the menagerie. Peter, the hawk guy, takes care of our more feathery, cuddly, or reptilian friends."

He beckons to me, a simple hand outstretched and a waggle of his sexy fingers, and all I can do is follow. He leads Blaze into one of the stalls, turning the horse and then backing him in like he's parallel parking. "There's not much to it, really. We have to feed them, groom them, and make sure they get their exercise. We bathe them when they're muddy, which is where Richard and Grant are for sure. They can't resist running through the mud and splattering the crowd."

I make a mental note to stand far back from the barriers after a hard rain. "So Blaze is yours?"

Christian pauses, stroking Blaze's thick neck. "He's technically King Geoffrey's property. He's used all year round for the various festivals on site. But I think of him as mine. We've been together for the past three years, haven't we, buddy? And it's for the best. He doesn't respond well to anyone but me."

He leans his head against the horse and it makes me melt that this cool, collected knight cares so much about his animal.

"He does have good taste, then," I say with a wink.

"Of course, and look at him. Have you seen a prettier horse? He can afford to choose whoever he wants." Christian looks at me, his gaze on me like the way I'd see Kyle size up the goal at a lacrosse game. "Want to help me groom him?"

"Sure," I say. "What do I do?"

Christian leans down, undoing something on Blaze's saddle so that he can lift it off the horse's back and put it on a rail close by. The horse's hair is gleaming white, though there's a darker patch where he had sweated underneath the saddle. Christian runs a hand through his own hair, pulling a sour face.

"You and I could both use a good brushing, huh, boy?"

Christian bends down, digging through a plastic bucket in the corner of the stall. I take the opportunity to study the way his tunic pulls taut over his back, his riding pants accenting a feature I hadn't had the chance to inspect before now—his butt.

Christian stands and I look away quickly (though I'm sure that image will be burned into my memory for a long time, thank goodness), and he holds out a brush to me. It's about the size of my hand and oval, with yellow bristles. It looks more like something you'd use to scrub the floors than brush a horse.

Christian slips a thick elastic strap over the back of my hand, the small contact with his skin nearly making me gasp. He takes my hand, lifts it so the bristles are against Blaze's skin and his hand is over mine, and whispers to me, "He likes a lot of pressure. Don't be afraid to brush hard."

Then Christian pushes my hand under his, showing me exactly how much pressure, and in tandem, we begin to move the brush in long strokes across the horse's body.

"See? He loves it," Christian murmurs when Blaze lets out a soft whinny. "You're good at this."

It's just brushing a horse, but I'm proud of myself, and happy that Christian approves. He moves closer behind me, his chest flush against my back, and I let myself lean into him as we continue to brush the horse, his hand on mine. For a moment we don't speak, just breathe, the sweet, tangy smell of the stables and the heat of his body becoming the only thoughts in my head as we fall into a steady but lazy pattern of brush strokes.

"Ro?" I hear him ask me, breaking my reverie. His voice sounds a bit strained, and I pride myself on that, too.

"Hmm?"

Christian turns me, gently but with purpose, so that my back is against Blaze. He's looking at me with purpose as well, and I suck in a breath, knowing this is it: He's going to kiss me. For real this time. I close my eyes and wait for his delicious lips to touch mine.

"Yo, Christian! You okay? I thought I may have accidentally caught you with my lance."

My eyes fly open and I turn back around, my brush on the horse again, as if that's what I'd been doing all along. I'm happy to hear Christian let out of a low groan of frustration.

Sage pulls her horse up to our stall—Big Red, if I remember right. It's a pretty chestnut-colored horse, but nowhere near as lovely as Blaze. If Sage has any idea what she just interrupted, she doesn't let on. She smiles wide at me and runs a hand through her fiery hair.

"Hey, Ro. Learning how to groom?"

"Um, yeah." I glance at Christian nervously. "Just helping a little."

"You didn't hurt me," Christian says to Sage, his voice cutting.

"Of course not," Sage says, making a face at him. "No one could hurt you, you big hunk of man, you. Sorry for suggesting you were vulnerable."

Christian looks at her, his frustration and anger softening slightly. "That's more like it."

Sage rolls her eyes and looks over at me. "Men," she says, and I nod as if I totally understand. "He's just sore because I'm better with a sword than he is."

"In your dreams, O'Brien," Christian taunts, and Sage merely grins at him.

"Care to put your money where your mouth is? Eddie dropped off two new swords at the encampment this morning. They could use some breaking in."

Christian looks over at me and although I can tell he's just as annoyed as I am that we didn't get to kiss, I can also tell he's looking for permission.

"Go ahead," I say to him, playing along. "You can't let her run her mouth like that."

"You sure?"

I nod, dropping my voice lower so that maybe Sage won't hear. "It's okay. Maybe I'll see you later and we can pick up where we left off?"

I toss my hair over my shoulder and give him my most smoldering look, and I have the brief thought that Suze would be proud of me right now.

"Can't wait," Christian says, and gives me a smoldering look right back, so that I feel it long after he's gone, standing there like an idiot with a horse brush on my hand, unkissed and abandoned.

Last night, I was surrounded by nearly fifty people, all laughing and loud and boisterous. Tonight, I'm alone in my tent. The difference is staggering, and for the first time since arriving, I feel a little homesick.

Suze is off with Grant, hanging out or . . . whatever. She told me not to wait up. I brought the B.A.B. back with me so I could look over the designs and maybe practice some of them, but I'm definitely not in the mood right now. I keep thinking about Christian and our almost-kiss today and last night.

"Lock it down," Suze said. Locking it down is proving to be infinitely harder than I imagined. We need to be somewhere far away from other people who rudely interrupt, and without any cell phones that rudely interrupt. Completely alone.

At the thought of a cell phone, I take out my own. Three days without talking to Kara and Meg is pretty much an eternity in our universe, and I'm still not sure how mad they are at me. The guilt over my last words to Kara has been hiding these past few days, waiting for the right time to spring and remind me what a jerk I am. With the solitude tonight, however, there's nothing to hold it back. It wells up inside me, giving my stomach a permanent sinking feeling and making my throat tight.

It's been two days without electricity and my cell phone is dead, leaving me without a way to call Kara and apologize for being a royal asshat. I put the phone down, right on my pair of flip-flops, so I won't forget to take it and look for a place to charge it tomorrow.

At a loss, I spend a few minutes tidying up my small living space, which seems to have somehow exploded into utter chaos in the past day. Then I spend an even longer time trying to make my hair somewhat manageable. I haven't washed it since my last shower at home, which means it looks like a hawk has built a nest on my head. I practice twisting the sides back, like Suze did yesterday at the tavern, and it's while I'm tying it back with an elastic that I hear the soft footsteps of boots on dried grass.

Will pops his head into my tent, and the relief at seeing a familiar face is almost overwhelming. "Hey!" I greet him, waving him inside. "What are you up to?"

Will takes my invitation and quickly makes himself at home on Suze's air mattress. He's wearing glasses again, and he adjusts them before explaining his sudden appearance. "Bored. Searching out people to annoy."

"Do your worst, Fuller," I say, and he accepts the challenge.

"Well, I could start with 'Ninety-Nine Bottles of Beer on

the Wall.' Then move on to the 'Song That Never Ends.' Then I could run through my list of favorite Christmas carols."

I jab a finger in his direction. "Two can play at this game, you know. I can recite the entire Constitution and the Gettysburg Address. Plus, I think I still remember half the periodic table of elements. Hydrogen, lithium, sodium . . ."

"Oh dear God, no." Will holds his hands up in surrender. "Make it stop. Besides, I've had the periodic table of elements memorized since sixth grade and I could probably say them a lot faster than you."

We stick our tongues out at each other and hold that pose for a long moment, and that's when I realize: I like the glasses. They look kind of natural on him, really, as if they're just part of his face.

"I didn't know you wore glasses."

Will taps on the frames. "Yeah. Jeff doesn't like them during the day."

"Because eyeglasses were invented after the Renaissance?"

"*During* the Renaissance, actually," he corrects with fake haughtiness. "But mine look a little too modern."

"You could get another pair."

Will shrugs me off. "Contacts are useful during the day. What's this?"

Will reaches across the walkway and takes the B.A.B. in hand, flipping through the pages with mild interest. "Are these the patterns you're supposed to follow?"

"Yeah," I say. "They're easy. I'm kind of bored with them, although I think Cassie's going to give birth to kittens if I keep going off-book."

Will's lips twist into a smirk. "You're too good for the book, huh?"

"I didn't mean it to come out that way," I say, but then consider his words. "Yeah, I am. I really don't mean to brag, but the book is easy stuff. I've been doing more complicated things since I was a freshman."

"Can I see?"

The question surprises me. I hadn't expected anyone to ask to see my art except Jeff. Kara and Meg are sometimes interested back at home, if they know I'm working on something involving them, but Kyle's eyes would glaze over if I started talking about it, and if I brought it up to my parents, they would usually smile and nod and then ask how AP English was going.

"Um, sure. I didn't really bring anything completed with me," I say as an excuse, or an apology, or a little of both. "But I figured I'd have a lot of time to work on a few pieces."

I open a separate bag in my suitcase, a large vinyl one that holds all my art supplies and my sketchbook. I pull out the sketchbook and hand it to Will, my stomach tightening into a sickening knot. It was one thing for Jeff to look at the completed art on my phone. It's another entirely to let Will see something I haven't finished.

He opens it, pausing on the first page for a long moment

before turning to the next. He repeats that for every page, for all six of my uncompleted works, lingering over each picture until finally moving on without a word. When he's done he looks up at me, surprise coating his voice.

"You're good."

"You sound shocked."

"Well, no offense, but you don't need to be Picasso to be a face painter," Will says. He glances back down at my sketchbook. "You should go talk to Robbie. She's a great artist and I bet she'd love the company."

"Sure thing," I promise.

Will flips through the pages again, eyes flicking over the images quickly. "So are you going to major in art in college?"

"No," I say, a little more short with him than I mean to be. I take the sketchbook out of his hands and set it on the mattress next to me. "I think I'm going to Boston College. If I get in. I have to write all these essays, and the test scores they expect . . ."

"High?"

"Impossible," I answer. "No, not impossible, just higher than I think I can get."

"Study. That's what I did, and it paid off."

I cock my head at Will, studying him. "Oh, really? And what were your test scores?"

Will flushes at my rude question and deftly sidesteps it. "Good enough to get into MIT."

I gawk at him. "You're serious, aren't you?"

"Yeah. I'm into physics. I really like how balanced everything is, you know? The equal and opposite reaction. And how there are so many rules of the universe, but so much we still don't know." Will looks up at me, embarrassed at himself. "Sorry, I'm rambling. You get me talking physics and you'll have me here all night."

"No, that's cool," I say, totally taken aback by this new information. I mean, I wouldn't have called any of his friends brainiacs, certainly, and I had assumed Will was the same. And what's more surprising than his choice of major is how passionate he is about it. "It's great that you're into something that way. I have no idea what I'm going to major in. Heck, I don't even know what to write about in my admission essays."

Will wrinkles his nose. "They're always about life-changing experiences or moments of self-realization, right?"

"Yeah, cheesy stuff."

Will laughs. "Mine were about my upbringing. About how my parents have always been nomads, traveling from festivals to faires to circuses and back again, and how that affected my relationships."

"Must have been hard, always moving," I say gently.

"I guess it was, but I didn't know any different. And I learned a lot from them. My dad is an entertainer; my mom is a seamstress like Lindy. So when I got old enough to work on my own, I wanted someplace familiar. I found King Geoffrey's, made some friends here like Davis, and stuck around." Will grins. "Seems normal, right? If you can call being friends with Davis normal."

I laugh, but sober quickly. "The whole reason my parents let me come out here was because they thought I could write an essay about it."

"I'm sure the admission board at Boston would love to hear all about Jeff's anal-retentive demands for historical accuracy. Or maybe you can center the whole thing around the theories about Ramón's mystery stew, make it an analogy for your own self-discoveries. 'Secret Ingredients to Rowena Duncan's Soul Stew.'"

"You're ridiculous."

"So I'm told." Will makes a grab for my sketchbook before I can stop him, and flips to a colorful page I started a few weeks ago, a watercolor of my favorite spot at the beach. It makes me long for the beach, long for my friends, and long for Kyle. I look away.

"You shouldn't be shy about showing this to people," Will says. "You're really great, Ro. This especially. It's so realistic. How did you do that?"

I jerk my shoulder, still not looking at the painting. "It's not hard."

Will gives me a look that says he thinks I'm full of it.

"What? It's not. I'll show you, if you want."

Will ducks down so that I'm forced to look at him. "I'd like that."

I take the sketchpad from him and find a blank page before giving it back to him. Will arranges it on his lap like it's an infant he cannot drop. Then I take out my watercolor set and a brush with a blunt tip. "What color do you want to use?"

"Green," Will answers right away, causing me to smile. I hand him my paintbrush and the palette of watercolors and he holds them in the same cautious way he holds the sketchpad. Amused, I begin my instruction.

"So watercolors are, well, runny. When you use them, they all tend to drip and meld together, so instead of working against that, we work with it." I place my hand over his, lowering it until he can dip the paint brush into the green. "Sometimes what we intend to happen doesn't happen at all. Shapes come out fuzzy, colors mix together wrong, but you've got to just roll with it and explore where the watercolors take you, no matter how screwed up it seems. My art teacher calls them happy accidents."

"Happy accidents are my favorite kind of accidents," Will says. "Far better than miserable accidents, or painful accidents."

"Indeed." I take his paintbrush hand and move it close to the sketchpad. "So start with a shape and see what happens."

Will contemplates the paint, the brush, and the sketchbook seriously, lifts his hand, and promptly paints the tip of my nose.

"How's that for a starting shape?"

"You, sir . . ."

"Not a knight."

"You, *my lord*, have just started a battle you cannot possibly win."

"Oh?" Will asks, brandishing his paintbrush in front of my face like a weapon. "I don't think so. Face painter or not, you don't have to be skilled to make a mess."

"No," I say and reach behind myself, pulling three tubes of paint from the folds of my blanket. "But I have more paint."

Will has just enough time to mutter "Oh crap" before I lunge.

9

WEEK 1—THURSDAY

When I wake up the next morning, Suze's bed is empty. Although I'm happy for her that she found a fairemance, I also find myself missing someone to chat with, especially since it's clear that I need to shower and I have no idea what awaits me in the showers at King Geoffrey's Faire. If it's anything like the tents, there could be bugs everywhere, and minimal privacy, and neither of those things are particularly inviting this early in the morning. Or any time.

Regardless, I can't put off showering anymore even if I wanted to. There's a layer of what I can only call "faire grime" on my skin. Not just dirt, but paints and bonfire smells and, after yesterday, horse. It was totally worth it, but now that I'm smelling myself, I know there's no way Christian would ever invite me to repeat it if he got close enough.

I grab my towel and my little bucket of toiletries and head

toward the showers. They're in a long, narrow building, and to my relief, it's all separate stalls and they're relatively clean. Bonus: I only see one bug, and it's spinning a web on one of the doors that lead outside, not anywhere close to my feet.

When I'm done, gloriously clean and smelling like my favorite rose body wash, I wrap myself in the towel and head back to the tent, smiling. It seems like it might be a great day, much better than yesterday, since I'm not hung over, and with my hair wet, I might be able to do something fun with it for once.

A nail sticking out of the doorframe seems to have other ideas. It catches my towel. There's a horrifying ripping sound and I look down.

About half my towel is gone, shredded apart from the rest of it, so that nothing but fringe hangs down over my thighs.

The curse I let out bounces around the walls of the showers and comes back at me angrily. I try to adjust, moving the towel down slightly so that my butt isn't hanging out in the back, but then the front is *way* too low. I have no other choice but to use one hand to pull down the back, and the other to pull up the front, which bends my body into a misshapen Z and makes me walk like a pigeon. It's not until I step out onto the grass that the magnitude of the situation hits me, full force.

Walking. Pigeon-toed. Almost naked. Across the camp. If there ever was a time to think about a quick cup of mead for courage, this is it.

I take a deep breath, grimace at the indignity of it all, and make toward my tent.

I almost make it to my tent unseen, by some miracle of the Renaissance Faire gods. Almost. But just as I'm entering the clearing the worst possible thing happens, and I mean The Worst.

Christian and Grant are on the path, heading in the direction of breakfast. I don't have time to jump behind a bush or a tree or anything like that, because Grant's already spotted me, calling out my name followed by several chuckles. All I can do is own it. So I straighten myself a bit (but just a bit, otherwise those boys would be getting a real show), and acknowledge them with a nod of my head. "Hey, guys."

Christian purses his lips as if he'd like to laugh but knows better, and Grant says, "I think you might need a new towel."

Christian looks me up and down, and I think I might melt into a pile of embarrassment and shame. Christian catches my eye, and there's a wicked twinkle in his. "I don't know, Grant. I kind of like this towel."

Oh God, please kill me now. Strike me dead.

"Can't complain," Grant says. "Maybe we'll see more of you at breakfast, Ro. Not that there's much left to see . . ."

Because God or the universe or whatever isn't compassionate enough to answer my pleas, all I can do is nod and desperately try to avoid eye contact as they both pass me by. Christian keeps his gaze on me the whole time, so potent that I can feel it on my skin.

Humiliated, I resign myself to a sucky day and pigeon-walk back to my tent.

Thanks to my accidental near–peep show this morning, I'm ten minutes late to the face painting tent. I'm running toward it, unladylike, skirts hiked up and flip-flops obvious, when I catch a flash of shiny auburn hair in the sunlight, the exact shade that has been burned into my brain forever, ever since I saw Kyle twist it around his fingers.

Lacey. It had to be. And unless I'm hallucinating, she was walking with someone, a someone whose hair I'd twisted around my own fingers a time or two.

So many emotions battle inside me that all I can do is stand there in the middle of the busy Renaissance Faire street, utterly useless, completely in shock.

"Ro?" Will's voice is warm but concerned, and I turn to him, full of gratitude. He's ten paces from me but he closes the distance quickly, jogging across the grass. "You okay? Jeff didn't get to you, did he?"

"I'm . . . I'm okay," I lie. Will obviously doesn't believe me because he reaches out and runs a hand along my arm, rubbing some warmth into my clammy skin. "You haven't seen a silver Saab in the parking lot today, have you?"

Will's eyebrows scrunch together. "No. I can keep an eye out if you want. But please tell me what's got you so spooked."

I try to laugh off his concern, but my laugh sounds shallow

and tinny, even to my own ears. "It's nothing. I thought I saw my ex-boyfriend, that's all."

Will's face contorts into an expression that is either confusion or anger, I can't be sure. "I take it you two didn't part on good terms?"

"I think he's here with the girl he cheated on me with."

"Oh." Will squeezes my arm. "I'll definitely look for the Saab and let you know. Want me to slash his tires?"

I force a smile. "Nah. But thanks for offering."

"Any time."

Will pauses, studying me for a moment, his eyes boring deeply enough to see the sadness I've tried in vain to hide there. Then he leaves, off toward the parking lot, and I take a moment to gather myself and tuck away the embarrassment and nerves. When I reach the face painting tent, Cassie looks at me with disapproval and then nods toward the small line of children waiting to get their faces painted. I motion the first one toward my chair and plaster on a bright smile, hoping that painting some kitty whiskers or a Spiderman mask will at least make *someone's* day less sucky.

Late is apparently my theme for the day. I dash into the tavern, almost knocking over a few innocent patrons who had the misfortune to be in my way. Suze is swamped, which makes me feel even guiltier about my tardiness. It's not my fault; an unruly child thought the face painting tent was more a game of war, and put his whole hand in my collection of greens, trying to fingerpaint everything within his grasp. His mortified father tipped me a whole twenty, but I had to scrub my face and hands before my shift at the tavern.

Still, when I see Suze carrying a huge tray full of food and barking at the busboy to help her out, I feel like the rottenest person ever.

She's Suze, though, not Cassie, and she merely gives me a grateful smile and points me toward a table in the corner, mouthing, "Thank you!" at me as I pass by.

I pull out a notepad and pen from my skirt and saunter up to the table. I'm not in the wench groove just yet, so instead of flirting, I try for sass.

"What'll it be?" I ask, marking the table number at the top of a new sheet.

"Ro?"

At the sound of his voice, my heart plummets into my stomach. I lower the notepad, revealing Kyle's familiar face and Lacey's shocked expression.

There's nothing I can do but pretend he's not the boy who made me cry for a week solid, and she's not the reason why he did it. I smile through gritted teeth.

"Hi, Kyle. Lacey."

"You work here?"

No. I just love the stress of waiting on demanding, drunk idiots all day long.

I nod. "Yep. Just started this week. What can I get you?"

"Ro," Kyle says. His voice is cautious, low, and anxious. It's the voice he'd use when we'd had a disagreement and he was trying to make sure I wasn't pissed enough at him to break up.

But that's the thing—Kyle and I only had disagreements, not fights, and he always made sure I was okay. That's a big part of the reason why his cheating was a total shock. Kyle just never seemed like the type.

But it's obvious he's just good at acting. Liars and cheaters need to be, I suppose.

"I didn't know. If I'd have known . . . ," Kyle says, and I glare at him, daring him to finish that sentence.

What? If you'd have known, you wouldn't have paraded your new girlfriend in front of me? You wouldn't have been a total asshole? Just what are you trying to say, Kyle?

"I mean, Brian said Kara was all upset about you working outside the city this summer, but he never mentioned where. I'm so sorry."

I hate that he truly looks like he's sorry.

"Yeah, we didn't know," Lacey says. She doesn't look nearly as earnest as Kyle, but she's just started dating him. Maybe his sleaziness hasn't rubbed off yet. "Kyle just wanted to bring me out for my birthday. He thought it would be fun to see the joust, since I'm such a geek about *Game of Thrones.*"

Lacey likes *Game of Thrones?* Of course she does. It's that weird show Kyle was always trying to get me to watch, raving about how it was the best show ever made. And why is she trying to make conversation? Can she not feel the awkward vibes pouring off me and Kyle? Obviously not, as she continues on, oblivious. "We thought we'd check out the Fairie Queen's Revel in August. Do you know if it's really as fun as everyone says it is?"

"It's fun, yeah," I say, not thinking to lie and tell her it's the worst, most boring party ever so that they won't come. "So what do you want to eat?"

Lacey frowns and looks down at her menu. "Want to split the ribs and fried potatoes?"

"Sure, baby," Kyle replies, then winces, I assume because he's used a term of endearment in front of me. No matter, I winced too.

I write it down and walk away without another word, and instead of going into the kitchen, I signal to Suze and she sets her empty tray aside and meets me behind the bar.

"Emergency," I say to her. My voice is surprisingly steady, considering how much I'm shaking, inside and out. "That's Kyle. With his new girlfriend."

"That jerk," Suze says, and looks over at them, eyes narrowed to slits. "He had the audacity to come in here with *her*?"

"He didn't know," I say, but then I realize I shouldn't be defending him. "Can you just take that table for me?"

"Of course! And I will spit in his food."

I can't help myself, I smile at that. What is it about Renaissance Faire workers that make them so inclined to revenge?

I take Suze's tables, trying hard to keep my back to Lacey and Kyle until they leave, but it's no use. I still see them smiling, laughing with each other, spooning food into each other's mouths. They look so happy. It's salt in the wound, and I have to sniff back a few tears nearly every time I look at them.

When they're getting ready to leave, Suze drags me into the kitchen. Amidst the cooks tossing food to one another and the smoke and rising steam, I can see Ramón glare at us.

"You two, work. Not gossip," he says, irritated, then grumbles something in Spanish.

Suze looks over her shoulder, eyes narrowed at Ramón. "We're in the middle of a crisis, Ramón." Then Suze leans in close so he can't hear. "She's totally not as pretty as you."

I smile at Suze's loyalty and say, "She's prettier."

Suze shrugs. "Only if you go for the vapid, vacant stare type."

I giggle at that, although I'm not sure Lacey qualifies now, not if she geeks out over TV shows with Kyle.

"Who is waiting tables if you two are in here?" Ramón calls. "Crisis is over. Out! Now!"

We both bite down on our lips so we don't laugh, then continue to ignore Ramón. Suze drapes an arm around my shoulders. "You okay?"

"I think so."

"You're okay, she's okay, we're all okay, but there are hungry people out there who are not okay!" Ramón barks. He shovels turkey legs and mashed potatoes onto two plates and holds them out, one for each of us. "Get. Before you make me angry."

I blink at Suze. "This isn't angry?"

"You haven't seen anything yet."

That is apparently the last straw, because Ramón balls his hands into fists and his face turns a violent shade of red. "NOW!" he roars.

Suze and I give Ramón a snappy military salute before scrambling back out into the tavern, which, in spite of everything, puts a smile on my face.

I take my time walking from the tavern to my face painting shift, not caring if Cassie shoots me another dirty look.

Kyle and Lacey left quickly, not dawdling, and for that I was thankful. But I couldn't get the image of the two of them out of my head, sitting there so happily. I don't think I ever saw them quiet when I looked over, as if they always had something to say, and they never stopped smiling.

Out of pity for me—I don't dare call it kindness—they hadn't kissed or anything, at least.

The rest of my shift was a blur. As much as Suze's presence had helped me, it was harder than usual to flirt with the guests. Suze gave me a huge hug as my shift ended and invited me to dinner at her parents' wagon tonight. I was so grateful for the invite that I got a little teary.

I'm just about to lift the tent flaps and face Cassie when a hand clamps down on my shoulder. I gasp and turn around. Jeff.

"I don't believe proper ladies wore flip-flops in the Renaissance . . ."

He scowls down at my feet. My rainbow toes poke out from beneath the folds of my dress. "I know. I need to get some sandals from The Bone Needle, but there hasn't been time."

Jeff holds a hand up in my face to make me stop speaking. The urge to slap it away is so strong that I have to knot my hands together behind my back so I won't. "This is a strike on your record, Rowena."

I can't believe it. Of course Jeff would find me today of all days, just to put icing on the cake of walking through camp nearly naked and seeing my ex with his new girl. Never mind that I see the cooks on their cell phones all the time, or the vendors using calculators, or Cassie pulling out lip balm every other minute.

I screw up my face, wanting to show him my righteous indignation, even if I can't speak it out loud. "Okay. Sorry."

Jeff, unfazed, launches into a lecture about the importance of historical accuracy, and I stand there pretending to listen. Over his know-it-all voice and the angry thoughts in my head, though, there's the hum of a distant melody. It's pretty but unfamiliar, and I can't imagine where it's coming from. It's not the musicians, who are probably parading around the square at the moment. It's too deep and powerful, and it's coming closer.

Leaving Jeff mid-speech, spittle gathering in the corners

of his mouth, I walk around to the other side of the tent, toward the direction of the hum. Cassie comes out the front and stands next to me, barking, "What is that racket?"

I shrug just as the answer comes into view. Rounding the bend where the bridge with the trolls is, about ten men come, all in matching gambesons of red and gold. They each have their lips pressed together, humming louder than it should be possible, and they're coming up the hill, straight toward us.

Jeff steps behind us, sneering. "I suppose one of your boyfriends hired the troubadours. You should know that employee relationships must be filed in my office. As article twelve of the employment agreement states—"

"Shhh," Cassie hisses at Jeff. "They're going to sing."

The troubadours—very dapper-looking gentlemen with toothy smiles—stop humming all at once, at some unseen cue. Then, again from an unseen cue, they all sink down to one knee and hold their arms out in my direction, and it's only then that I understand what's going on. The troubadours are going to sing. For *me*. And if Jeff's right, someone hired them to do so, and I'd bet a hundred dollars I know who hired them.

I giggle, half delighted, half embarrassed, and Cassie's head snaps in my direction.

"What?" she demands.

I shrug and try not to look too proud of myself. "Christian must have sent them. He's so sweet."

Cassie is not nearly as impressed with that as she should

be, but I don't care because one of the troubadours sounds a note on a pitch pipe and suddenly ten strong, beautiful voices are singing to me. It takes me a moment to recognize the lyrics of the old Renaissance tune, but when I do, I blush even more furiously.

"Alas my love you do me wrong to cast me off discourteously," one of them croons, and then another joins in, his tenor overlapping the baritone of the first.

"For I have loved you well and long, delighting in your company," he sings, and then all the troubadours join in, adding layer upon layer of harmony, so pleasing to my ears that it feels like a caress.

"Greensleeves was all my joy, Greensleeves was my delight. Greensleeves was my heart of gold, and who but my lady Greensleeves."

One of the men moves toward me, taking my hand in his and pulling me onto his knee. I gasp and then laugh at myself, then settle in while the man croons to me. Cassie and Jeff watch with expressions of mild disgust, but I don't care. No one has ever sung to me before, and this is definitely baptism by fire. The power of the blush in my cheeks makes my whole face tingly.

But then, as I listen to his strong, slightly operatic voice, the words he's singing level me. I guess I'd never paid much attention to the lyrics of Greensleeves, or I would have realized how heartbreaking they are. The song, which I had merely guessed was a tribute to a girl in green sleeves, much like my own dress today, is actually about unrequited love. The man is pleading for the lady in green to give him a chance and love him.

By the time the troubadours reach the last verse, where the narrator is praying to God that the lady in green will notice him, the troubadour is singing with such longing that I can't help but be moved. My eyes have filled and I have to wipe tears from my cheeks as the troubadours finish with a low bow. I thank them, calling it out as they walk away, and they respond with nods and tips of their hats.

When they've disappeared over the bridge, I turn back to Cassie and Jeff. "That was so beautiful," I say.

Cassie looks bored. "It was okay. I'm going to get back to work." She gives Jeff what can only be called a suck-up smile as she walks by him, and then calls back over her shoulder, "We've been slow this morning so brace yourself. The afternoon is going to be hell."

"Okay, thanks for the warning," I mumble.

Jeff is looking at me, half disgruntled, half like he's trying to figure me out. "Find shoes, Rowena, and remember what I said about filing a report. It's against faire policy to have an undisclosed relationship."

I open my mouth to protest; after all, I wouldn't qualify what Christian and I have as a relationship. Not yet. But Jeff holds up a hand, and I stop myself.

"Please. If someone's sending troubadours to sing 'Greensleeves,' I have to take it seriously."

He walks off, his whole body crouched as if he's stalking the faire, which isn't far from the truth.

Normally, I'd laugh at Jeff's reaction to Christian's song choice, like that particular tune holds some sort of mystic Renaissance symbolism that makes it more important than the others he could have chosen. That said, the words to it have taken root inside me, tugging at all the heartstrings I possess.

Is Christian really feeling so strongly about me? And is he nervous that I won't return those feelings?

That thought gives me a deliciously hopeful feeling, which is great after the day I've had. I doubt anything could bring my mood down now, even the thought of Kyle and Lacey stumbling into the face painting tent.

With a bounce in my step, I head back to work.

10

I step into the stables, trying to keep my footfall as silent as I can so I don't spook the animals. I'm hoping to see Christian so I can thank him for the troubadours, but there's no one but the camel and a few sheep in here, and they give me dull looks before going back to their straw. I'm torn between leaving or hanging around and waiting, and possibly looking desperate while I'm at it.

"Hey, Ro."

I jump at Sage's voice as she comes in, Big Red trailing behind her.

"Hey," I say to Sage and try to act like I'm in the stables every day, nothing out of the ordinary. "How was the joust?"

She grins wide, making her look like she's about twelve years old. "Great. I won. Got to knock old man Richard off his horse."

I watch as Sage puts her horse in the stall and untacks his saddle. If she's back, Christian should be here soon. Hopefully.

"Waiting on someone?" Sage asks me when she's done. There's a hint of mischief in her eyes, the same as I saw when she handed over her cards to me at the bonfire, and I know she's trying to get me to admit why I'm here.

"Oh, well, not really. I just . . . like the animals," I fib because I can't let her win. I'm too stubborn for that.

"Do you ride?" I glance at her horse, and I must have looked fearful enough that Sage knows the answer. She laughs. "I can teach you if you want."

"That's okay," I say, forceful and, I hope, final.

She blinks, then there's a slow smile as she pushes me more. "It's easy. And relaxing. You'd love it."

I stare at her, hating that she's calling my bluff, but trapped regardless. "I guess I could use some relaxation."

"Thatta girl," Sage says, and smacks her horse's butt. I detest the triumphant look in her eyes when she adds, "I'll take Big Red here, but how about we start with a pony for you?"

"That's fine," I can't help but grumble, and soon Sage has a peanut butter–colored pony saddled up for me. Sage tells me how to get on the horse by swinging my leg over its back, which is undignified and unladylike in my skirt and flip-flops. My skirt scrunches around my thighs and my feet look strange in the stirrups with the flip-flops on, and I'm positive this is the most ridiculous I've looked since arriving at the faire.

Sage stands back, inspecting, lips twitching. "Okay, so mental note . . . wear jeans or pants next time, got it? And an actual shoe. Boots if you can. Don't want your foot to slip through the stirrup, or worse, lose a shoe out on the trail."

I sigh. "Sure."

"This is Jiffy, the sweetest pony we have. He's used to kids riding him so he pretty much follows the path, but we'll get him on a gallop out in the field and let him cut loose for a while." Sage climbs onto her horse like the pro she is, making me feel completely inadequate, and frumpy to boot. Tomboy or not, on a horse, Sage looks cute and sassy, her back straight and a confident air about her. I look like what I am: a girl who doesn't want to be there, on a horse for the first time ever.

But then Jiffy lets out a soft whinny and turns his head back, making eye contact with one of his huge horsey eyes. He looks kind of sweet, truth be told, so I reach out and pet his long neck and as a reward for my effort, he whinnies again.

"Aww, you've made a friend," Sage coos, and it's as if at least for that moment, we've both forgotten this whole thing is a ruse.

I pat Jiffy's neck and smile at Sage. "So how do I make him go?"

"Just a little kick in his ribs." At my horrified face, Sage laughs. "A gentle one! You don't have to kick hard. Think of it as a small poke to get his attention."

Sage demonstrates and Big Red starts out of the stables,

leaving me with no choice but to kick Jiffy (gently!) in the ribs. The pony lazily begins to walk, following Big Red as if he knows that horse is the leader and his job is only to follow.

As we pass through the doors and the sunshine hits my face, I have to admit, this might be fun. That happy thought slams on its brakes in my head, though, when I see Christian riding up the hill toward us. I look down at myself, skirts hiked up and rainbow toes bright and obnoxious. Great.

Oh well. He saw more of me this morning, and I think this might be the less embarrassing of the two scenarios.

Sage calls out to him and I give a feeble little wave in his direction. He rides up to us, and Jiffy backs away a little, as if he's intimidated by Blaze.

"Going riding?" he asks, looking at me and not Sage.

"She wants to learn," Sage answers anyway, and Christian keeps his gaze on me.

"Oh, really?"

I can only hope my blush doesn't call my bluff. "Yeah. So Sage said she'd teach me."

"Well, don't let Jiffy run off on you. He's a wild one," Christian says, smirking, and with a swift kick to Blaze's ribs, he's gone.

"Dang, he's got a nice backside," Sage whispers, leaning forward on her horse to get a better view as Christian rides off. She settles back in her saddle and winks at me, daring me one last time to come clean with my reason for being in the stables. When I don't, she shrugs. "Let's get going. The trail's long."

As soon as Jiffy and I reach the path, I'm glad I bluffed and Sage took me along. Even just a few steps in, the path is quieter than the rest of the faire, more peaceful, even. The trees are thicker here, the density blocking out the sounds of the Renaissance instruments, the children yelling, and the crowds clapping at Patsy and Quagmire's show. It's cooler too, somehow, and the many layers of my dress don't seem as constricting.

The path is narrow, considering that it's meant for horses, and between the quiet and the steady sway of Jiffy, I find all my stress left over from the day fading away. The towel incident, seeing Kyle and Lacey, being zinged by Jeff—I just breathe and let my mind wander, enjoying the flickering sun as it darts between the leaves, the steady thump of hooves on the dry ground, and the sweet, clean air.

Sage doesn't talk much. She tells me to pull out on Jiffy's reins if I want him to turn, and to pull back on them if I want him to stop, but for the most part Jiffy just follows Big Red, and Sage seems to be as lost in the nature around us as I am.

When we loop around and come back into the faire grounds, I'm sad it's over, and I tell Sage so.

"Best way to relax around here," Sage says to me, wise and proud. "I'm glad you liked it. If you want to go some other time . . . ?"

"Sure!" I find myself agreeing, and we spend the next few minutes untacking our horses in the same congenial silence we shared on the ride. Sage slips out the doors before I can thank her, which is just as well. It probably would have embarrassed both of us, and I've got to head straight to Suze's parents' place for dinner. The ride took longer than I thought and there's no time for a shower.

I look down at myself. There's horse hair on my skirt and my toes are caked with dirt, plus I'm pretty sure the smell of the horse is clinging to both my dress and my skin. I may not mind the smell of the stables *in* the stable, but outside of it . . . let's just say that eau de Jiffy is not pleasant.

So much for a good impression with Suze's family.

Suze told me her parents live on the very edge of the faire property, in a little corner they have all to themselves because they've been involved with the faire for so long. "Lifers," I'd heard both Suze and Will call them. Which meant Suze was a lifer too and the faire was her natural habitat.

I follow the written instructions Suze scrawled on a napkin at the tavern, which says simply, "Go to the edge of the village and follow the wall through the forest until you reach the corner." It seems simple enough, but after I step off the main road and start into the forest, time seems to slow to a crawl. If I wasn't following the fence line, I'd have figured I was walking in circles. All the trees and the rocks look the same; heck, I even pass two identical wooden bridges, small and almost useless, save for getting you over the tiniest trickle of a creek.

When I finally see the Mulligan family home in the distance, I have to wonder if I've somehow been following the wrong wall.

The Mulligan's home is a wagon. I was picturing an RV, maybe even a trailer like Jeff's, but this is an honest to goodness wagon, the kind you might have seen a hundred years ago that traveled in the circuses. It's huge, like the caboose of a train and just as sturdy, and it's painted a luxurious deep red, with fancy gold, fading lettering on the side that reads, MULLIGAN'S FANTASTICAL CREATURES. All of that is made even more lovely by soft white Christmas lights that tangle in gently glowing icicles from the top and sides. I guess since this is a residence and it's way off the beaten path of tourists, Jeff doesn't mind the generator that hums quietly in the back.

Suze steps out onto the stair that hangs down from the front door. "You found us!"

"Suze, this place is awesome! It looks like a gypsy caravan or a circus wagon."

Suze swings out, looking at the wagon herself. "Yeah, they did a circus once, but Dad was really upset over the way they treated their animals, so they went back to the Ren Faire circuit really quickly."

I blink at her. "You're serious, aren't you?"

"Very."

"I love it."

"I'm glad," Suze says, clearly amused that I'm so enthralled. "So do you want to go in or just stand outside staring?"

I roll my eyes at her impatience and hoist myself into the wagon. The first thing I do, after being introduced to Suze's dad, Peter, is apologize to everyone for smelling like a horse.

"Eh, nothing to it," Peter says, waving me off. "Nine days out of ten, I come home covered in bird poop. We're no strangers to animal smells around here."

The inside of the wagon is small but tidy, with just enough room for Peter to stand without bumping his head. A table with chairs sits in the corner, right next to the smallest stove I've ever seen. There's a bed with velvety embroidered pillows piled on it, and in between there's a row of shelves with drawers at the bottom. Books about animal training and costume-making are displayed, but I also notice a lot of classics: Dickens, Brontë, Hugo, the complete works of Shakespeare, some children's favorites like *Peter Pan* and *The Little Prince* in French. Propping up some of these books and other knickknacks, like a large brass compass, are Lindy's dolls and a few hand-carved trolls, much like the one I saw on the post that led me to the faire.

I'm about to inquire if Peter whittled them when Lindy takes the top off a pot that's boiling on the stove and releases steam that smells so good my mouth waters. "I hope you're not a vegetarian, dear."

"Never. I'd die without cheeseburgers," I say, and Suze laughs.

"Just don't feed her any turkey legs, Mom. I thought she was going to hurl when that group of guys ordered a dozen of them today and sat there chewing with their mouths open."

I wince just thinking about it. "That was so nasty."

Lindy laughs. "Don't worry. No turkey legs. Strict rule in

the Mulligan cabin: no faire food. I made my famous chili."

"*My* famous chili," Peter corrects, wrapping his arms around her from behind. She turns and kisses him on the mouth before stirring the contents of the pot. "The whole thing was my idea."

"Nonsense. You added more jalapeños, that's it," Lindy says. When Peter reaches over to swipe a bean from her wooden spoon, she bats his hand away playfully and he pouts, prompting her to give him another kiss.

They're sweet, and for two adults, they're obviously still as in love as they were when they were teenagers. It's so unlike my household and my parents. It's not as if my parents don't love each other, but they're never affectionate, at least not in front of me.

I watch as Lindy dips her spoon back into the chili, emerges with a decent-size bite, and blows on it to cool it down before feeding it to her husband. I look over at Suze, smiling, but she just rolls her eyes. It's clear she's not irritated, though. The expression on her face is too warm and happy. I'm a little jealous that this is how she grew up, with affectionate parents and a cool wagon and a life half lived in fairy tale. I'm also a little jealous of how in love Lindy and Peter are. I never quite felt that way with Kyle, but I thought I was close. Maybe it would have happened if he hadn't cheated.

Someday, I tell myself. *Maybe sooner than you think.*

We tuck in around the table and the chili is served (just the right amount of kick, I think, and I make a point to tell

Peter so), and for nearly two hours the conversation doesn't stop. Lindy tells me about the first time she saw Peter at the Austin, Texas, Renaissance Faire, nearly twenty years ago, how he was only an apprentice back then and she bandaged his finger when one of his hawks got surly. I learn about how Peter worked his way up from apprentice to overseeing his own menagerie, and they tell me how Suze was almost born in this very wagon, but a friend let them borrow their car to get to the hospital and it was a stick shift that Peter couldn't drive, so she was born in the car instead. Suze talks about an interesting girl she met at the tavern today who works for rock bands doing pyrotechnics, and, after dessert and a glass of cold mead, I share the story of how I walked scantily clad from the showers to the tents this morning, making Peter laugh so hard that he nearly chokes on his bite of strawberry shortcake.

At the end of the evening, Peter and Lindy both hug me and make me promise to come by for supper again soon. I thank them, once again astounded at their generosity, before Suze and I waddle home.

We flop down on our beds, exhausted and with bellies full of good food. I want nothing more than to fall blissfully asleep, but before I do, something soft lands on me, almost covering my entire body. Pulling it off me, I hold out the object for inspection.

"It's a bathrobe, genius," Suze chides as I stare blankly at it. "Please borrow it until we can get you into town to buy your own. As much as Grant and Christian probably enjoyed it, I'd rather not see you stumbling through camp buck naked, thank you very much."

I give her a sardonic look but thank her anyway, laying the bathrobe out between our two air mattresses. Then I roll over on my side and watch her as she braids her hair. She always puts it into one long braid before sleeping, just to keep it tame until she braids it again for work in the morning.

"So, regardless of the towel incident and Kyle, the day wasn't a total loss. I think Christian sent me the troubadours."

Suze sits up dramatically, flailing in her surprise. "What? And you've been holding this juicy little chunk of information from me all day long? *Spill it*."

I do, telling her about the song Christian chose, what the troubadours did, and Jeff's overreaction. I even mention Cassie's complete indifference.

"Oh, well, Cassie . . . ," Suze starts, but doesn't finish.

"Cassie what?" I say, reaching over to poke Suze in the knee. "What about her?"

"She had a thing with Christian is all," Suze says, and I can tell she's trying to make her tone light. "That's it. Fairemance. They were a thing, and then the season ended and it fizzled out."

I prod her for more. "Are you sure? There's nothing between them now?"

"Please. If there was, she'd be parading him around the village square. She'd probably rent the billboard off the highway to proclaim it. Trust me, she definitely made sure everyone knew about them last summer." Suze's lips scrunch together all duck-like, and she makes a "pfft" sound dismissively. "You've got nothing to worry about."

"Good," I say, crawling under my blanket. "Because Lacey said she and Kyle are going to the Revel."

"Then it will be just tragic for him when he sees you on the arm of a hot knight."

"My thoughts exactly." I snuggle as deep into the air mattress as its inflation level will allow. "Good night, Suze, you saucy wench."

"Good night, fair Rowena. Sleep well."

11

The next morning at breakfast I arrive bright-eyed, bushy-tailed, and clean. The shower this morning was glorious—warm and long, and when I went back to the tent I was dressed in Suze's bathrobe, completely covered up.

I help myself to Ramón's bacon and a waffle, and park myself at Will's table, since Suze is spending some time with Grant and Christian isn't there. Will pushes a bottle of maple syrup toward me and I thank him before pouring a healthy dose on my waffle. Except for Ramón, the group is engaged in conversation, rapid and energetic, despite the earliness of the hour.

Quagmire and Patsy are the loudest of all and I have to wonder how long their argument has been escalating. The debate seems to be about horror movies and the quantity of blood needed to make them scary, but I don't get to hear much more because suddenly Will butts in.

"I don't know," Will says while forking sausage into his mouth. He doesn't bother chewing and swallowing before saying very seriously to Quagmire, "Patsy's right. I think that really, nothing beats a good Hitchcock."

"See?" Patsy says, as if Will's support is the deciding factor. "Hitchcock relied on mystery and tension. Not chainsaws and screaming teenage girls."

"Terrible taste, the whole lot of you," Quagmire mutters. "Especially you, Indy."

"Aww, sore loser," Will chides and bites into his sausage, chewing triumphantly, and Patsy beams while Quagmire scrapes the scrambled eggs around on his plate, sulking quietly.

I take the moment of reprieve to poke the prongs of my fork into Will's hand. He turns back to me, scowling. "Hey. That hurt."

"You're such a baby. It did not."

"Okay, no, but you got syrup on me."

"Whatever," I say. "Why do they call you Indy?"

Will raises his hand to his mouth and licks, and it's kind of cute the way his pink tongue darts out in search of the sticky syrup. He's wearing his glasses again, and he adjusts them as if stalling. "I'm not just the parking lot attendant. I do other things here."

"What other things?"

Davis leans across Will so that I can hear him. "He's a whip cracker."

"A whip cracker? What's that?"

Davis and Will both mime flicking a whip, and make the "whip-pash!" sound effect to go along with it.

I'm still not following. "Like, with the horses?"

"Ha. No. The knights would kill him if he got near their precious horses with that thing," Davis says, and Will shrugs. I can't tell if he's smug or embarrassed that we're talking about him.

"I do a show. Whip tricks. Hence, Indy. Indiana Jones."

I nod as if I understand. "So you just . . . whip things? In your show?"

Will waves his fork. "Nah. It's more than that. Flicking things out of my assistant's hands. Swinging from it. That sort of thing. There's fire and stuff."

"Fire?" I eye him, not sure how to reconcile the unassuming Will I know with a person who knows how to wield a whip on fire. "How on earth did you get into that?"

"It's a Fuller family talent. My dad cracked the whip, and his dad before him. I guess you could say I come by it honestly."

"He's funny, Ro," Patsy adds from across the table. "Hilarious. I can't believe you haven't seen his show yet."

"He never told me about it," I say to her, shaming Will

some in the process. I add for good measure, "Maybe he didn't want me to see it."

"I want you to see it," Will says softly. "My stage is close to your tent, actually. I do shows at the odd-numbered hours."

Now that he's mentioned it, I remember hearing cracks off in the distance, but I always thought it was the little snapping fireworks they sell in the toy shop, and that certainly explains why he walks through the kids' section frequently.

"Well, I'm coming to see you today," I tell him in a tone that means he's not getting out of it.

"Looking forward to it," Will says, but it doesn't have his usual swagger, and I have to wonder if he really means it.

Cassie's in the tavern today, leaving me on my own, which I've decided is my new favorite thing. When she's not around, I don't feel any obligation to stick to the B.A.B., and I do things the way I want. I even clean the brushes the way I want, taking my time to rinse out every little bristle and hum along with the distant minstrels while I do it.

Today a boy wanders in, probably not more than six years old. His older brother has clearly been given the task of escorting him into the tent and looks as bored as can be, tugging on the child's hand as if to lead him out of the tent.

"Come on, Colin. Let's go see the sword fighters or something," his brother urges, but the younger boy looks absolutely miserable at the thought of leaving my tent. His eyes are wide as he looks around, taking in all the Polaroids I've taken of my previous customers, the B.A.B., which lies open on Cassie's station, and the rows and rows of paints.

"Do you like the colors?" I ask him, and he turns to me, sucking in a breath as if he's been caught doing something terrible. I give him my softest, friendliest smile, and he timidly returns it. "Which color is your favorite?"

He doesn't give me a verbal answer, but he points toward a fantastically bright fuchsia.

His brother snorts. "Of course you'd like pink . . ."

I wish sometimes that looks could kill, because this child's brother would have keeled over right then from the cold stare I give him. I smile at the child again. "That's fuchsia. Do you want me to use that color?"

The boy nods, much to the chagrin of his brother, and I pat the chair opposite me. The boy is so small that his feet don't touch the ground beneath us.

"What would you like to be?"

Again, the boy doesn't use words but points instead at the painting hanging above Cassie's station. It's a dragon of the Chinese variety, and it's incredibly detailed and gorgeous. The name scribbled at the bottom says "Janet." When I'd read that, I'd sighed a huge sigh of relief that it was my predecessor and not Cassie who had painted such a marvelous creature.

"Okay," I say, and as his brother grumbles something about

how at least the kid chose a cool animal, I vow to do my best. I pick up my thickest brush and get to work painting his whole face fuchsia. "I'm Ro. What's your name?"

"Colin," he says, his voice just as small and timid as he is. "I'm six and a half."

"I'm seventeen and three-quarters," I say back, which earns me a surprised grin. "You want big scales and scary eyes?"

He looks unsure, so I lean close to his ear and whisper, "Maybe you could scare your brother if you had scary eyes."

Colin nods emphatically, but presses his lips together tight, making sure it's just our little secret.

By the time I'm finished with him, I've used not just the fuchsia but some purples, blues, and golds to make some shaded scales, and his eyes come out to dark black points almost above his ears. It's similar to an idea I saw in the B.A.B., but with an Asian twist and a lot of color and detail. I stand back and admire it before taking a Polaroid. It's really good, even if it's my own work and I'm probably biased. I've never done anything quite that intricate, especially not on a face, and I've managed to make him look both fierce and beautiful.

I feel puffed up with pride, and when I show Colin the Polaroid, I can tell he feels the same way. He holds it in his small hand, smiling at the fierce creature he sees as the gray image darkens into color. I want him to remember this feeling for a long time, so when he tries to hand the picture back

I tell him to keep it and snap another picture of him. He's smiling in this shot, all that pride coming out in one giant, crooked grin.

His brother hastily hands me a ten, wanting to get a move on, but even he seems astounded when Colin turns to show him. He quickly recovers from his shock and grumbles, "Dad's gonna hate that."

Colin doesn't say thank you to me as his brother pulls him out of the tent, but the shy wave and that giant grin are all the thanks I need.

Cassie was not pleased when I excused myself hurriedly for a break at five till three and dashed out of the tent while tossing a careless, "Going to Will's show. Sorry if I'm not back in twenty!" over my shoulder. I could feel her dislike for me burning a hole in my back as I scurried down the hill, in the opposite direction from the stables, but I don't care. There's no way I'm going to miss this.

There's a small crowd gathered around a stage that can't be more than fifteen feet long. The curtains look like a few canvases woven together, very homespun, and in pointed calligraphy, the title of the show is written large and looming:

WHIP CRACKER JACQUES

I don't know whether to groan or chuckle.

The crowd is decent: definitely smaller than the number of people you see at the jousting match, but a whole lot more than the acrobats and Patsy and Quagmire manage to pull together, combined. There's a large group of preteen girls gathered by the edge of the stage, whispering to one another, several men who look like they mistook the faire for a Viking festival, and some young boys who are playing with the toy weapons they must have just purchased. One of them, I can see, has bought a whip.

When the curtains open and Will steps out onstage, I'm glad the audience cheers and claps because I'm a little too dumbstruck to do anything myself.

Will has combed his hair down with what looks like a metric ton of gel (how does Jeff let that go?), and it's slicked back and up like a pompadour. He's also pencilled in a hilariously fake mustache, the handlebar variety, with the ends curling tightly like scrolls. Someone offstage tosses him a whip, which he unfurls with great flair and then launches into a story about how he, Jacques, came all the way from "old Paree" to be with us today. His accent is over-the-top fake, and he plays up the French snob act. He sees me standing in the back, and although he doesn't break character, the ends of his mustache rise up with a slight smile.

But then he starts a sequence of whipping and fancy foot-work that is a complete contrast to his goofy persona, skilled and precise. He takes aim at a beam that holds the curtains up and swings himself, in true Indiana Jones style, out over the audience and to the other side of the stage. Then he daringly cracks the whip at various targets, getting progressively harder until he finally whips an apple off of a volunteer's head.

And during all these dangerous feats, he tosses out clever jokes so quickly that if you don't listen up, you'll miss a chuckle.

I listen. I'm giggling like a maniac by the time he asks for someone from the audience who might want to learn how to crack a whip.

I'm pleased when Will selects the boy standing close to me who bought a whip from the toy store, and asks his father to come up as well. The boy clambers up onto the stage, so excited that he's bouncing when he stands next to Will.

Will does this whole routine where Jacques insists the boy will be able to, on the first try, knock an apple off his father's head with the whip. The dad gets really into acting scared of being accidentally whipped and not believing Jacques's comical reassurances that since he is the best whip cracker in the world, so are his pupils.

"I assure you, zere ees no way 'e will fail with my ex-*pert* guidance," Jacques says, the father shaking his head exaggeratedly back and forth. Jacques tries to make the father sit still, and twice the father scrambles up to leave and Jacques has to race after him and drag him to the chair.

"You must trust Jacques," he says to the father with a flourish of his hand. "Ze best whip cracker in ze world. Only three people 'ave ever died on my stage. Ze odds are good, no?"

Before the father can protest any further, Jacques sets the apple on his head and hands a whip to the boy.

The joke is that the boy's whip is too short to reach the

father, but behind him, Will flicks his own whip and knocks the apple straight off, and the boy thinks he's done it. The crowd cheers and applauds as he bows, and then Will begins the second part of his show—with flames.

It's mesmerizing to watch the blue-orange flames of the whip dance around Will as the slightest movements from his hand control it. He's precise but smooth, and he begins to move with the whip, in and around it, so I can't tell if he's dancing around the whip or it's dancing around him. It's all so fluid that my brain can barely comprehend that he and the whip are separate beings; the whip seems merely an extension of him, some rare kind of magic he was born with.

The audience oohs and ahhs, and I find myself doing it as well. Then, with one final flaming flourish and several campy bows that would have made a diva look reasonable, Will disappears behind the curtain again.

Unlike the rest of the crowd, which scatters to the far ends of the faire, I walk directly behind the stage and duck, without hesitation, behind the ropes. Will is sitting on the stairs, laughing with a small crowd of boys with toy whips. He's still in character, using his French accent, and when he sees me he winks at the boys and says, "Oui, all ze ladies love Jacques. You want a pretty girl? Zen whip cracking is ze job for you, yes? Go and practice and remember what ze great Cracker Jacques said: Eet eez all in ze wrist!"

Will and I watch as the boys scamper off, shouting to one another about how cool Jacques is. When they're out of sight,

Will picks up a small mirror and starts to wipe off his mustache.

"Eyebrow pencil?" I ask, and Will makes a sound of agreement. "Eye makeup remover or Vaseline would work better."

"Vaseline? Really?"

"Yeah, it works great. It always makes me break out, though," I say, then wonder why I decided to bring up my acne problems with him. Gross. I add hastily, "You know, I could paint a much better mustache for you, if you wanted."

Will stops fussing with the mirror and paper towel and looks at me, expression surprised and soft. "I'd like that," he says, then laughs a bit. "As long as it's not realistic. Part of the joke is how fake Jacques is."

"Oh, I can make you a fantastically fake mustache," I promise. I clear my throat and add, "Jacques is rather funny. Really funny, actually."

Will sets down the paper towel and mirror and asks, with a note of uncertainty that seems very un-Will to me, "Did you really like it?"

"Yeah," I say. "I mean, it's funny, and it's a great act, but beside that I was super impressed with all the whip stuff. I didn't realize it was so . . . artistic."

He nods, emphatic, and I know I've said exactly the right thing. "The flame part? It's my favorite. I wrote that whole sequence myself, and it took a lot of time to get it right. I had to practice it for months so I wouldn't burn myself in the process. It's all just very precise physics, you know? Every move an equation so that the snap comes at exactly the right second, and the flames have a moment to breathe so they won't go out. I'm considering doing my dissertation on the physics of whip cracking. You know, if I make it beyond undergrad."

Will squeezes his eyes shut and pinches the bridge of his nose. "I'm sorry. I can't shut up about it once I get going . . ."

"It's okay, I get that," I reassure him. "Ask me about my art and I'd do the same."

"I'll have to remember that." Will's gaze captures mine. "Do you think about it all the time? Dream about it when you sleep?"

I think for a moment, adding up all these moments in my life: moments of practicing my lines and shading, of thinking about how to change designs or capture things I see around me on a canvas, of the way my hands seem to always be longing to hold a paintbrush. All together, the sum is pretty staggering.

"Yes, actually," I tell him, more than a little surprised.

"Me too. All the time." Will pauses, then corrects himself. "About physics, not art, of course. Why aren't you majoring in art, again?"

"It's just not an option in the Duncan household," I admit, though I have no idea why I'm telling him that, because my parents haven't ever said that to me. Not in those exact words. But my father's been obsessed with me going to his alma mater for as long as I can remember, and when I asked for private art lessons two years ago, they decided it was a waste of money. That was all the answer I needed, and that's why I can't even consider art as a career choice.

The look he gives me is so full of pity that I turn away for a second to gather myself. Then, as a distraction, I pick up the paper towel he was using and sit next to him. He takes the hint and turns his face toward me, and I run the paper towel gently over his skin, wiping away the last traces of his mustache. "So how many times did you burn yourself learning that routine?"

"Only a few hundred," Will says. "No biggie."

"Of course not. First-degree burns? Child's play," I say, nudging his knee with my own. "Seriously, I was impressed. I can't believe you didn't tell me to come watch the first day."

Will doesn't respond to that, but cocks his head at me. He's still really close to me, his face mere inches from my own. His brown eyes are bright with the mischief I'm used to seeing from him, and for the first time I notice that they have little gold flecks in them, all around his pupils, like the bottom of a miner's pan after a good haul.

"So, Cracker Jacques, want to teach me a few tricks so I can keep the unruly tavern patrons in line?"

Will laughs. "Sure, I could teach you a few tricks, if you want."

"I'd love that." I wad up the paper towel and hand it to him. "And I'm holding you to that mustache."

He snorts at that, then we both get quiet. I sit there stupidly, not sure of what else I can say, but then the bell tower dings once, long and somberly, and I realize I've been away from the face painting tent for a whole half hour. "Shoot. I'd better go or Cassie will give birth to dragons."

"Now that I'd like to see," Will says. "Thanks for coming."

"Thanks for finally inviting me, Jacques. See you later." I bump my knee into his again before I go, and he bumps mine back with a shy laugh.

"Bye, Rainbow Ro."

12

WEEK 1—FRIDAY

The afternoon passes in a pleasant blur after that, one nice thing blending into the other.

I spend the rest of my shift painting well-behaved children's faces without incident, using some of the B.A.B.'s ideas to work from, but adding my own personal touch.

A small group of boys wander in at some point, rambunctious and hyped up on sugar and all the awesome things they've seen at the faire. They look to be around ten years old, and though I wonder where their parents are, I don't blame them at all for letting the boys roam around so they can have some time on their own.

Cassie takes two and I take two, and maybe I'm biased, but they're the best two I could have chosen. The first boy, who has bought a wooden replica of Richard's sword (Richard must have won the championship today), wants the royal crest on his cheek, and thank goodness I am a good faire worker and memorized the brochure like Will suggested. Although his cheek is a small surface area to work with for such a detailed design, when I show the finished product to him in the mirror, he reacts by exclaiming, "Whoa! Guys, check this out! It's even got a dragon on it!" and the boys clamor around him, agreeing about its awesomeness.

When the second boy sits down, I ask him if he wants the same. I'm relieved and wholeheartedly approve when he tells me he wants a mustache like Jacques.

"Did you like Jacques?" I ask, and all of the boys answer.

"He was so cool!"

"Did you see how big the flames got?"

"I bet I could swing on a whip like that . . ."

I smile down at the boy in my chair and grab a thin brush and some brown paint. "I like Jacques too. He's funny."

The boy nods and lets me paint the scrolling mustache on him. He looks kind of like a mini Will when I'm done with him.

When Cassie and I are done with the boys and they've paid, I sit back in my chair, satisfaction coursing through me. I wonder if Will has any idea how his performances affect people, or really, if any of the performers realize. Richard's obviously affected that kid today, and my first day, Grant's did the same to the child who wanted to be a badger. It's fascinating and so cool to see these kids react, imagine, and dream.

I have to wonder if my face painting has the same effect,

and my mind drifts naturally to the boy earlier with his fuchsia dragon. I loved seeing him smile, loved giving him something his older brother's harsh words couldn't take away. Maybe my art can inspire people, just like the knights' performances, just like Will's. Maybe my art can change people, or help them see things about themselves, or help them heal. It's a gratifying thought, but heavy at the same time. To think I could do something that could change someone, even if it's just temporarily making their day a little brighter, is a mind-blowing thing. There's a lot of responsibility in that. The troubadours changed my mood almost instantly yesterday, and to have that kind of effect on people is a gift.

The thought of the troubadours brings me back to reality. I still haven't thanked Christian for that, so as soon as my shift is over, I head down to the stables.

Thankfully, Christian's there, untacking his horse. Unfortunately, Richard and Grant are also there, but it doesn't matter. All I can think about is Christian and the last time we were in the stables together. The memory of his hand over mine, brushing the horse's soft coat, is enough to make my insides heat up like mead on a chilly summer night.

"Hey," he says simply when he sees me, and that heat inside me gets a little warmer.

"Hey," I say back. I rub Blaze's muzzle and get a soft whinny of gratitude in response. "Thanks for yesterday, Christian."

"Yesterday? What was yesterday?"

"Just . . . you know, the troubadours. It was a completely

awful day. You have no idea how much it cheered me up."

Christian looks at me strangely, as if I'm speaking another language or maybe I've got a piece of spinach caught in my teeth. "The troubadours?"

"The troubadours," I say louder, like that might help. I reach over and squeeze his forearm, which is delightfully muscular. "You know . . ."

"Oh, uh, sure," he says, half laughing. "I'm glad it made you feel better."

"It really did." I smile at him. "So, what are you up to?"

Christian looks over at Blaze's stall. "I've got to do some squire training right now. The little boys need to be shown how to ride with a lance. Hopefully, we'll knight one of them before the season's out."

"You actually knight them?"

"Well, no. Not me. King Geoffrey. But yeah, we love our ceremonies here, fake as they are. Besides, if a guy goes through enough training to pull off our stunts, he deserves a title." Christian reaches up and brushes a rogue curl from my cheek. It's not a sexy move, not like the other day when he was wrapped all around me, his mouth pressed to my ear, but it's so intimate that it makes me dizzy. "Will I see you at the campfire Sunday?"

I completely forgot that campfires were a weekly thing, but thank goodness they are. A campfire means another chance to hang out with Christian, and hopefully this time he'll kiss me.

"Of course," I tell him. "I had a great time at the last one."

Christian gives a slight nod. "Unfortunately, this one is officially sanctioned, so . . . best behavior and all that."

"Well, I'd love to go, even if I have to be on my best behavior," I say quickly.

"Me too," Christian says, and then his voice dips low. "Maybe we'll misbehave a little anyway?"

He doesn't wait for my answer. Probably because he already knows what it is. He slides his fingers over my hair as he passes on his way out the door, giving me goose bumps, and in response I make a hideous gurgling noise that I pray he doesn't hear. I walk out of the stables, trying hard not to capture the attention of Richard and Grant, who, thankfully, are too involved with what they're doing to notice my presence.

It's only been a few days at this place and already I'm so filled with news and secrets that I might explode if I keep them all bottled up. And although Suze has been great to talk to, I desperately need to spill my guts to Kara and Meg. Nearly a week has gone by without hearing from them or talking to them, and not knowing if they're still pissed at me. It's like I'm homesick for them and only them because, in truth, I haven't missed my actual home much. This place easily settled into that void. But Kara and Meg? Irreplaceable.

I need to make a phone call that's long overdue, and even though it's almost time for the faire to close, I don't want to risk being caught by Jeff. That leaves me with only one choice:

It's time for a little road trip.

• • •

It only takes me a few minutes to throw on some modern clothes and pack my purse with my phone, phone charger, keys, and a few dollars. I tell Suze what I'm up to, and she promises to squirrel away some dinner for me. In return, I vow to bring her something tasty from Starbucks.

Soon I'm in my car, phone plugged into the charger, the radio cranked to the first modern music I've heard in what feels like forever. After only a few minutes, though, the never-ending beat grates on my nerves, and by the time I've pulled out onto the country road that leads to the faire, I've switched the music off. I guess after only a week I've gotten used to the quiet of the campgrounds, and the melodious, calming music played by the lutes. It's kind of a scary thought that I've adapted so fast, but at the same time it makes me smile. Maybe the remote community of artists suits me even better than I'd hoped.

Suze had given me directions into the nearest town, a small place called Sugar Grove, which is short on stoplights but long on everything we might need. It has a Starbucks inside the lone supermarket, a strip mall where the faire workers sometimes get their hair cut at a salon chain, a laundromat, a Target, and a dollar store.

As soon as I reach the town, I recognize it: It's where Suze took me to get the air mattress my first night. We'd been too busy gabbing for me to note the town's name, or even notice much of what was around me. I smile at that, thinking about how we were instantly friends.

When I pull into the supermarket parking lot, the miraculous happens: My phone gets service. Texts ding in, so long withheld, one right after another. It's so fast that it sounds like Morse code. They're all from Meg and Kara, about twenty of them total.

I read them as I walk into the market, slowly, savoring each one as precious contact and connection to the best friends I've had since elementary school.

Kara Tuesday 8:43am: I'm so sorry. I know you're still sick over Kyle. I shouldn't have said anything.

Meg Tuesday 9:29am: Ro, answer me, dammit. Kara's a mess that you're fighting.

Kara Tuesday 12:03pm: Are you still angry? I hate fighting. I don't know how to fight with you! We don't fight!

There are a few more messages from earlier in the week, pleading with me to get in touch as soon as I can. Guilt wells up inside me over that. Then, the messages continue.

Meg Wednesday 5:40pm: OMG RO. Is it true? Did Kyle go to your Renaissance thingy? Did you see him? Was he with that awful freshman chick?

Kara Wednesday 5:42pm: Ro . . . I'm so sorry! I didn't know Kyle and Lacey were planning on going to the Renaissance Faire. Ugh, you didn't see them, did you? I would have told them the whole place was infested with fleas if I'd known they were going.

I find the Starbucks inside the market, order an iced tea

to beat the heat and a giant Rice Krispies treat to satisfy my sweet tooth, and find a seat at a round table by the window. I hit number one on my speed dial and Kara answers.

"ROWENA DUNCAN!"

I laugh. "I've missed you!"

"ME TOO!"

Excitement isn't quite the reason why Kara's yelling, although I can tell she's psyched that we're talking. There's loud music in the background on her end, the syncopated thump-tha-thump of a deep bass line, and voices shouting and laughing. "Are you at a party?"

"WHAT? YEAH." There's some rustling, a thunk, and the music dies down a little, like perhaps Kara's either gone into another room or she's outside. When she speaks again, it's with a much calmer voice. "We're at Sylvia Reynolds's place by the beach."

The beach. Where I could have been with them as much as we wanted all summer, if the TK's schedule worked out that way.

I don't ask her if Kyle's there. I know he is. Kyle doesn't miss beach parties. Instead, I start my apology, and Kara jumps in, our sentences overlapping like they do when we're both really emotional, or when we both agree completely about something.

"I'm really sorry about what I said to you," I say, voice soft. "I like Brian, you know I do."

"I know, and I shouldn't have pressed you about Kyle."

"No, you should have. I was running away from Kyle and you knew that."

"But I shouldn't have judged you for that. I was just worried."

"And I was angry that you could see right through me."

"Well, I should have just let you do what you needed to do instead of trying to make you stay here and see him every day, practically."

"I miss you," I say, and it's the most truthful thing of all. It's heavy, too, hovering sadly between us somewhere above our heads in the cell phone towers, and it completely stops the momentum of the whole conversation. "I wish I could be at the beach with you guys tonight."

"Do you hate it there?"

"No, actually. I love it." I settle deep into my chair. "I'm learning how to paint better. And there's a knight who . . . I don't know. He's just so hot."

Usually that would have gotten Kara all nosy and excited, and she would have pressed me for more, but suddenly there's the thumping bass and voices in the background again, as if someone's opened the door back into the party. There's some murmuring, and then it's relatively quiet again.

"Shoot, Ro. I've got to go. Everyone's jumping in the water," she says, and I know she didn't hear my last words. I suppose it's just as well. That conversation is going to take a while, and it's Friday night there, even though it's a work night for me.

"Okay," I say, and try to mask my disappointment. "Tell Meg I'll call soon. I just wanted to call you first, you know, to make sure everything was okay."

"Oh yeah. Meg will understand. We miss you. I'll talk to you later!"

"Bye!" I say, and hear a couple of shouts (one of them unmistakably Meg, the other Brian) before Kara ends the call.

Let down, though relieved that we got to talk at all, I resign myself to calling my parents and making good on the promise to call weekly to check up. My mother answers, then insists my father pick up the other phone in the den so we can all talk together. Mom asks me if I'm getting enough to eat and if the tents are warm enough at night. Dad asks me if the job is bringing in good tips.

I try to tell them about my art and how I've made some kids feel really good about themselves with my work, but they seem to ignore the point.

"That's great, dear. You can put that in your essays when you apply for colleges."

"Yes," my father agrees. "Did you bring your laptop? You could get to work on it while it's all fresh in your mind."

"No, Dad. Even if I had, there's not exactly electricity out here."

"The old-fashioned way, then!" he exclaims, too excited about the concept for my taste. "Paper and ink."

We make plans for their visit the last Sunday of the summer, but after a while I end the call, mumbling some excuse about needing to get back to the faire. Emptiness floods my insides. Did everything have to lead back to college applications?

I order a mocha with a splash of caramel for Suze and head out. Before I climb into my car, though, I look around at Sugar Grove. There's a pizza joint up ahead, and beyond that, a little store that advertises homemade jewelry at great prices. For a moment I'm almost tempted, but then I remember that whatever Ramón is cooking is going to be better than some pizza joint, and the silversmith's rings and earrings at the faire are probably prettier and better made than what the store might have. I get in my car and turn toward home—at least, the place that's truly beginning to feel like home.

Suze practically explodes with gratefulness when I hand her the mocha, and she trades me for a plate of fried chicken and green beans. We eat and drink, and I fill her in on my phone calls, the conversation coming to rest on my parents.

"I don't know how to make them understand about art. They seem to think it's only about how it'll make me look on college applications."

Suze takes a long, thoughtful drink of her mocha and says, "So, what is it about, if not that?"

That gives me pause. "I don't know," I admit. "I just like it. I like helping people see the world a little differently, I guess. I like how it makes me feel when I do it."

Suze studies me for a long moment, enough for me to

grow anxious. She looks as if she might say something, some-thing important, but then thinks better of it. A smile blossoms on her face and she raises her paper cup in my direction, like she's toasting me. "Thanks for this. I swear. I can give up everything about the modern world but a Starbucks mocha." We share a laugh. "I'm going to head over to Grant's."

I know what that means. It means she won't be back tonight, which means I've got some time alone again. Unlike the other night, though, when I felt bored and lonely, this time I'm looking forward to some quiet time.

I tell her to have a good time, and as soon as she's out of sight, I push my dinner plate away and drag out my art supplies. After that conversation with my parents, I need to draw something. I spread the supplies out all over my air mat-tress, contemplating what I want to do. I've been using paints so much for my job that it's been a while since I've used oil pastels, or even just my charcoal pencils, and I'm longing to make some bold, defined lines again.

I choose a pencil and set to work. If there's anything I've wanted to capture perfectly with my art, it's Christian's face, so I try that, starting with his chin and the strong cut of his jaw. I get the shadowing perfectly and move on to his fea-tures, creating the swooping curve of his lips and the gentle slope of his nose.

But when I get to his eyes, something is off. It's not at all like that sketch of Kara, where I'd managed to show her personality in the light within them. With Christian's sketch, nothing I try seems to get it right. Everything I draw looks lifeless or worse, sad or angry. Frustrated, I give up and reach for my oil pastels instead, turning to a new page in my sketch-book. I look down at the box, the varying shades daring me to unleash all the emotions I've got swirling around within, and I know that this time I've chosen the right medium.

Although all the colors call to me, it's the yellows, blues, and oranges that are the loudest, and I start with those. Soon I'm lost in a daydream of paints, the colors twisting to make tongues of flame, burning in the long, curving lines of a whip.

13

WEEK 2—SUNDAY

It's no wonder I had trouble drawing Christian two nights ago. I've barely seen him.

It's Sunday, a.k.a. Campfire Day at King Geoffrey's Faire. I caught sight of him only briefly yesterday, as he exited the stables after the last joust. He was scowling, clearly not in the mood for company, so I kept my distance, and I hadn't seen him since.

"Some family thing," Sage said after breakfast this morning, as she and I walked in the direction of the tents. I inquired as casually as I could about Christian's absence because paranoia was beginning to set in that maybe he was avoiding me. "He'll be back before the noon joust."

Sage's words weren't nearly as comforting as they could have been, and I spent most of my shift at the tavern and the face painting tent wondering if I'd get to see Christian tonight, and selfishly, if his "family thing" would interfere with him finally kissing me and officially locking it down.

"You did a great job on that last kid."

Cassie's voice, which is surprisingly kind, pulls me out of my own neuroses. The kid she's referring to was a girl who wanted to look like a flower. Instead of just drawing a bright center on her nose and some petals, I drew an entire bouquet, stretching from the right side of her chin to the left part of her forehead and fanning out across her cheeks.

"Thanks," I say. In truth, that girl wasn't the only one who got a Rowena Duncan special design. Ever since that scared little boy who wanted the fuchsia dragon, I'd become braver myself, hardly sticking to the B.A.B. at all. Every customer I'd had the past two days exited the tent with a huge smile on their face, and I was pocketing some great tips. As they got happier, my designs got bolder, more whimsical. In fact, I was thinking about perhaps altering some of the B.A.B.'s designs, or adding to them.

The village clock tower chimes, letting Cassie and me know it's time to close down shop for the evening. Until Tuesday, to be exact.

A trill of excitement zips through my belly. Campfire tonight. With Christian.

As we straighten our supplies and wash out our brushes, my gaze falls on the B.A.B., and I think of the alterations I have in mind.

"Hey, Cassie? Mind if I take this back to my tent? I'd like

to study it. You know, see if I can copy some of the harder ones."

"Sure!" Cassie says, rather chipper. She pulls out her lip balm and applies several heavy coats, studying me while she does it. Then, to my utter astonishment, she holds out the tube to me. "Want some?"

I can't believe it. She's offering me her precious lip balm. I don't know what that means. Maybe she respects my artistic ability. Maybe she got hit over the head with a turkey leg. Maybe somewhere pigs have sprouted wings. Whatever the case may be, in Cassie language, this is a big deal, and I can't refuse now.

So I take the lip balm, put on a liberal coat, and thank her with a big smile before we head off to our respective tents. As I walk, the lip balm starts to tingle, tickling my lips in a fun, pleasant way. It's minty, creamy, and really luxurious, and I make a mental note to myself to cough up some extra moola to spring for this stuff at the mall next time. After all, I'm making some great tips now, I can afford to splurge a little, and wouldn't it be great to kiss Christian with this on? If I make him tingle half as much as he's done to me the last few days, he'll ask me to the Revel for sure, and then we can kiss like that on the dance floor.

I imagine Kyle in the corner, miserably watching the whole spectacle and lamenting that he ever broke up with me, and I almost float back to my tent.

• • •

Part of me was nervous that the second bonfire wouldn't be as magical as the first, that seeing it all again would make it feel ordinary.

How naive of me.

As Suze and I make our way through the woods, my stomach tight with anxiousness, the stars that dot the twilit sky nearly take my breath away. It's like they know tonight is special, and decided to mark the occasion by sparkling twice as brightly as ever before. I even make Suze stop and stare at them with me, and she points out a few constellations that mean a lot to her: the Little Dipper, because her father once told her that the little one was hers and the big one was his, and her zodiac sign, Aquarius.

The campfire seems even more magical, and it has everything to do with the feeling around it. Last time, at my welcoming party, the crowd was loud and raucous. Tonight the mood is infinitely more mellow. People are in small groups, chatting quietly, and there's no hard liquor in sight (save for Quagmire and Ramón, who are sitting on a log together close to the fire and sharing a bottle of what looks to be gin). People have cups of warm mead and the acrobats are being generous with the wine that one of them had shipped in from France.

"Classy," I say to Suze, and she agrees.

The classiest of all is the music. The minstrels aren't playing tonight, so there's none of the chuckle-worthy arrangements of classic rock and pop songs on their lutes and sackbuts.

Instead, Christian is sitting on a log by the crackling fire, a guitar tucked under his arm.

Of course he plays guitar, I muse. Of course he does. He's gorgeous and muscular and charming, so why would God have stopped there? Might as well throw in some musical talent just for good measure, so that no woman alive would be able to resist. I feel my mouth curve into a sappy, ridiculous smile.

"Go get him," Suze urges, though I'm not sure it's because she really wants me to be with Christian as much as it's that Grant has just made an entrance, and she's ready to get cozy with him by the fire.

We wish each other luck and part, and I head straight toward Christian. He's surrounded by people, but it's no matter. With a slight jerk of his head, Christian indicates that he wants me to sit next to him, and Richard gives up his seat, no questions asked. I whisper my thanks to Richard as he settles on the ground next to my feet and I sit down next to my knight.

Christian looks my way for only a moment, a smile touching his lips briefly before he turns his concentration back to the song. I don't know much about music; it always seems like such a foreign art form to me, though I'm jealous of people who understand it and can move others to tears with the sound of their voice or their instrument. It's the kind of thing I'd love to do with paint, to express that much emotion, but I've come to believe that musicians trump artists in this regard. There's just something about the dips and crescendos of music that speak directly to the soul, as if the notes enter the ear and go right to the heart, that can't be matched by merely gazing at a painting. There have been many paintings that have moved me, but music has a way of making itself at home inside you.

When he strums the last chord and lets it ring, a few people across from us clap, and all I really want is to tell them to go away so I can have Christian all to myself.

"Your hands are empty," Christian remarks. To the disappointment of everyone around us, and me as well, he sets the guitar aside. "How about I get you a drink?"

I nod, and he stands, making his way toward the acrobats. Without him next to me, I can feel how much I was taking his body heat for granted, and it occurs to me that we were sitting close enough that I felt his warmth. I'd sat down and pressed myself against him, naturally. Like that's where I was supposed to be.

I hold out my hands and warm them with the fire's heat, then rub my arms. I'll have to remember a sweatshirt next time, or at least sleeves. But I certainly hadn't chosen to wear my lacy tank top for my own well-being.

Then Christian's beside me again, handing me a cup of red wine, and it has a hint of berry in it. It's good. Too good. So I sip it. There's no way I'm going to get tipsy again and feel the wrath of a hangover all day long tomorrow.

"So, are the bonfires usually more like this?" I ask.

"Like what?"

"Mellow."

Christian smiles into his cup and takes a drink. "You could say that. Last week we sort of wanted to throw you in, you know? Hit you up with all the crazy at once to see how you handled it."

"I threw up in the woods and felt sick all the next day."

Christian laughs. "We overdid it a bit, I guess."

We sip for a moment in silence, watching the flames bend and sway. Then I take a deep breath and ask, "Did you have to go home yesterday?"

Christian turns to me, eyes narrowing, and something dark passes in his expression. "Yeah, I did. Who told you that?"

"Sage," I say, hoping I sound casual enough to combat his sudden seriousness.

"Oh." Christian leans back, stretching out his long legs. "Yeah. Family stuff. It was stupid."

"Everything okay?"

He jerks one shoulder, his mouth turning down. "Okay as it's ever going to be, I think."

He doesn't say any more, and he really doesn't seem as if he wants to talk about it, so I don't press him for more information. After a moment he hands me his cup and takes up his guitar again, this time starting in on a song I'm very familiar with, a song that sets my teeth on edge.

I used to like this song. Kyle once found a box of CDs

in his attic, old stuff his parents listened to when they were in college. The box was a treasure trove of grunge and post-grunge, alternative, and even folky stuff. Kyle and I would listen to those CDs as we cruised around town, congratulating ourselves for being so cool for knowing these bands from a bygone era. This song, in particular, was a favorite of ours, and this is the first time I've heard it without Kyle sitting beside me, driving along and singing along, our voices nowhere close to the tune. Now that I'm listening, I can't stand it—not the melancholy guitar, not the pretty chords, and especially not the words.

But it's clear I'm the only one around the campfire who feels that way, and some of the acrobat girls start singing along with Christian's guitar, giggling when they mess up the lyrics.

I excuse myself with a pat on Christian's shoulder and a mumbled explanation of "Bathroom," but I don't go to the bathroom. I step out beyond the firelight and stare at the stars again, impressing myself when I find the Little Dipper like Suze taught me, and Orion's belt.

I sit at the foot of a tree, not caring that I'm getting my jeans dirty, and just enjoy the solitude. I can still hear them singing but I'm far enough away that it's a pleasant accompaniment to the night, not a method of torture designed only for my ears. Alone like this, without anything to impede it like hectic work schedules, the steady steps of the horses, fidgety children, and the voices of my new friends, thoughts fill my head. Thoughts of Kyle that I can't stop.

On a night like this, we'd be down at the beach, or maybe just driving. It never seemed to matter what Kyle and I were doing, we always had fun. He had this way of making me laugh, mostly at his own expense, and we could talk for hours, passing the time going seamlessly from one subject to the next. He would always surprise me with trivia about some obscure thing I'd never heard of, or he'd fascinate me with his ideas and his thoughts about the deeper questions of life. Kyle somehow always made me feel like I was the only thing in the world he could see, and even though I knew I was lucky to have a boyfriend who made me feel that way, he always insisted he was the lucky one.

I miss that. I miss our nights at the beach, or on the coast, or driving. I miss hanging out with our friends, the whole big group of us, having fun and getting into shenanigans. I miss his kisses and his sweet words and promises. But most of all I miss that connection we had, the same kind of connection that maybe he has with Lacey now, and I'm scared I won't ever have it again.

Someone in the distance says Christian's name and it yanks me out of my thoughts. It's jarring to go from these sweet memories to the present reality, and once I get my bearings there's an immediate sense of guilt and anger at myself. I've been out here thinking of Kyle when a gorgeous boy is playing guitar by firelight—a gorgeous boy who might be a new start.

I need to get back to the campfire and lock this thing down

with Christian, and get over Kyle and his stupid off-key singing and the stupid way he'd kiss me until I forgot my own
name.

Determined, I push myself up from the ground and brush
away the dirt. When I reach the campfire, though, the crowd
seems to have dispersed. The acrobat girls are gone, and so
is Christian, guitar and all. I do a full circle around the clearing, searching for him through the trees, but he's nowhere to
be seen. Vanished into the night, and no one I speak to has
seen him. When I stumble on Grant and Suze making out
against a tree, I apologize profusely, staring down at my shoes
in embarrassment.

"Looking for Christian?" Grant guesses, smirking at my
sudden shyness, and I nod. "I think he had to take a phone
call."

"Oh," I say, disappointed. "His family?"

"Don't know," Grant says. He slides his arm back around
Suze's waist, and she looks mighty proud of herself. "I was
otherwise engaged when I saw him pass."

"Of course," I say, and allow myself a laugh. "Thanks,
guys."

I walk away quickly, steering myself back toward the fire.
There are more people in the clearing than before now. It's
Will, and he's brought his crew. One of them is Davis, and he
notices me approaching first.

"Hey, puke girl," he says to me.

"Hey, pee boy," I say back.

Will looks between us, eyebrows raised, a you-two-are-so-weird expression on his face, but then he must read something on my face because he ducks close to me, whispering into my ear, "All right?"

"Yeah. It's been a weird night," I whisper back.

Will nods as if he understands. "Well, you know the cure for that, right?"

I squint at him, unsure of what he's getting at, and that's when he holds up his hands to reveal a bag of giant marshmallows and a tree branch sharpened to a point on one end.

"Toasted marshmallows?"

"Yes. Or s'mores. We have graham crackers. And chocolate. At least we did." Will clears his throat and directs a loud voice to the other side of the fire, where Davis has parked himself next to a box of chocolate bars. "If Davis hasn't eaten them all by now."

A muffled, "Shuddup, Indy," comes from the direction of Davis, which sounds distinctly like it might have been said around a mouthful of chocolate.

Will turns back to me, his expression a perfect balance of amusement and irritation. "Seriously. Nothing can cheer you up like a toasted marshmallow. I'll make you one. I have a patented, foolproof Fuller family method."

I let myself smile. "Oh? And what's the patented, foolproof Fuller family method?"

"Light it on fire and then wave it around like a lunatic until it stops burning, of course."

"Mmmm, I love that charcoal flavor," Davis chips in.

"Nice and smoky." Will smiles at me, and then dips his hand into the bag, retrieving a marshmallow. He harpoons it on his stick.

"I don't know if the Fuller family method will work for me. I don't like the burnt ones," I tell Will, and raise my nose in the air. "I like mine toasted, golden brown all over."

Will narrows his eyes at me and shakes his head like he's absolutely disgusted. "Marshmallow snob."

"Cretin."

At that, Will unceremoniously lowers his marshmallow into the fire and waits until it catches. Then, true to his word, he whips it out and waves it back and forth frantically, cursing at it, until the fire goes out.

He blows on it, glances at me with triumph, and bites into it. The charred black sugar crunches and the gooey, melted insides drip down his chin. I watch, amused, as he tries to wipe the goo off his skin, then licks his fingers.

"See?" he says, as if all the chaos of the last few minutes totally proved his method. "I win."

"You have marshmallow on your nose," I say, and Davis guffaws behind us, his own marshmallow totally aflame.

Will wipes at his nose where, sure enough, a bit of sticky marshmallow has landed. "Fine," he says, pride obviously wounded. "Show me how to make the perfect marshmallow, O Wise Marshmallow Guru."

I stick my nose even higher into the air and take his stick

and a marshmallow. I step toward the fire, lowering my marshmallow so that it's just over the flames. It takes a while, but then, perfection always takes time. I turn my stick like a rotisserie, toasting each side until the whole thing is a warm, golden brown, no charring in sight. I point my stick at Will, offering him the marshmallow, and he pulls it off the end and sniffs it suspiciously before popping the entire thing in his mouth. His eyes go wide, and he emits a sound that seems to be pure pleasure.

"My God," he says to Davis around the fluff in his mouth. "The woman is a genius."

"Give me that," Davis says, and snatches the marshmallows from Will, eager to try my method out for himself.

My method lasts all of ten minutes before the boys get impatient and start burning the marshmallows to a crisp again, although they still hold that my method produces higher quality marshmallows. Soon we have a crowd around us and we break into the chocolate and graham crackers. We lose ourselves in sugary, s'more heaven until the air is far too chilly and our stomachs are regretting our gluttony. Christian hasn't reappeared, but I ignore the itch of irritation under my skin about it and focus on having a good time without him. It's only when people start making excuses to leave, taking a final s'more for the road, that I realize how tired and full I feel, and I just want to lie down and sleep until the breakfast bell in the morning.

I plunk down on a fallen tree. "So full. Need to sleep."

"Aye," Will replies. He's sitting at the foot of a tree and he leans back, rubbing his aching stomach. "Shouldn't have had that last one."

"I shouldn't have had the last four," I say, and he chuckles tiredly at that. "I'll see you at breakfast? Thanks for the marsh-mallows."

Will exhales loudly and stands, stretching. "I'll walk you back."

"You don't have to," I say, feeling a little pathetic. It should have been Christian offering, and now I'm just the poor loser who is going to wander through the woods alone.

"I'm walking with you. A gentleman would not leave a lady alone in the woods."

A gentleman indeed. Where was Christian's concern for my well-being? He's left me in the woods twice now. Aren't knights supposed to be chivalrous?

"Thanks," I tell Will. I smile at him and accept his arm when he offers it. We walk in silence, save for the occasional groan when a dip in the path or a protruding tree root jostles our stomachs. Will walks close as if he's afraid I might fall (and okay, maybe he's right about that), and twice his arms fly out, trying to catch me as I stumble.

"I'm sorry," I mumble to him. "Tired. And drunk on sugar."

Will laughs. "Worse than mead."

When we near the tent, though, Will reaches out and grabs my arm, halting us. "What?" I ask.

He jerks his head toward my tent and I listen, fully expecting to hear the rustling of some wild animal or the like.

Well, it does sound a little like a wild animal. Two wild animals. It's very clear that Suze and Grant are having a *fantastic* time in my tent.

I clamp my hands over my mouth to keep from laughing, although Will doesn't bother. He motions for me to follow him, and we make our way back to the other side of camp, giggling and laughing like children all the way. We stop in front of another ring of tents, and that's when Will turns to me with a wicked gleam in his eye.

"Oh, Sir Grant, you brawny hunk of a man," Will says, his voice pitched high in a falsetto that doesn't sound like Suze at all, but is hilarious nonetheless. "Take me now!"

I drop my voice down low and gruff in my own impersonation of Grant. "Say please, you sassy wench!"

"Please, sir, please!" Will answers in falsetto, and I lose it, laughing so hard that there's no way I can continue our bit. Will's right there with me, and we both plop ourselves down on the ground, since laughter has rendered us unable to walk.

It seems to take us forever to collect ourselves, and Will reaches over and pats my knee. "You could crash with us. Davis won't mind."

The invitation makes me blush, even though it's as innocent as can be. But I don't know where else to go. I can't go to Cassie's, that would just be awkward, and showing up at Christian's is a step I'm not ready to take yet. I nod to Will, shy to accept, and he smiles just as shyly back.

Will pulls me into his tent, and Davis looks up from a comic book with irritation. "Dude. We have a deal. If you want to bring a girl back to the tent, use the code word so I can get out of here before—"

"Dude yourself," Will says to him, smiling. "Ro's tentmate is getting down with a knight right now, so she's crashing here. Unless you've got a problem with that."

Davis looks at me, jerking his chin once in my direction. "Nah. No offense, Pukey. I just thought . . . well, you know. At least I was hoping for his sake. But I should have known. Will's a complete disaster when it comes to women."

"Is that so?" I ask, just as Will launches one of his pillows at Davis's head. Davis smoothly dodges it and grins at me.

"Very so."

Maybe it's his way of challenging Davis's remarks, or maybe Davis is wrong about him, but Will does two awesome things for me after that. The first is that he gives me his sweatshirt, which is from a quiz bowl competition he participated in during high school. IT'S ALL SO TRIVIAL it reads on the front, and there's a list of quiz team members on the back, with a drawing of a brain set in the background. I see Will's name nearly at the top, with only an Adams and a Fitzpatrick above him.

The second is that he gives me his air mattress and lies down in the small space on the floor. After an argument, in which I politely refuse to take his bed and he politely refuses to let me refuse, I give in and slip on his sweatshirt before making myself at home in his bed. His pillow is soft, and the sheets feel a lot more worn in and comfortable than my own. I pull the sleeves of his sweatshirt up around my hands and press them to my face, breathing in.

It smells like him—leather and lighter fluid and Irish Spring, and it makes me feel right at home.

"Good night, Will," I say as I burrow my head into the pillow.

"Good night, Rainbow Ro."

"Good night, Will," Davis says, then adds, "and good night, Pukey McPukerson. Or should I call you Vomit McGee?"

This time, Will's pillow lands successfully on Davis's face and he finally shuts up.

14

When I wake up, Davis is sprawled on his stomach, snoring loudly. Will, on the other hand, is still and quiet on the floor between the air mattresses. He's used another sweatshirt as a pillow and a blanket is draped around him like a toga, crossing from his shoulder across his torso, where it wraps around his waist and legs.

He's not wearing a shirt, which surprises me. When I fell asleep he was wearing one, but maybe he got too hot with three people in the tent.

Wait.

Will's not wearing a shirt.

I lift myself up on my elbows to get a better view, half ashamed of myself and feeling like a peeping Tom, but too curious not to look. He's . . . not bad at all. He's got definition to his chest and, from what I can tell, his stomach too. Not like

Kyle, who lifted weights quite a bit for lacrosse, and maybe not like I imagine Christian is after all that knight training, but it's enough. And there's something extra nice about knowing that he's gotten it naturally, not in a gym or in a contest to be the most threatening on a field.

Good lord, Ro. You're checking out the whip cracker.

I think this place might be starting to mess with my mental health. I shake my head at myself and slip out of bed as quietly as I can, folding Will's sweatshirt neatly and setting it on the foot of his mattress. Both boys are still sleeping soundly as I exit the tent.

The sun is up, faint but growing stronger, and it's clearly going to be a hot day. It's already warm and humid enough that the lacy tank I'm wearing from last night is comfortable. I estimate that it's about eight o'clock, smiling proudly at myself for even guessing. I'm probably not as accurate at telling the time by the sun's position as Will and Lindy are, but I bet I'm close.

Since the faire is closed today, most of the employees are still sleeping, taking advantage of the hours off. Ramón will serve breakfast, but later, making it more like brunch. I have a while. I could take a nice long shower, fix my hair, and perhaps work on some of my watercolors, and all before my first meal. That is, if Grant has gone home and isn't still in our tent.

"Have a good night?"

I whirl around, and Christian is behind me. He looks from me, pointedly, to Will's tent, and back again.

I feel my skin prickle and flush, like I've been caught, only I haven't really been caught at anything. "I . . . I had to spend the night with Will because Grant was in my tent with Suze."

He cocks his head at me and I rush to clarify. "Not *with* Will. Just. You know. On his floor. We're just friends."

Christian studies me as if trying to find the cracks in my story, and I'm not entirely sure there aren't some there. I can feel myself shrinking, bit by bit, as he looks at me. I hate the feeling, so I try to shift our focus. "Where did you go last night?"

Christian looks away, and I immediately wish I would have used a nicer tone, a less accusatory tone. "Just drama again," he says, resigned.

"Everything okay?"

He shrugs. "I guess." He glances at Will's tent again, and there's a glint of something dangerous in his eyes. "So the whip cracker—"

"Just a friend," I rush to say. "So you don't have to defend my honor, sir knight."

Christian, finally, smiles at my cheek. "I thought we'd been over this. Your honor's no good around me."

He moves close to me, and though he doesn't put his arms around me, I can still feel the heat pouring off his skin, I can still smell his clean scent. He reaches out, sliding a finger from my collarbone over my throat to my chin, lifting it slightly. He pauses, searching my eyes, and I gaze back, wondering if he's finally going to kiss me and holding my breath like I've never held it in my life.

The crunching of dried grass and leaves makes us both turn slowly, reluctantly, toward the source. Grant is heading our way, amused.

"Tent's free," Grant says to me, looking rather proud of himself. "And Suze said something about wanting to go to breakfast with you. Sorry for kind of kicking you out last night."

"That's all right. She spent the night with the whip cracker," Christian says. His voice seems somewhat mocking, and it makes me bristle.

"We're just friends," I repeat in my defense.

"Of course. I stay the night in friends' tents all the time. No big deal, right?" Christian says, and I know for sure then that he doesn't quite believe me. My heart sinks. Have I just screwed up my chance with Christian?

"And Christian does have a lot of friends," Grant says, and his smirk blossoms into an expression of pure delight. "I think Fuller made him jealous."

"There's no reason for him to be jealous," I say, but I'm ignored as Christian talks over me.

"Please. Will Fuller?" Christian sneers. "What kind of talent is waving a whip around, anyway? He probably couldn't even lift one of our swords."

"There's an art to whip cracking. It takes a lot of skill," I say in Will's defense before I realize how that sounds to Christian. When I look at him, his lip is curled in disgust.

"Hear that, Christian? Fuller's got skills."

Christian shoots Grant a look that's downright murderous—a look that he shifts to me in a somewhat less potent form before he turns and walks away, leaving Grant and me alone on the path.

I mutter a curse and rub my temples with my fingers, fighting an oncoming headache that just might rival a mead hangover. When I open my eyes, Grant's looking at me, his expression fixed solidly between sadistic joy and concern.

"I really screwed that up," I say, and Grant chuckles.

"How? You should be given some prize, at least a gold medal."

I scrunch my brows together in confusion, and Grant rolls his eyes like he can't believe I don't get what he's saying. "What? Why?"

"I've never seen him jealous like that. Ever."

"And that's a good thing?" I ask, even though I know the answer. My heart flutters like a hummingbird. Christian's jealous. Over *me*.

"For you, maybe," Grant says. "For Fuller? Not so much."

Grant leaves me with that rather interesting—and somewhat concerning—tidbit of information, and I hurry back to my tent, wanting to get out of these clothes and get a shower.

Suze has other ideas, however, and chucks shorts and a T-shirt at me. "Put these on," she says, eyes sparkling. "Dad's making omelets. Trust me, you do not want to miss this."

If Suze says I don't want to miss something, I definitely don't, so I throw on the outfit she's picked out for me and tie my hair back into a somewhat respectable ponytail. We fill each other in on our nights as we walk to the wagon, Suze going into a little too much detail and me blushing the whole time.

Inside the wagon, something smells delightful. Peter's at the small stove, waving a spatula over a skillet like it's some sort of magic wand, and Lindy's cutting up ingredients and placing them into separate bowls.

Lindy greets me and Suze with a kiss on our cheeks and tells us to take whatever we want for our omelets. As Suze and I help ourselves to tomatoes, cheese, green peppers, and mushrooms, Peter hums a happy tune, shaking his hips to his own beat as he lets the eggs cook to a delicious yellow.

"How was the campfire last night?" Lindy asks, and Suze and I both rush to say, "Fine!" and look away in case we laugh.

"Uh-huh," Lindy says, as if she knows exactly what goes on at the campfires. Considering she and Peter are lifers, she probably has some personal experience to draw from.

"What are you guys up to today?" Suze says, changing the subject.

"Omelets. Then I'm going to see a man about a pair of trained ravens," Peter says, and I can't help but chuckle a little that trained ravens are just normal conversation for the Mulligans. He takes my plate from me, adds my choices to the pan, and flips the egg over on itself. He makes a big show of letting the whole thing slide from the skillet onto my plate and hands it back to me with a little bow. I thank him and grab a fork.

"And I'm going to head into town because the craft store has a sale on fabric," Lindy says. "You girls could come with me if you want."

"Nah, I'll just hang around here," Suze says, and I know what she means is that she and Grant have plans. Lindy looks to me.

"I was actually going to work on some art," I say, hoping I'm not disappointing her too much.

Luckily, she doesn't seem at all put off by it. "You should drop by Robbie's. Have you met her yet? She's quite talented. She'd love another artist to talk with."

Another artist. The simple acknowledgment that I'm an artist makes me beam.

"I've been meaning to go see her. That sounds like a great plan." Excited about the idea, I sit back and enjoy my omelet quietly as the Mulligans chatter about trained ravens and dress fabric.

Robbie's shop door is locked when I arrive, but I can see her inside through the window so I tap on the glass. She looks up from her work, grinning, and calls out, "Be right there!" She opens the door wide and welcomes me in. She's not dressed in Renaissance clothing, but her clothes aren't exactly modern either. She's wearing a long skirt with a linen blouse and a scarf in her hair. Her smile is as kind as Lindy's and as quirky as Meg's.

"I completely forgot to unlock the door. How unfriendly of me," she says. "Ro, right? The face painter?"

"Yes, I hope you don't mind me dropping by."

"I was hoping you would! Would you like some tea?"

I look around her small shop, which is filled to the point of claustrophobia with painted teapots and teacups and serving trays, and just about every type of furniture you could imagine that could be used for a display.

"Which teacups do you actually use?" I ask, not meaning to sound rude in any way.

"Oh!" Robbie exclaims, and starts laughing, her round body shaking with it. "Well, I don't use the fancy ones myself. I keep a few in the back that are rather embarrassing. Have a seat, I'll brew us a cup."

As she disappears into a back room, I sit on a chair that looks like it might be part of a display, but it's the only chair that's as easily accessible as the one Robbie was using. Hers sits behind a table no bigger than the desks we have at school, and there's a set of teacups on it that look only partially finished. Next to that, like my station at the face painting tent, are jars of brushes and different palettes of paints. Tucked behind her jars and paints are a few carved trolls, peeking out at me like little mischievous spies. I wonder if maybe they *are* magical, since I see so many of them around here. Maybe they watch over the faire folk.

I smile at my ridiculousness as Robbie emerges with two steaming mugs, and hands one to me. The tea is Earl Grey, and despite the heat of the day and the warm air inside the shop, it tastes delicious.

"Your work is beautiful," I tell her, and she looks around her shop at her work.

"I'm pleased you think so. I hear you're quite the artist."

"I do okay with faces," I say.

"I meant your sketches. Will tells me they're quite beautiful."

I pick up my tea and hold it in front of my mouth to hide my smile. "Will talks to everyone, doesn't he?"

"He's basically our town crier," Robbie says with a wink. "But he doesn't lie. If he says you're good, you're good."

"I think I'm getting better. This summer I've really started to pay attention, you know? To see things around me in a new way."

Robbie completely gets what I'm saying. She nods emphatically. "Yes, when you start to see everything around you like a painting, that's when you know."

"Know what?"

"Know you're toast," Robbie says, laughing. "Once painting has its claws in you, you're never the same again."

"Sounds painful," I muse.

"Only if you fight it," Robbie says. She pauses like she's expecting me to say something else, but I don't, so she gestures to her teacups. "Ever paint a teacup? Quite different from a canvas, though it might not be that different from a face."

I pick up one of her teacups and study the design she's

started on it. It's a vine of blue and green, curling around the cup as if growing up its sides.

"When I paint faces, I kind of work with their features. Long noses lend themselves to badgers and superheroes, tiny noses to cats and rabbits." I set down the teacup. "I'm sure each teacup has its own story to tell, too. Its own possibility."

Robbie says nothing to that, but after a moment of looking at me with a rather intense sort of scrutiny, she gets up and disappears into the back again. When she comes out she has a wooden wine goblet in her hands. She hands it to me, takes a seat, and smiles in my direction.

"What is its story?"

I grin and select a small, slanted-bristle brush from her collection and get to work. She takes up her brush and starts back on her vines and we work in silence until she figures out that I'm painting the stages of the moon all the way around in a looping design. That gets her asking questions about my art lessons, and in turn I ask about how she learned, and what seems like only minutes later, we've each painted about six drinking vessels and it feels like we're old friends. It's only when the bell tower chimes that we realize we've been sitting there for three hours.

I pick up the goblet with the moons on it, which is now fully dry. The grays and blues swirl wonderfully on it, and I'm proud of my shadowing.

"You should keep that," Robbie says. "Or . . ."

"Or . . . ?"

"Or you could sell it. I could display it here, and if some-one buys it, I'll give you the money."

"Sell something I've painted?" I ask doubtfully.

Robbie gets a kick out of that. She laughs, rolling back in her chair. "You sell your paintings every day! They're just on people's faces instead of cups or goblets."

"I guess, but . . ." I make a face. "This is so different."

"You *can* make a living being an artist, you know. I know from experience. And trust me, these will sell." She ges-tures to my goblets and teacups, which, honestly, look pretty decent. "You just have to promise me one thing, if I sell these for you."

"Sure, what's that?"

"That you'll let me see some of those sketches Will was raving about."

"Deal," I say. "Maybe I can stop by Wednesday after my tavern shift?"

"I'll look forward to it," Robbie promises, and I leave her with her teacups and mine, beautiful and ready for a buyer.

Ramón is busy basting and marinading and stirring when I stop by the tavern kitchen. His day off, I have learned, com-prises doing any and every task in the kitchen that can be done ahead of time, to save himself the hassle during the week.

He barely looks up at me before shoving a raw turkey leg

in a vat of something I can't identify and then throwing it into a large Ziploc bag with the others.

"Need help?" I ask.

"No."

I sit on a stool next to his counter space. "Can I make a sandwich?"

Ramón slowly turns his head to me, his right eyebrow arching toward the ceiling. "Now the truth comes out. There's ham in the fridge."

The tavern has about five fridges and two freezers in the back room, but I take a wild guess and find the correct fridge on my third try. I set the ham on the counter, pull out a bun from the gigantic supply of them in the cabinet, and set to work layering ham until it's stacked the way I want it. When I open up the fridge and pull out a jar of mayonnaise, a hand closes over mine.

"Over my dead body. Here." Ramón shoves a container of a brownish-gold substance at me and I curl my lip up at it. "My homemade dijon. You will not assault my smoked ham with mayonnaise."

Ramón gives me a death glare when I remove the lid of the container and poke my finger in the dijon to taste it. I smile brightly. "It's good."

"I know it's good, that's why I told you to use it. Now make your sandwich and get out."

I slather it on my sandwich and sit back on the stool, happily eating while Ramón works.

"I told you to leave."

I smile brighter. "I like watching you."

Ramón grunts in response then turns, grabbing another bun. He slaps a few pieces of ham on it, gives the other side a nice layer of dijon, squishes it together and hands it to me. "Will is down by the menagerie practicing. Go eat your sandwich with him. He's hungry."

"How do you know he's hungry?" I ask. I take the sandwich and wrap it in one of the wax paper liners we put under turkey legs so the grease won't soak through the paper plates.

"Because he wanted a sandwich and I told him to go away. Like I told you." Ramón picks up another raw turkey leg and points it at me. "Now go. Before I get angry."

"Are you sure *this* isn't angry?"

"ROWENA."

"I'm leaving, I'm leaving."

I'm done with my sandwich by the time I reach the menagerie, except for a small part of my bun, which I throw to the goats. The sun is glaring down, strong and hot, and the rest of the animals are smart enough to stay away from me and keep their places in the shade of the barn on the other side of the pen.

Will is in the center of the menagerie ring. He's got one whip uncurled and dangling from around his neck, and another rolled tightly around his shoulder. When he sees me, he comes right over.

I hand him the sandwich. "Ramón said you'd be hungry."

"Ramón kicked me out. How did you manage to get a sandwich?"

"He likes my particular brand of pestering, I can tell," I say, smirking. Will digs into the sandwich, stopping only to compliment the dijon. When he's finished, he thanks me again and rolls the wax paper into a ball that he slips in his pocket.

Then, without warning, he shrugs out of the whip on his shoulder and tosses it to me.

I catch it with a gasp. It's heavier than I imagined, and I file that little tidbit of information away for later, if Christian makes another wisecrack about Will's strength.

Will doesn't say anything, so I find the handle of the whip and let the other end drop, and it coils at my feet like a snake. The handle is about three times as thick as the end, and there's leather stitching on both sides of it, creating tight seams like a baseball glove. It's taken someone ages to get it that perfect.

"Feels good in your hand, right?"

I jerk my head up, surprised to see Will's been watching me. "It does. Makes me feel like a lion tamer."

"That's my next act."

"Ha," I say, but I'm distracted, still running my fingers over the stitching. "Did you make this yourself?"

"Yes. I mean, I wove it. I didn't make the leather. Davis made that at The Bone Needle. Well, and the cow made it before that. So I can't take all the credit."

"The cow is a very important ingredient, I'd say." With a

sly look in Will's direction, I raise my hand, bringing the handle of the whip over my head, and try to crack it like I've seen so many actors do in the movies. The result is not like the movies. In the slightest. The end of the whip barely moves, and the rest of it flops lazily, hardly coming up higher than my shoulders.

I turn to Will and I feel the pout on my lips. He coughs to hide a laugh.

"It's all about momentum. And . . ."—he looks at me apologetically—"strength, too. It's going to take some muscle to get the whip above your head."

I look down at my arms, which are thin and kind of scrawny. I'm still having some trouble lifting big trays of food at the tavern, even though after just one week, it's better than it used to be. Kyle used to tease me about my arms, since his were always so thick and built from his lacrosse playing. He used to ask me to flex, and then pull up the skin on my biceps to make me look bigger, like Popeye on spinach.

"What are you talking about? I'm huge!" I flex with one arm and use the other hand to pull up my skin, just like Kyle used to do to me. Will finds this hopelessly amusing.

"I know. You're a giant. But even giants need some help with a whip at first." Will pushes up the short sleeves of his shirt. It occurs to me that this is only the third time I've seen him without a billowy peasant shirt and a leather vest, but he looks equally at home in that as he does in a T-shirt and jeans, which is probably why I didn't notice his street clothes at first. His T-shirt is green and it's got a sketch in blue and white of two robots holding hands. There are hearts over their heads and it says under their feet ROBOT LOVE. There's a brownish-black stain on one of the robot's faces, and I don't know if it's leather oil or chocolate, but both seem like equal possibilities.

Will shoves his sleeves farther up and removes the whip that's dangling around his neck. "So really, whip cracking is all about momentum. Physics," he adds with a grin. "You're breaking the sound barrier each time that whip cracks, and it takes a certain speed, a certain curvature, a certain motion . . ."

Will talks as he demonstrates, making sure he's far enough away from me that I'm not in any danger as the whip sails through the air. Even without the fire, with only basic, straightforward moves, it's impressive. The end of the whip never touches the ground, but creates beautiful shapes as it floats—curves and loops and infinity symbols. He seems to create a song, too, the faster cracks making higher sounds than the slower ones, building a staccato melody as he moves. But as intriguing as the whip is, what's even more intriguing is the arm at the end of the whip, guiding it.

Christian definitely had no idea what he was talking about when he was acting so jealous this morning. Will would have absolutely no trouble with a sword. His arm is flexed, and deep lines of muscle in impressive peaks and valleys glide under his skin as he works the whip through the air.

I stare. Dumbly. I can't help myself. Even this morning,

seeing him sleeping without a shirt . . . heck, even at the whip show, I never suspected his arms would be like that when flexed.

"So it's basically perpetual motion," Will's saying, and I snap my gaze away from his lifted arm to his face. Luckily, he's not watching me at all but concentrating on the movement of the whip. "I mean, what you've got to do is get the motion right and just keep it going."

I nod as if what he's saying isn't all just Greek to me, and raise my own arm to give it a try. After watching the motion he's making for a few more seconds, I give it a try myself. It's sort of like a helicopter with one propeller. I whirl it around and around in a circle.

"What?" I ask when I hear Will snicker. He's let his whip fall to the ground and is motioning for me to stop. I do, and thank goodness, because the helicopter motion alone is winding me.

"It's not a lasso," he says, still laughing to himself about my lack of skill.

I scowl at him. "I was doing what you were doing."

"It's really cute that you think so," he says, and I deepen my scowl. This only makes Will crack up more. "Here, let me show you."

Will moves behind me and places his arm on top of mine, lacing his fingers in the gaps that mine have created around the whip handle. He raises our arms together, and as he does, I have to sort of lean back into him so I won't lose my balance.

His body is blazing hot against me, competing well with the noonday sun, and I can tell through the thin material of my tank top that his chest is just as muscled as his arms. Will pulls our arms back and then snaps them quickly forward, and the whip sails over our heads through the air. At the last second, he pulls our arms back, and a satisfying "crack" echoes around us like a gunshot.

"Sorry," he whispers to me. "I should have said it's not just about perpetual movement, but quick movements, too. You can't get a crack if you don't have a good snap."

Even though the whip has dropped to the ground, he's still close to me, his arm over mine, his chest flush with my back. It's like Christian in the stables, but . . . it's not at all like Christian, either. Because Christian was using grooming his horse as a way to touch me, and I was using it as a way to touch him. And now, here, with Will, it's different.

At least, I think it's different. Arm muscles aside, and never mind my peeping at his bare chest this morning in his tent, it's different. Will's just a friend. Just a guy teaching me how to crack a whip. A guy who I happen to think is really funny, and has great arms, and smells really good; a guy whose tent I slept in, whose sweatshirt I'd worn all night, who I defended to an incredibly sexy knight that morning at the risk of losing my chance at a fairemance.

"Ro?"

My name brings me back to the present, and I almost laugh at my own absurdity. This is *Will*. Of course I'm fixating on all this because it's all just so odd and my brain is having trouble computing.

"Sorry," I say, twisting my neck so I can see his face. He's really close like this, and I feel a little lost as I look at him. "I think I get it. Thank you."

"Want to try again?"

His arm flexes over mine, his hand spreads over my fingers. It makes me feel like if he moves again, or gets any closer, I could jump out of my skin. Just the anticipation of it is enough to make me feel prickly, like the chills you get when someone else is braiding your hair.

And I can't deal with that. Not right now. It's too much, too weird. I step out of his grasp. "Mind if I try it by myself?"

The brightness in Will's eyes dulls a bit, but he nods and steps away so I have enough space. I manage to make the whip give a feeble crack, and I'm proud of it regardless. I hand it back to him, avoiding his gaze the best I can, and mumble some excuse about needing to paint.

"Of course," I hear him say as I turn to go. "But you should try again. Sometime soon."

I yell over my shoulder that I will, and I have no idea if I sound sincere or not. I have no idea if I am.

A bottle of nail polish hits my air mattress and bounces into my lap, right on top of my sketchpad. I pick it up and glance at Suze, who's doing her best to look innocent. She falls woefully short.

"Do something more useful. Paint your toes instead. They're looking rough."

"Gee, thanks." I look down at my toes. The rainbow paint job I did the day I interviewed for this job is mostly gone, chipped off by a week of wandering around a Renaissance Faire in my flip-flops. "Bring any nail polish remover?" I ask, relenting.

She tosses a bottle of that to me, as well as a cotton pad, and I set to work removing the rainbow. When I'm done I look at the bottle of polish Suze threw at me.

It's bright green. Kermit the Frog green. So long, rainbow, I guess, and that kind of makes me sad. I wonder if Will will continue to use my nickname if I have monochromatic toes.

I unscrew the cap and start with my big toe. "Hey, Suze? Can I ask you a weird question?"

"I live for weird questions."

Weird or not, I'm not sure she's prepared for this. "What do you think of Will Fuller?"

"Indy?" Suze lifts up her hand and blows on her fingers, trying to get them to dry. "He's all right. Pretty eyes. Strange sense of humor, though."

"Yeah," I agree, even though I actually like Will's sense of humor. But then, people always think I'm odd when I laugh at certain things, like the tense part of the movie or an uncomfortable silence.

"Besides, I'd say what really matters is what you think of Will Fuller," Suze says. She gives me a look that says that I am not going to get out of the impending conversation—no way, no how. "And what *do* you think of him? Does Christian have competition? Will there be a showdown with whips versus swords? 'Cause I'm not gonna lie. That would be hot."

"No, no. Nothing like that." I finish up one foot and move on to the other. "It's just . . . he was teaching me how to crack a whip today—"

"Mmmm, yeah. Really hot."

"Suze! Let me finish. Anyways, he had his arm on mine and he was all close to me and . . . I don't know. It's not like I like him that way. He's just a friend."

"You sure about that?" Suze asks, and I can't raise my eyes to meet hers.

"Yeah. Of course." I paint my smallest toe and put the cap back on the bottle. "It was just a weird moment or something. I don't know."

Suze hums. "And how are things going with Christian?"

"He hasn't even kissed me yet," I say, sighing. "Or asked me to the Revel. Then this morning he saw me leaving Will's tent and got all pissy."

Suze cackles. "Christian doesn't like to lose."

Christian doesn't like to lose. That's true, on the jousting field or off. But I'm not sure that means anything good for me. Grant seemed to think it did, but maybe he's reading too much into it. Maybe I am, too.

"What do I do, Suze?"

"Well, if you're telling the truth and you don't like Will,

then there's not much you can do, right? Keep flirting with Christian. Come on. He's tried to kiss you twice, right? He likes you." Suze gathers her hair into three sections and starts to braid. "Unless you want to go for Davis or something."

"Davis is kind of hilarious."

Suze shakes her head at me, disgusted. "He thinks it's funny to light his farts on fire."

"Noted."

We chat on as I wait for my nails to dry, then give them another coat. Suze begins to twist my hair into a configuration that will last all day tomorrow, even through a hectic tavern shift. We gab about everything. She also updates me on the gossip around the faire. Apparently Magda and Ramón hooked up again last night, though they're both denying it, which could explain Ramón's particularly sour mood today. Richard was seen leaving the campfire with one of the cuter squires, and a couple of the acrobats decided to toilet paper Jeff's trailer, and of course they were so stealthy Jeff slept soundly through the whole thing.

Suze pulls back on my hair so that I'm looking up into her face. "So how was your day, other than working up some major tension with the whip cracker?"

I stick my tongue out at her and she pushes my head back down, continuing my updo. "Hmmm, well. It was kind of awesome. I bugged Ramón for a while."

"Oh, I bet he loved that."

"He let me have a sandwich, with his homemade dijon."

I feel Suze shaking her head behind me. "How did you get on his good side?"

I snort. "I sat with Robbie and painted for a while, which was fun. She's really good, and it's nice having another artist around. Then it was the whipping lesson. After that I stopped in at The Bone Needle and finally got my sandals."

At that, Suze completely drops my hair and goes in search of the new sandals, which she deems adorable, considering they're historically accurate. They do have the look of a ballet slipper instead of a gladiator sandal, so I am grateful, and Davis hardly charged me anything for them.

Suze resumes fixing my hair, and I resume my recount of the day.

"As I was coming back here before dinner, your mom pulled me into her shop to show me some of the fabric she got, and . . . we had a conversation."

"That doesn't sound good. What exactly did my mother say to you?"

I shrug off Suze's concern, cursing myself for even mentioning Lindy at all when I could have easily left out that bit of my day. The whole conversation upset me so much (way more than the awkward moment with Will) that I hadn't even meant to bring it up.

"Rowena," Suze says, and it's exactly the stern voice her mother used on me that afternoon.

I sigh, and Suze tugs tighter on my hair. I yelp and confess before she tugs on it again. "She asked me what I want to do with my life."

"Yeah? So?"

"So . . . ," I say, exasperated. "So I don't have a clue. I mean, my parents want me to go to college and major in something respectable, so I guess that's what I'll do."

"Well, to hell with your parents," Suze says. "What do you want to do?"

"You sound just like your mother."

"My mother is seldom wrong." Suze wrinkles her nose. "Please don't tell her I said that."

In spite of the confusion inside me, I laugh at that, but sober quickly. This conversation is remarkably similar to the one I had with Suze's mom hours ago, when Lindy had asked me what I would do with my life if I didn't have any restrictions. I started to think about my art, and about how much just silly face painting means to me, and how quickly time seems to pass when I slip into that other world and just paint, like this morning with Robbie.

"What do *you* want to do?" I ask Suze after a moment.

Suze begins to braid. "It's so geeky . . ."

I smile. I can't imagine Suze doing anything geeky. She could make pocket protectors cool. "Spill."

"I want to major in history. Renaissance history." She sighs at herself. "I know. Like I haven't spent enough time on the Renaissance already."

"I think that's awesome," I tell her, and I can feel her relief at my approval. Which makes me wonder if she's faced some disapproval about it at one point in her life. "What did your parents think?" I ask cautiously.

Suze laughs, but it's not genuine. "Well, they just about exploded. They couldn't get why I didn't want to be a lifer forever like them."

"But now they do?"

Suze is quiet for a moment, and then, "I don't know if they get it, but they're okay with it. They realize that I'm different from them, even if I'm their daughter. And they're proud that I got into Amherst. They're just proud in general, you know?"

Suze's words feel directed at me, even if she didn't mean to do it. I try to keep the focus on her. "So do you want to teach or work in a museum?"

"I'm not sure yet. Probably teach. But you're avoiding the question."

"Am not." I sniff indignantly, even though I am totally avoiding the question.

"Then answer it. What do you want to do?"

"Will is majoring in physics," I say in reply. Suze growls at my nonanswer in exasperation, but I go on, determined to make a point. "Did you know that? He's going to MIT. He's that smart. And he's so passionate. I didn't know people could be passionate about physics, but he is. He really loves it. You should hear him talk about it."

"And you should hear yourself talking about Will," Suze teases. She gathers my hair up again and starts to do her magic with it. "But you're just friends, right?"

"Quiet, you." I'm smiling as I say it. "Anyway, I guess I want something like that. Something I can talk about endlessly, something I'm totally in love with."

"You talk about art like that," Suze says quietly. "During our break yesterday you talked about some watercolor thing you did for nearly the whole twenty minutes. I thought Ramón was going to kill us."

"I did, didn't I?" I ask, and I grin like a goon as I realize it. "I'm sorry."

"It's okay. It was far more interesting than complaining about Ramón's stew." Suze finishes up my hair with one last twist and a snap of my elastic. "All I'm saying is that if you want to do something you're in love with, maybe you should stop listening to your parents and listen to your heart instead."

Suze hops onto her own air mattress and wiggles under her blanket. She leans over and grabs hold of the knob on the gas lamp, turning the flame down low. "And it wouldn't hurt to do the same about Indy. You have a week until the Revel. Plenty of listening time."

"He's just a friend," I say, as stubborn as Patsy when she's arguing with Quagmire. "It's Christian I want."

"Everyone wants Christian. That's not the question," Suze says. "What's important is what you *need*."

I repeat those words in my head, memorizing them for later, when I'm not so tired and confused that I might actually be able to make sense out of them, and lean over to turn the lamp the rest of the way down. As I do, I spy my Kermit the Frog–colored toes. It's one thing to hope Jeff might miss my multicolored toes; it's just plain idiotic to hope he won't see bright neon green.

"Hey, Suze? Should we take the polish off? What if Jeff—"

"Oh, screw Jeff," Suze mumbles, already half asleep. "He can eat my dainty slippers . . ."

Laughing, I turn out the light and go to sleep.

WEEK 3—MONDAY

The upside to having my car at the faire is that I can leave any time I want. The downside is that since you can leave any time you want, people often want to leave with you.

Which is how, on my second day off at King Geoffrey's Faire, I ended up with Suze and Will and three baskets full of laundry in my car, headed into Sugar Grove to wash our clothes.

Not that I minded them coming along. I got up and showered that morning, only to realize I didn't have a single clean pair of underwear in the tent. I looked over to Suze, who was rifling through what remained of her clean clothes, and I could read it on her face as well: The underwear situation was dire. We would have to act now.

Then Will saw the two of us making our way to the car, laundry in tow, and he begged to come as well.

"My shirts," he complained, grimacing at some remembered smell. "I'm making myself gag."

Which is why he is in my back seat, sitting dangerously close to my dirty underwear. Yes, he's just a friend—and this whole week all but proved that; I'd seen him only a handful of times, and each time? Not a whiff of any sort of attraction to him. And no awkward moments involving whips, either—but still, a boy that close to my underwear seemed just a little too intimate for my taste.

When we reach the laundromat, I make a dash toward the washer at the end of the row, hoping I can get my undies in without Will seeing that I have a few scandalous red lacy pairs, a few that have Hello Kitty on them, and worse, ones that read, right across the butt, ALL THIS AND BRAINS TOO. Luckily, he seems just as embarrassed by his own dirty clothes and heads off in the opposite direction. Suze, who is never embarrassed about anything, plops right down in the middle and sorts her dark thongs out from her whites.

As soon as all the washers are spinning around in tandem, we meet at a rickety old table in the center of the laundromat and sit down.

Will sighs, a satisfied and somewhat smug grin on his face. "Ah, I've missed that clean detergent smell. And the fabric softener. And machines that work on both indoor plumbing and electricity."

Suze lets out an unladylike snort. "I've missed McDonald's. And Starbucks. And movies. Remember movies, guys? I mean,

I think it's been four months since I've seen a movie, unless you count Jeff's safety training videos."

Suze and Will turn to me expectantly, and I realize they're waiting on me to voice my complaints. I clear my throat. "I, um . . ."

"Wait a minute. She isn't bitching and complaining. Could it be?" Will asks Suze. "Is the newbie in love with the faire?"

I feel my face redden, and I look down at my hands. "I do love it," I admit to my friends. "I haven't missed electricity like I thought I would. Maybe texting and talking to my friends, but I haven't missed Facebook, or TV, and I certainly haven't missed my job at the mall."

Will and Suze exchange a glance that I can't read. I go on in my own defense. "Besides, it's giving me time to work on art. I've been painting so much, and not just faces and teacups. In fact, I should probably see if I can buy another sketchpad here in town."

"She's gotten so much better at flirting with the customers, too, Indy. You should see her." Suze beams like a proud mama. "Sassy and efficient, all at once."

"And Sage says she's getting good at horseback riding. She told me you took Jiffy on a trot the other day." Will wipes a pretend tear from his eye and leans in to Suze, choking out, "Our little baby's all grown up!"

"I have," I say, accepting their teasing as a compliment, because it's not untrue. I add, with a good dose of pride, "And Robbie says my teacups are practically her bestsellers."

Suze looks at Will with fake concern. "I think our Ro may have drunk ye olde Kool-Aid."

Will nods solemnly. "Yep, she's one of us now."

One of us. I smile at that. Everything *does* seem to be falling into place. Everything, that is, except for the Revel date situation. Or lack thereof. And one other small, minor detail that has been gnawing at my brain like one of the horses with an apple: my future. I had been so content, just marching straight on the path my parents laid out for me, and then Suze, Will, Lindy, and even Robbie started putting all these thoughts in my head about majoring in art. They're getting my hopes up, showing me new paths, making me want other things . . . things I can't have.

"Earth to Ro . . ."

My head jerks up and Will and Suze are staring at me. Will waves in my face. "You still with us?"

"Um, yeah," I say, and try to shake myself out of my thoughts. "Sorry. I guess I must be tired. Still worn out from the tavern shift yesterday."

I laugh, but no one else does. Will's eyebrows scrunch together. "Are you okay?"

Warmth spreads throughout my chest at his concern, and I give him a half smile. "Yes," I lie.

"Liar," Suze says. She purses her lips. "You're obviously not okay."

"It's nothing," I tell her, but she's not buying it, and from the way Will's eyebrows come together in a V across his forehead, I can tell he's not either. "Really, guys. It's nothing."

"Oh, come on, Ro. Spill," Suze says, and I've never been able to keep things from Suze, even when it's embarrassing to talk about, so I tell her.

"It's just that you guys know exactly what you want to do with your lives, and I'm so jealous of that. I have no clue what I want to do."

Suze quirks a brow at me, her lips making a flat line. "Bull. You know what you want to do. Doesn't she, Will?"

Will looks uncomfortable, like he'd really rather not be brought into this conversation. He gives me a gentle smile before he speaks. "I think she does."

I roll my eyes at them and tease, "Okay then, wise career gurus, what do I want to do?"

"Art," Suze says simply. "You love it."

"I like art. What's your point?" I say. My tone is a bit sharp, but Suze and I have been down this road all too often lately and there's not much more I can say. She's been pestering me about it ever since our conversation the other night. Tirelessly. And I keep repeating the same stuff back, rather fatigued. I hate that she's bringing it up again, in front of Will, no less.

"You know it's not an option for me, Suze," I say, and hope that's the end of it. I plaster on a smile, which I hope looks casual, not strained. "So I was thinking maybe communications, or perhaps even pre-law. I don't really see myself in a courtroom, but I'd be great at legal research."

"You don't see yourself in a courtroom because you see

yourself in front of a canvas," Suze says. "I wish you'd just tell your parents. You should at least try." Suze looks to Will for support. "She loves it, so she should go for it, right?"

Will looks at me, and I can see something pass in his golden brown eyes. He nods once. "I think you should, Ro." He tries to smile at me. "I mean, if it's what you really love, you need to try. I think if you gave up art, you'd regret it."

"I don't have to give it up. I can still paint no matter what I major in," I snap at him, and he blinks, stunned. It's the first time I've ever even sounded angry at him, and honestly, it surprises me too.

"It's not the same," he argues, keeping his voice quiet and level.

I look between them, Will with his pitying eyes and Suze with her smug grin because she's right. Of course she's right. I love art. I liked it before, but I didn't understand how much, and now, with this summer experience, I know I've fallen in love with it. It's just like Will said when he was talking about physics: I think about it all the time. I dream about it when I sleep. I can't get it out of my head.

"You know Indy's right," Suze says, catching my gaze with her own, trapping me. "They want you to be happy, I'm sure, and I bet they'll surprise you. Lindy and Peter sure surprised the hell out of me when I told them I didn't want to be a lifer. I don't understand why you won't just tell them."

Suze's words strike a dissonant chord within me—a bitter, jealous chord. Suze's parents are wonderful. They are loving and affectionate, they are happy with what they have, they are artistic and strange and they love others who are artistic and strange. They don't care about their image; they don't care if they aren't rich. They count their friends and talents as successes, not their house or their car or their status in their social circle.

They are the exact opposites of my parents.

So how could Suze understand? How could she possibly know what it feels like to be afraid of disappointing her parents? To feel like she isn't good enough? To feel like she can't veer from the path they have created for her?

"Of course you don't understand, Suze," I tell her. "Your parents are different than mine."

Suze leans back into the rickety chair, crossing her arms over her considerable chest. "So?"

"So . . . ," I start, impatiently. "My mother is a lawyer. My dad's a partner in an accounting firm."

Suze's eyes narrow. "I'm failing to see your point."

I shrug. "I just mean that they're important people, and they want me to do something just as important."

"I see," Suze says. Her voice is tight and eerily flat. "So they're more important than my parents."

"That's not what I'm saying."

"Then what exactly are you saying?"

I take a breath and try to regroup. This conversation has gone off the rails a bit, heading toward a dangerous place, and I've got to get it back on track. I try to choose my next words carefully.

"I'm just saying that they expect a lot more from me."

"Because they're so important. And mine don't expect much from me, since they're unimportant," Suze says.

"No," I protest. "Stop. You're putting words in my mouth. All I'm saying is that it's easier for you because all they do is go around to Renaissance Faires. I mean, they wanted you to be a lifer instead of going to college. They don't have high expectations for you like mine do for me."

Suze looks at Will, nodding as if she understands what I'm saying completely. And for a moment, I'm relieved that she might understand. But then she starts speaking again, her tone acidic, and my stomach drops.

"You hear that, Indy? Being a lifer isn't a high expectation for Ro. It's not good enough. Because, apparently, all my parents do is go around to Renaissance Faires." Suze turns her sharp gaze at me. "I'm sorry my family's not important enough for you, Ro."

"Suze . . . that's not what I meant," I say, but Suze has pushed back from the table and is standing.

"Isn't it? You said it yourself. Being a lifer isn't good enough for you." Suze shakes her head, slowly and with disgust.

"No. I was talking about my parents. What my parents think. Being an artist won't be good enough for them. That's what I meant."

"Oh, I know what you meant, Ro. And I suppose being a seamstress or a falconer or a whip cracker probably isn't good enough either." Suze laughs, but it's without mirth. "I can't believe you. After all my mom has done for you . . . no, you know what? I'm glad I found out what you really think of us. I won't waste any more time with you."

"Suze . . ."

But Suze stalks off toward the laundromat exit, mumbling over her shoulder. "I'll walk back. Wouldn't want you to have to drive around a lowly Renaissance Faire worker . . ."

The bells on the laundromat door tinkle and Will stands, his eyes following Suze out to the parking lot. "I'll walk with her," he says, not looking at me at all, and I reach out, putting my hand on his forearm. He doesn't jerk away, but he looks down at my hand like it's done something offensive, and I pull back.

"I didn't mean that. I was just trying to say that my parents are stricter. And they have all these plans for me. That's all I was trying to say."

Will looks at me then, and I almost wish he hadn't. His brown eyes are dull, his shoulders are slumped, and the worst part is that he isn't angry or hurt, just disappointed. His family is deep in the Renaissance Faire circuit; he had no other choice than to take my words the same way Suze had.

"See you back at the faire," Will says, and takes off after Suze. I watch as he jogs to her and wraps her up in a hug. I can tell from the way she's hunched over and the way she's covering her face that she's crying, and that hits me hard. It feels like the fight with Kara all over again, maybe even worse. At least with Kara, I had faith that she'd come around no matter what and we'd forgive each other. With Suze, she doesn't have to forgive me and be my friend again. She can find a new tent to crash in and never speak to me again if she wants. And what about Will? Another new friend I might have just lost because I was too angry and jealous and proud to see that they were trying to help me.

I watch them until they disappear behind a building down the street. It's almost three miles back to the faire, as the crow flies, longer if they don't cut through the woods. I should get in my car and go after them, but then again, if I know Suze, she needs some time to cool down before she'll hear me out. And maybe by then, Will can convince her I didn't mean it the way she thought.

If he believes that himself.

I spend the next hour watching the clothes spin around in the dryer. When they're done I take them out and meticulously fold all of Suze and Will's things, because it's the least I can do.

Storm clouds are gathering as I pack all the laundry into my car, and I hope Will and Suze are already back at the campgrounds, safe and dry. It's barely past noon, though, and I can't face going back to the faire and seeing their hurt faces again, or worse, going back to the tent to see Suze packing up and moving out. So, like the coward I am, I go to the nearby grocery store with the Starbucks in it and have some coffee. I sit at a table by the window and watch the gray clouds swirl and roll, the wind blowing grocery bags around in shopper's hands, but it hasn't yet started to rain. I figure I could wait out the storm, maybe have another cup of coffee, but the truth is that it doesn't taste as good as Ramón's black sludge, and I don't even want the cupcake I bought to go along with it. To make things worse, the caffeine is making me feel jittery. I'm not sure if it's the coffee or my anxiety that's making my hands tremble, or a little bit of both.

After staring a bit longer out into the oncoming storm, I pick up my cupcake with trembling hands and set off toward the faire.

When I get back to the tent, Suze isn't there, as much as I hoped she would be. To kill some time, and to give myself a chance to think, I decide to take a long, hot shower. It helps more than I expect it to. The steam calms me, the warmth of the water soothes my aching muscles and makes the chill I felt under my skin fade slightly. Every time I think about the fight, though, the chill comes back with a vengeance and I'm left with goose bumps all over my skin.

But as I step out of the shower and wrap myself in a robe—Suze's robe—I feel guiltier than ever.

I have to apologize. That's all there is to it. And as quickly as possible, too. I can't let this go on the way I did with Kara and Meg, and worry for days about the things we said or should have said. I can't do that with Suze; it'll drive me to madness.

I tighten the belt on the robe and play out the scenario

in my head. I'll go get dressed, find Suze, apologize, try to explain if she'll hear me out, and of course, beg forgiveness. Then maybe I can find Will and do the same, if they're not together, talking about what a horrible person I am and questioning how they could have ever accepted me as a friend.

I push open the wooden door of the showers and I'm hit with a different kind of water. It is *pouring*. The storm that had threatened all day, looming over me like my guilt and regret, finally broke. Clutching my shower caddy, I do what any reasonable girl would do: I take off toward my tent at a dead sprint, awkwardly running through the mud in my flip-flops, squealing like an idiot.

But the rain is coming down so hard that it's made my shower practically useless. The bathrobe is weighing me down, and I'm soaked and miserable and defeated after only a few paces. With no thought in my head but getting to shelter, I run toward the closest tent I know, the only one I can think to go to right now: Christian's.

He's alone, luckily. I couldn't have dealt with more commentary about my bathrobe from Grant. I pull back the tent flaps and let them fall behind me as I enter. He's got his back turned to me, and what a great back it is.

"Hey," he says, his deep voice sultry. "Wondered what was taking you so long."

"I didn't know you were expecting me," I say, and he turns at the sound of my voice. The surprise on his face melts into a slow, sexy smile. "Waiting on someone?"

"Not anymore," he says. "I guess the rain is leaving people stranded. I love the rain."

Flattered, I feel myself blush. I reach up and smooth down my hair, only to realize how soaked it is and how drowned rat–like I must look. "I was showering. I guess that was pointless."

"I could tell from the robe," he says, making a little motion with his hand toward my sole piece of clothing. "I suppose some would call this an improvement over the towel."

"Not you?"

He chuckles, dark and wicked. "Not me."

I flush again and then curse myself for being such a little girl about it. "Mind if I wait out the storm, then?"

"Not at all." He sits on his air mattress and pats the space beside him, and I take my cue, trying to sit as gracefully as I can in the soaked robe.

He's not in his knightly attire today. He's just wearing jeans and a white shirt, and yet, he still looks like a prince. The jeans are perfect on him, definitely designer, probably better than even the kind Kyle liked to wear, and they look, some-how, like they've been tailored to his body. His hair has a bit of a wave in it today, probably from all the humidity, and it curls around his ears like a Greek sculpture.

How one person can look that good has to be some sort of weird anomaly in the universe. I'm sure somewhere there are several truly ugly people walking around so that nature can balance out all the attractiveness Christian got.

And here I am, next to him. Wearing a bathrobe that's not

even mine, hair wet and stringy, and no makeup at all.

"I thought maybe you were mad at me," I tell him. "I haven't seen you around much this week."

"Why would I be mad at you?" he asks, amused, and I wonder then why I thought he was. Maybe I'm so used to feeling like people are mad at me, it's just my default setting now. Or maybe I've been so upset that he hasn't asked me to the Revel that I was taking it the wrong way. Or maybe my confusion over Will has just made me feel guilty.

"Just being paranoid, I guess," I admit. "But Sage says you've been dealing with family stuff."

"Sage," Christian mumbles, then snorts, shaking his head. "Well, here I am, and we're finally alone, and it's storming so everyone's stuck where they are. So we should probably take advantage."

"How should we take advantage, do you suppose?" I say, trying to be coy.

"I have a few ideas . . ."

Christian leans close and touches his lips to mine. Somewhere in the back of my mind, I know that his arms are moving around me, ensnaring me and drawing me closer to him, that I'm pressed up against him, my bare legs vulnerable to the brush of his designer jeans, that his soft mouth is gently working mine open, more insistent and with more purpose than I ever remember Kyle having. But I can't really grasp all that. Not beyond the basic level, because all I can think is *finally*.

Finally, Christian is kissing me. Christian the knight. Prince Charming. *Finally*.

And it's so worth the wait. He's good at this. Skilled, even if he is a little impatient. His lips slide against mine, sensuous and firm, and when I feel his tongue touch my own, I hum at the thrill of it, and his voice joins mine.

Christian shifts, and I find myself being eased down onto his air mattress. It's so fast, so practiced, that it makes me dizzy, and a rush not unlike a shot of adrenaline shoots through me. It's not quite the feeling I'd hoped for—not the tingling of pleasure but the prickling of alarm instead.

No, wait. There is a tingling, but it's coming from my lips. It's like I've just been to the dentist and the numbing shot is wearing off.

Christian presses his mouth against mine harder and the tingling gets worse, and now I taste it, too. Minty. Like toothpaste or mints or . . .

Lip balm.

Tingly, expensive lip balm from the mall.

It takes more effort than it should to push Christian away because he's gotten so handsy in the last ten seconds, and I'm relieved when he's not touching me anymore.

"Have you been kissing Cassie?" I ask, wiping at my mouth.

"What? No. You really are paranoid, aren't you? Crazy, even."

I am utterly astounded. "Are you really trying to turn this around on me? You're wearing her lip balm."

Christian moves away from me, shaking his head like I'm the unreasonable one. "Yes, I was kissing Cassie. So what?"

"When?"

Christian bites at his thumbnail. "She was here before you."

His words as I entered the tent hit me like a sack of fertilizer: *Wondered what was taking you so long.*

"You were waiting on her when I came in, weren't you?" Christian doesn't deny it, but bites down hard on his thumbnail. "I can't believe it. Her and then me? All on the same day?"

Christian takes my disgust in stride. "Come on, Ro. It's not like you're my girlfriend or something."

"No, that's Cassie, right?" I snap, and Christian emits a laugh that's half nervous, half surprised.

"No, she's not my girlfriend either."

I stare at him, all the hurt and confusion swirling around in my head making it hard to comprehend what he's saying. Then it all clicks into place in one loud, resounding crack. The phone calls he just had to take, disappearing in the evenings, the same old tired story of "family stuff"—it can only mean one thing:

"You have a girlfriend, too, don't you? That's why you were always going off to answer your phone." I dig my fingers into my brow bones, trying to ward off the inevitable headache. "And you're cheating on her with Cassie. And me."

Christian looks rather smug when he says, "Well, not you until today. Technically."

I stand, my head touching the canvas roof of the tent. "And you're proud of that, aren't you?"

He doesn't answer but he doesn't have to. The expression on his face says it all.

"You've been lying to me this whole time." I say it more to myself than him, as if I have to say it out loud to understand it, and maybe accept it as well.

"I haven't been lying." I stare at him, and he merely shrugs. "So I didn't tell you about Cassie, and I didn't tell you I had a girlfriend. So what? You said yourself you just wanted to have fun."

My words from the bonfire three weeks ago come back to bite me right in the butt. I offer up a weak argument. "There's a difference between having a casual thing and messing around with two girls behind your girlfriend's back."

I can't believe it. Christian rolls his eyes at me. Like, legitimately rolls them, as if I'm the pesky little kid saying stupid stuff whom he can't get rid of. "*You* were the one who started this. You came on to me. You said you wanted to have some fun and you've been following me around—"

"I have not!"

Christian barely acknowledges that I've spoken. "You follow me to the stables, you sit by me when I play guitar, you come to the jousts, and now, here you are. In my tent. In only a bathrobe, I might add. Come on, Ro. I'm not an idiot. I know what you're after. This isn't the first time a girl's shown up at my tent half naked."

Well, if I'd had any doubt as to what state of dress Cassie was in earlier, it's gone now.

"But you flirted back," I protest, unwilling to let him convince me this is all my fault. "You acted like you wanted me."

"And that wasn't a lie," Christian says, and he says it in a way that could almost be sexy, if every syllable didn't make me feel like a low-life home wrecker.

And that's really what I am, because Christian hasn't said anything untrue. I did come on to him first. I did follow him around. I did pursue this. I did make it clear to him that I wasn't looking for something serious. Sure, I didn't know that he had a girlfriend, but that doesn't matter. In the end, I'm the "other woman" in this situation. I'm the Lacey.

Oh no. I'm the Lacey.

That realization on top of everything else makes tears come, unbidden and unstoppable. I wipe at my face but it's no use, Christian's seen them.

"Hey," he says. His voice is gentle and he drapes an arm across my shoulders. To anyone else this might seem soothing, but now I see right through it. It's fake, just a lie like everything else, and goodness knows his idea of "comforting" isn't what I need right now. "Don't get so worked up. It's just what everyone does out here, you know?"

"What everyone does?" I ask dumbly.

"Yeah. I know you're new, but I kind of already thought you got it, with you hooking up with Fuller and all. It's all just summer stuff. No feelings." Christian pulls back, looking at me meaningfully. "Fun stuff, like you said."

Fairemances. Suze warned me. Only this wasn't quite what I had in mind. There are two types of summer flings, I guess. A fling who doesn't care and a fling who cares, and I guess I wanted one who cared.

And I thought Christian did. At least a little bit. He sent me the troubadours, after all.

"But . . . ," I say to him. "If you don't have feelings for me, then how come you sent me the troubadours that day I was so upset because my ex was here?"

"I never sent you any troubadours." Christian squints. "That is a great idea, though. Should have thought of it."

"But if you didn't send them, who . . ." I don't have to finish the question because I know the answer now.

Will.

Will was the only one I told about Kyle, except for Suze. And Suze wouldn't have sent me troubadours. That's not something friends do for each other. That's something boyfriends do.

Or boys who want to be boyfriends.

I look at Christian. Maybe it's just my imagination, but he's nowhere near as beautiful now. He looks perfect still, maybe, but in a cold way. Aloof and uncaring. Not at all like Will, who always has a smile for me, except for today, when I insulted his whole existence.

"I didn't hook up with Will," I explain, though I have no idea why I even care what this cheater thinks of me. "But maybe I should have."

I walk out of the tent. Christian calls after me, but I can't hear what he's saying because of the rain. Even though it is coming down harder than ever, I walk slowly back to my tent, too dazed to go fast.

My tent is vacant, and although I hate that Suze is avoiding me, I'm grateful there's no one there. I sink down onto my mattress, my thoughts as muddy as my feet, and let myself cry.

16

WEEK 3 — TUESDAY

I'm in birthday party hell.

Little girl after little girl sits in my chair, all of them requesting butterflies or fairies or unicorns, all of them chattering about ice cream and knights and dragons.

A party of eight-year-old girls celebrating a birthday and talking constantly in their squeaky voices is irritating, but it beats the hell out of the cold stares Cassie's been giving me. I'm sure she and Christian had a good laugh at my expense last night, and they've been having good laughs since. When the birthday party moves on to the petting zoo, I almost beg to come with them just so I can get away, but I've got a job to do. So I spend what's left of the day in uncomfortable silence with Cassie, and run out the door as soon as the bell in the tower chimes.

Unfortunately, the bell tower chime also signals that the

last joust is soon, which means that in half an hour Sage will be expecting me for our riding lesson. There is absolutely no chance I can risk running into Christian in the stables, and there's no point in going riding today anyway. I'm too much of a mess. Even Jiffy's steady trot and the stillness of the forest won't help me now—in fact, all that quiet time is just the thing I need to avoid.

And since Suze still isn't talking to me, and I have to assume Will isn't either, all I've got is quiet time.

Impulse and desperation lead me to the kitchen behind the tavern, where I make myself useful peeling potatoes and rolling sporks and Wet-nap packets inside paper napkins. Ramón's disposition is equal to my own, and he doesn't question my motives when I hang around long after the joust is over. The boys in the kitchen try to remain classy for a few minutes, unused to a female presence, but it all goes to hell in a handbasket when one of them drops a whole tray of baked potatoes on the floor and they proceed to cuss one another out over who, exactly, is at fault. Somehow it makes me laugh, in spite of everything, and they relax around me and tease one another about their recent screwups, in the kitchen or otherwise.

A knock at the back door quiets their trash talking, and Ramón opens the door to reveal Sage. She looks past him to me, saying, "Hey, what's the big idea?"

I hop down off my stool by the sink and head outside, taking care to close the door behind me so the kitchen workers won't hear.

"Sorry. I just couldn't face the stables today."

"Why?"

I shrink slightly under Sage's interrogation.

"I found out about Christian. He has a girlfriend."

"So?"

"So . . ." I look at Sage. We're truly different people. This kind of thing would have just rolled off her back. Or maybe she would have challenged Christian to a sword fight and bullied him into submission. I don't know. All I know is that she won't really get this. "So he was lying to me. Flirting with me and trying to kiss me and all this time he had a girlfriend."

Sage kicks at the ground. "I know. He's a liar. Not your fault, though. So let's go riding."

"I really don't want to see him," I say again, as if the simple act of repeating it might make it sink into her thick head. Then what she said sinks into mine. "Wait. You knew?"

"Well, yeah," Sage says. "A guy like that? Yeah. Guys like Christian always have somebody."

"Why didn't you tell me?" I ask, and my voice rises up a few notches. "Were you covering for him? All that crap about family stuff?"

Sage has the decency to turn red and look generally uncomfortable. "I mean, I didn't exactly lie. I didn't know for sure, but I'd heard him talking to someone on the phone. But he said it was family stuff so . . ."

"That's your story and you're sticking to it?"

Sage makes a face. "It's the knight's code, dude. Sorry. I'm not going to rat out one of my brothers. It doesn't work that way."

"What a load of bull."

Sage's nostrils flare. "Hey, we have to be able to trust one another. If we can't trust one another off the field, someone's going to get hurt on the field. Know what I mean? It's faire loyalties and stuff."

"Faire loyalties," I scoff. "You know what I think? I think a lot of people use the faire as an excuse to act like assholes. I just didn't think you were one of them."

I whirl around, marching back into the kitchen, making sure to slam the screen door loud enough that Sage will hear it as she walks away. It's also loud enough to make everyone in the kitchen stop peeling potatoes or stirring sauces to stare at me. Their questioning eyes only make me feel worse, and tears cause my vision to go hazy.

Ramón's gruff voice saves me. "I think the steins need to be washed, and the dish towels could use some folding, and there's a whole floor out there that could use a good mopping."

When the workers don't move immediately, Ramón adds, "I wasn't saying it for my health. Get out of here."

The workers dash off, exiting from every door around us in a way that would be comical if I was in any mood to laugh.

Ramón sits down on a stool and pats the one next to it, and I take the hint. When he picks up a potato and a knife, I follow his lead. We shave off peels for a moment in silence.

"You and Sage fight?"

Ramón's voice is as rough as ever, but it's quieter, and that effort warms me. "Yes. But not just her. Suze and Will, too."

"It's been a busy summer for you."

I chuckle miserably. "It hasn't been all bad. But yesterday sucked."

Ramón grunts in understanding, but offers no advice or consolation. I set a fully peeled potato aside and reach out for another one, and that's when I realize Ramón isn't peeling the potato—he's carving it. A shape is emerging from its dirty white flesh, its form rustic and crude from the many scrapes of the small knife, but I recognize it immediately. A bulbous nose, comically large eyes, a droopy smile and a lazy twirl of mustache, the beginnings of a long, pointed hat.

"You make the trolls," I whisper, awed. "The wooden trolls I see in Lindy's shop, and sometimes The Bone Needle and even Robbie's place. You made the one that got me here."

I'm sure that last part doesn't make any sense to Ramón at all, but he nods and begins to shave out more potato, revealing more of the odd troll inside it. "I whittle. Sometimes. When the mood strikes me."

"They're really good," I tell him, hoping he doesn't catch the many notes of surprise in that phrase.

He doesn't acknowledge my compliment, but his voice is softer when he speaks again. "It took a long time to learn. A lot of scars."

Ramón sets his knife and potato aside and then holds his

hands out between us, flipping them palm side up so I can see them clearly in the harsh kitchen lights. His hands, which are knobby and cracked, also have deep gashes in them, old scars that have lost the angry red of wounds and are now silvery pink.

"Are all of those scars from woodworking?" Ramón nods. "But . . . why? Why do it if you cut your hands all the time?"

Ramón picks up his potato and knife. For a moment he doesn't speak, and I wonder if he's going to answer me. Then he sets back to carving and says to me, "When I cut myself, I learn. It's the pain that will make me remember not to do it again. It makes me mindful."

I think about that, and it leads my thoughts right back to Kara, Meg, and Suze. "I must need more pain then. I do stupid stuff and instead of learning from it, I do it again. You know, I had a fight with my friends before I came out here, then a fight with Suze for almost the same reason. And this guy, my boyfriend, hurt me a lot. He cheated on me and we broke up. And what did I do when I came out here? I spent the last three weeks flirting with Christian the cheater. The pain hasn't sunk into my thick head yet."

Ramón hums in agreement. "Sometimes it takes a lot of pain, *deep* pain, to remember. Sometimes we heal too quickly and we forget. That's why scars are so useful."

"Because they remind us of the pain?"

"Yes, but also because they remind us that we went on in spite of it. We healed. We forgave others; we forgave ourselves. We picked up a knife and whittled again."

There's a lot buried in that statement, ghosts and old memories, heartache and triumph, and it hangs heavily in the air, refusing to go unacknowledged.

I turn to him and I feel like I'm seeing him for the first time, seeing underneath the hard and distant exterior to the big heart and the melancholy spirit below. Ramón, the surly boss of the tavern, who whittles adorable trolls, who sometimes makes awful stew but whose baking could reduce you to tears, who has scars all over his hands and perhaps a few on his heart as well.

"Sounds like you're speaking from experience."

I don't dare ask him directly about Magda or any of the other rumors I may have heard, so this is the right thing to say: open-ended enough that he could tell me more if he's comfortable, or be completely vague if he wanted.

To my surprise, one corner of his mouth curls up. "I've done some living, I guess you could say."

I smile at that but I'm careful to keep my eyes on the potato. "I suppose scars can make a person more interesting."

"Of course. I wouldn't trust someone without them."

I laugh but then sober quickly. Setting down the knife and the potato, I turn my whole body toward him. He lowers the troll potato in his hands, which now has a complete hat, and his eyes meet mine.

"And what if you don't need to forgive someone, it's that they need to forgive you?"

Ramón stares at me for a moment, then grunts and begins

to work on the troll's backside. "Then you beg and plead and promise them you won't hurt them again."

Beg, plead, promise things. I can do that. I certainly never want to hurt Will or Suze again. There's just one catch.

"But what if they don't forgive me?"

"They will."

"But how can you be sure?"

Ramón shifts on his stool, and I can tell he's grown a bit irritated at my uncertainty. And probably all of my talking and questions. Regardless, he holds out his hands to me, showing me his scars again.

"Scars here," he says, using one hand to point at the other, "are not the same as they are here." He taps on his skinny chest. "Not the same at all. The heart is quick to forget the pain. To forgive. The heart wants to take another chance. Be friends again. Or perhaps," he adds with a sly smile, "fall in love again."

"Sounds like the heart is a dirty traitor," I say, startling a laugh from Ramón.

"Yes, it is a dirty traitor. The dirtiest. But it also tells the truth."

The truth. My heart has been so broken and bruised, so jealous and unfulfilled. But, I realize, it's also been honest with me. In spite of what happened with Kyle, and even with Christian, I want to be with someone again, I want to care about someone and hope they care about me. Even though I don't have a family like Suze's, even though my parents won't be supportive of my dreams, I paint anyway. I long for it anyway. I want to spend all my time learning and doing and being an artist. The truth is there, even if the flip side of it hurts.

"You're right," I tell Ramón. "I think my heart's been broken all summer, and yet here I am, still longing, chasing dreams, as if all the pain doesn't matter. It's still there, right along with the happiness."

Ramón nods, then sets back to work on his whittling. He leans close to me and whispers, "Healing takes time. Sometimes a lot of time."

"So what do I do?" I ask him. "How can I get it back to normal so that I only feel the good stuff?"

"You can't," Ramón says. He opens his hand and a completed troll stares up at me with its lopsided mouth and potato-white eyes. It's cute, and remarkably artistic and detailed for something made out of a vegetable. "Take the chance anyway. Risk the pain."

Take the chance anyway. I have to try to work things out with Will. And really, Will's not that big of a gamble as far as my heart is concerned. He's been here for me all summer, making me laugh, making sure I'm settled in at the faire, sending me troubadours when I feel down, roasting marshmallows for me when I'm all alone at the campfire. And, like Suze, he's been rooting for me to be an artist. No, my heart would be safe in Will's hands.

"There's just one problem," I say, blowing out a frustrated breath. "In order to take a chance, I've got to make a few things right first."

Ramón nods. "Will's heart is the same as yours—scarred, but wanting to heal."

I look at Ramón, impressed and charmed by his intuition. I haven't mentioned that it's Will I'm talking about, but somehow, he knew. I'd be willing to bet Ramón knows a lot more about what goes on at this faire than he lets on, sneaky man that he is. And I kind of adore him for it.

"Thank you," I whisper, overcome for a moment by his kindness, and Ramón lets out a startled noise that borders on a squeak when I drape myself around his shoulders and hug him. He hugs back, taking care to hold the knife far away from my skin.

Before I go, he supplies me with a sticky bun and a giant glass of milk.

"Sugar makes the heart heal faster," he says with a sparkle in his eye that I've not seen before.

I doubt sugar has anything to do with healing a heart, but one of Ramón's sticky buns can't hurt. There's a reason they call it comfort food, after all.

The workers are allowed back into the kitchen and they work around me as I sit and eat, and I formulate a plan amidst the hubbub: I'll find Will tonight and beg him to talk to me. Maybe he'll listen, even if he doesn't particularly want to hear. Hopefully, I can fix this thing with him, and fix myself a little in the process. I just hope Ramón's right about hearts.

Somehow, I don't doubt he is.

Dinner that night is worse than I expected. Ramón sees to it that I have an extra helping of mashed potatoes, but he is the only spot of warmth in the whole thing. Suze sits with Grant, refusing to acknowledge my presence, and there's no room at Will's table. He doesn't try to make room, either, so I ditch my tray and take my plate, planning on eating alone like the pathetic, friend-insulting loser that I am. But as I pass by Will I catch him looking at me, and so I bend next to him and whisper, "Can we talk later?"

He nods.

"Meet me by the menagerie after dinner?"

He nods again and I leave him to eat in peace. I head to the menagerie because I can wait for him there, but also because the goats and the ducks are better company than none at all. I force down most of the mashed potatoes out of gratitude for Ramón, but I can't stomach the green beans or the sausage. Instead of wasting it, I toss the scraps into the pen and watch as the ducks waddle over and battle for them, quacking and flapping their wings. They kind of remind me of the vendors battling for customers in the village, and the thought makes me giggle.

"Good to see you laughing." Will's voice makes me turn around. He's not inside the ring but is walking from the direction of the kitchen.

"It's a whole lot better than insulting my friends." We walk toward each other until we meet in the middle. His whip is looped around his shoulder, and he's in a shirt that I know I folded yesterday. "I'm really sorry about what I said."

"I know. And I know you didn't mean it like it came out."

I let out a breath that I might have been holding since yesterday. "I didn't. But still, I'm a crappy friend. I know you and Suze were just trying to help me. I'm just—"

"Scared?"

"Exactly. I mean, what if my parents say no? Or refuse to pay for college? Or worse, what if they're disappointed? Duncans aren't artists. Duncans are lawyers and accountants and business owners."

Will studies me, his face expressionless save for the hint of a sparkle in his eyes. "I think Duncans can probably be whatever they want to be. Even face-painting Picassos."

"I don't have to be Picasso to face paint," I say, parroting his words from days ago. "Besides, after I conquer your mustache I have much higher aspirations."

"Is that so?"

"Of course. Your backdrop needs a ton of work."

Will bursts out laughing. "Yeah, it really does. I think Davis might have painted it himself, actually. It looks like a six-year-old did it."

I watch him as his laughter dies away to a thoughtful smile. "So," I begin, "we're friends?"

"Friends."

"Is that all you want to be?"

Will's head jerks up. "What?"

"I know you sent the troubadours."

"Yeah, well . . ." He shrugs. "You were really upset. I didn't like seeing you upset."

"I think maybe it's more than that. Isn't it?"

Will doesn't say anything, and I can't tell what he's thinking. The ambiguity makes me nervous, throws me for a loop. I expected him to agree with me, or maybe to confess right away the reason why he sent the troubadours, but this particular scenario never played out once in my head.

Determined, I decide maybe it's best if I show him what I mean. I reach over and tug at the whip over his shoulder, bringing us close together until there's no space between us at all. Then I take a deep breath, tell myself to take the chance, and lean in.

My lips touch his and this . . . this is so much better than Christian. So much better than Kyle, even. His lips are warm and giving, not impatient, and I feel myself fall into the kiss, spinning headfirst into something inviting and wonderful.

But then it stops, his lips parting from mine too quickly, leaving me cold and bereft.

"No, Ro."

"What?" It comes out as a whisper, nearly as indecipherable as my thoughts.

Will is shaking his head, and it's like a dark cloud has passed over his face. "I said no."

Hearing it a second time is like a punch right to the gut, and I clutch my stomach in response. "So . . . you don't like me?"

"Are you kidding me?" Will laughs, but it's tuneless. "Ro, I liked you from the moment I saw you. Heck, that first time you rolled down your car window I wanted to kiss you like this."

"Then why . . ." I can't bring myself to ask him why he won't kiss me now.

"I've liked you all summer long," he says, swallowing thickly. "And I've watched you chase after Christian all summer long. I thought maybe it was okay, because every girl seems to like Christian, and I thought you'd see me eventually."

"I do!" I say. "I see you now."

"Yeah," he says, resigned. "*Now*. Because Christian's no longer an option."

I open my mouth to ask how he knows, but it doesn't matter. I shake my head. "It's not because of that. I was just confused because we were friends, that's all. It's you I want to be with."

Will nods in understanding, though that doesn't make him look any less miserable. "Maybe you do want to be with me. But I've spent weeks watching you go after him, and moping about your ex and I . . ."

Will closes the distance between us and takes my hands in his. "I'm sorry. I really like you. So much that it scares me a little, but that's why I don't want it this way. Because right now I feel like a stand-in. I don't want to be the stand-in. I want to be your first choice. That's all I've wanted this whole time."

"But . . ."

"I'm sorry, Ro. Maybe someday, but not now."

Will squeezes my hands and then lets them go before turning and walking away from me. I watch him, his shoulders drooping, his whip hanging from his arm, until he rounds behind the barn and disappears from sight. I hear the whip cracking, and maybe I'm just imagining it, but it sounds more melancholy than energetic today.

When I get back to my tent, I can tell Suze has been there and was rummaging through her things, but she's long gone. I want to cry but I can't. It's like I'm in shock. So I take out my supplies and start to paint something very abstract, a long streak of brown and then a few of orange and yellow, until I've painted a single flame. It's all alone against a gray sky, burning down to ashes.

17

WEEK 3—WEDNESDAY

"Oh. I thought you'd be at breakfast."

Suze's voice wakes me up from the only minutes of sleep I've had all night. After I painted, I spent most of the night thinking about Will and what he said, or Suze and what I did, or Ramón's advice. The result was near-sleeplessness, save for the few minutes right as the sun was coming up when I was too exhausted to think anymore.

I sit up and wipe at my eyes. Suze is bent over her stuff, grabbing at her clothes.

"Suze."

She reaches for a hairbrush.

"Suze. Please talk to me."

She tucks the hairbrush under her arm, hugs her clothes close to her, and turns to go. Before her foot can hit the stair, I blurt, "I kissed Will."

Suze straightens slowly and turns around. "What?"

"I kissed Will but he told me he didn't think we should be together yet, and I'm really sorry about the other day, Suze. Really sorry."

Suze steps back in and sinks down on her air mattress. She's scowling, but I see the curiosity in her eyes. Even mad at me, a story about kissing Will Fuller is too much to resist.

"Will, not Christian, huh?"

"Well, there was some Christian kissing too."

Suze's eyes widen so much it's almost comical, but she quickly trains her face into a blank expression. Almost. There's still too much curiosity in her eyes.

"Well, I'd certainly like to know how that happened." She crosses her arms over her chest and pins me with a stare. "But this doesn't mean I'm not angry anymore. It was a really crappy thing to say."

"It was, and I didn't mean it," I rush to tell her. "I'm just . . . jealous that your parents are so awesome about what you want to do."

"I know," Suze says. It's not exactly an acceptance of my apology, but I remember what Ramón said to me yesterday: Sometimes it takes time. I sit next to Suze and spill my guts, including every last humiliating detail.

"So let me get this straight," Suze says when I'm finished. "Christian has a girlfriend, and Cassie, *and* still tried to get with you, then you realized it was Will you should have been with all along—which, by the way, calls for a giant I Told You

So—and he didn't kiss you back and said maybe, but not now?"

"That about sums it up."

Suze reaches up and rubs at her temples. "This is a mess, Ro."

"The messiest." I grin at her. "But it was good to tell you. I've missed you."

"I've missed you too," Suze says. "It's been awful not talking to you. And Grant snores, so I haven't slept much at all."

I laugh, and it feels good rumbling around in my chest. I haven't laughed nearly enough these past few days. "Does that mean you forgive me?" I ask her.

"Of course, though if you ever say anything like that again I'm going to turn Mama Mulligan on you, and fairy doll-mother or not, she could kick your ass."

"I have absolutely no doubt about that," I say, laughing some more.

"Okay, I have to be at the tavern in about fifteen minutes or Ramón will have my head. It's bar cleaning day." Suze stands and drops her belongings back onto her air mattresses, signi-fying the end of her long self-imposed exile. "But why don't you come by the wagon for dinner tonight? It's Wednesday, which means meatloaf."

"I could never say no to Lindy's cooking," I say. After she leaves, I hurriedly dress and make my way to the face paint-ing tent, practically skipping with happiness. Will may not have said yes, but he didn't give me a hard no, either, and now Suze and I are back to normal. Maybe, with those things in mind, Cassie's mocking smirk won't be so hard to bear today.

Cassie's applying lip balm as I walk in, as per usual. She surely has to be running low on that tingly stuff by now.

We don't speak, which is for the best, and I organize my station in the silence until the first customers arrive. The silence continues all the way up to when Cassie leaves for her shift at the tavern, and I could swear that even the customers sense the tension. More than a few children cast nervous glances from me to Cassie, then back to me again, as if they're afraid World War III might break out between us.

But after Cassie leaves, all the tension and chill in the tent evaporates. Finally relaxed, I get up to stretch the strain out of my shoulders and back and my stomach rumbles. Almost time for Lindy's meatloaf. In fact, I haven't had a customer in a while. I could probably get away with turning the sign to closed and taking off for the night.

I'm about to do just that when a little girl wanders into the tent, destroying my hope of leaving early. She looks to be about eleven, and she's a tad overweight. She also has really curly hair, which I know from personal experience can be a pain in the butt.

I fix my frown into a smile and ignore my empty stomach. "I'm Ro, what's your name?"

"Anna," the girl replies. She bites hard on her lower lip.

"Do you want your face painted?" I ask, praying the answer is no.

"Maybe." Anna lowers her gaze to the ground.

I sigh. This might take a while. "Are your parents around?"

"Mom's in the jewelry shop with Mike."

I don't know if Mike is a brother, the girl's stepfather, or just the mother's boyfriend, but I have to wonder if Mom even notices Anna's gone.

"Does she know you're here?"

Anna worries her bottom lip between her teeth. "She told me to stay in here for a while."

Ah. So I'm a babysitter. Great.

I look at her, with her cute little dimples and her sad expression, almost like she wants to apologize to me for being such a bother, and my heart breaks for her. Suddenly my rumbling stomach doesn't matter and my impatience shames me.

"Well, Anna, that's fine. We're going to have a great time." Her face lights up, which makes me melt. "Why don't you come over here and pick out some colors you like? Once you have the colors, we can think of something to make out of them."

I lead her over to look at the colors on my desk. She takes a long moment, studying the colors with the kind of scrutiny I usually see only from my parents, or teachers, or Jeff. Then she points out three colors: orange, turquoise, and purple.

"Perfect," I say, and the approval of her choice makes her beam. I sit and motion her into the chair opposite me, then take the small tins of color out so I can arrange them close to my hands. I study her and an idea forms in my head, as clear as if someone had whispered it in my ear. She's got a pretty face, heart-shaped with a strong chin, and she's got lovely long eyelashes and a sprinkling of cute freckles over her cheekbones. I need to highlight that, show everyone how pretty she is, and make her feel important all at once.

"How about I make you a butterfly princess?"

The question is met with a small squeal and excited nodding, and I completely understand. I'm just as excited to get started.

I begin with purple over her left eye and draw the outline of a butterfly's body all the way down over her nose and right cheek, and then outline two large wings that take up the rest of her face. I shade that in with the orange, giving the outline of the butterfly's body and wings a sparse tinge. It's the turquoise I want to use the most.

When I lean over to get a cloth to wipe my brush, I balance myself on something thick and leathery, and I look down, realizing it's the B.A.B. I push it aside. It's just taking up space that I need for my paints. I don't need it. Not for the butterfly princess; not really for anything. I'm a better artist than that.

And it feels good to know it.

Anna and I chat as I work, bonding over our curly hair and our love of Ramón's sticky buns. In the end, I end up painting on a shimmering golden crown and even sticking on some rhinestones that I found in an old jar in the tent. When I'm done, Anna's in awe of how she looks, gaping at herself in the mirror for ages. Then she reaches into her pocket and pulls out a crumpled five-dollar bill.

"Is this enough?"

I take her bill and give her two dollars back, which will cover the paint and the rhinestones. "Yes. More than enough. You get the curly hair discount."

I wink at her, and she giggles. It's that giggle, shy but happy, that I capture in my Polaroid of her. I don't know if the camera will catch the pride there in Anna's face, but I don't need it to. I might just remember it forever.

As Anna scampers back out into the faire, I call after her, "Have fun! Go see Cracker Jacques. He's awesome!"

It's time for dinner at Lindy's, and I turn the sign to CLOSED, but before I leave I take a moment to just look around the tent and breathe. My hands are tired from gripping the paint brushes all day, the callouses prickly and sore. My lower back aches from sitting in a chair for so long, leaning forward to get close to my particular canvas. The tent is a mess of color, drips and splashes, looking thoroughly used and abused.

I'm tired. Exhausted, even. But as exhausted as I feel, there's an even bigger sense of accomplishment, of pride. Of feeling like I've found something I needed, or that maybe it's found me. And as I stand there, inhaling the scent of grass, dirt, and paint, I realize: I don't want to give this up. I want this always. I have to take a risk and major in art, even if it means disappointing my parents.

As I step out of the tent and head off toward the Mulligan

wagon, I have the feeling that, for the first time in my life, I know where I'm going.

Lindy sets down a plate of meatloaf and cheesy broccoli in front of me and my stomach makes a noise of appreciation. Or perhaps it's a demand.

Lindy hears and laughs. "You poor thing, spending most of your time all the way out in the kids' section, nothing but ice cream if you get hungry."

"Yeah, Mom, because ice cream is terrible," Suze says, hoisting a considerable chunk of meatloaf toward her mouth.

"It is if you want to stay healthy." Lindy tucks herself into the table but adds another slice of meatloaf to her husband's plate before she lifts her own fork. "Or fit into a dress for the Revel."

"I don't think that's going to be a problem, since I'm not going," I mutter.

"Nonsense. Of course you are," Lindy says, jabbing her fork in my direction. "You can't miss the Revel. It's so lovely, and everyone's there, all dressed up. . . .Tell her, Suze."

"She's right, you can't miss it," Suze says, grinning, knowing she's being no help whatsoever.

"I don't have a date," I say.

"Why don't you ask that Fuller boy? He's always seemed like such a sweetie," Lindy says, and Suze coughs, covering an errant giggle.

"Yeah, Ro. Why don't you ask the Fuller boy?" she asks, feigning innocence.

I kick at her under the table and miss, making her snort. I turn to Lindy and try my best to act ladylike. "It's . . . complicated with the Fuller boy."

Lindy barrels right over me, oblivious to Suze's and my exchanged looks and my obvious discomfort.

"I have always thought Will Fuller was handsome. He looks so much like his father. Suze, I know you don't remember his father from the circus days, but Jack Fuller? Rugged. Handsome. Always seemed like the type to do something crazy and adventurous, like run off to explore the rain forests or join the Peace Corps or something. He's so charming, too. You wouldn't believe the way he'd make us all laugh. Very charming, indeed."

"I am right here," Peter mutters around a mouthful of broccoli. "Your handsome husband who is also adventurous and rugged."

"Aww, sorry Pete. My love. My life," Lindy says, and when Peter's focus is back on his food, she mouths to us: "Seriously, Jack Fuller? Dreamy."

Suze and I giggle quietly, but then I grow melancholy. I frown at Suze, and she sticks out her bottom lip in sympathy. "Unfortunately, I think maybe I blew it, and I don't think Will will want to go with me. And I can't go dateless. I just can't face Kyle and Lacey if I'm a lonely loser."

"I wouldn't give up yet," Lindy says, and Suze agrees.

I shrug. "It's just as well. I don't have a dress anyway. I didn't bring any of my dresses with me."

Suze makes a face that says she's both shocked and disgusted. "Oh, you're such a newbie. I forgot. You can't wear modern clothes to the Revel anyway. The faire staff has to be in period dress. Jeff's rules."

My heart sinks. There's no way I can go to the Revel then, even if Will would go with me. None of my day-to-day costumes are fancy enough. I'd need a fairy godmother to make me a dress and turn a pumpkin into a carriage and turn Jiffy into . . . well, a bigger horse.

It's as if Lindy can read my mind. "Don't worry about that! I have just the thing for you in my shop. It'll take some hemming, but that's no problem."

Her offer nearly reduces me to tears, but I can't let her do that. She's been so kind to me, and I've done nothing but insult her to her daughter in return, however accidental it may have been.

"I don't want to take up your time," I tell her, the ball of guilt in my throat making it hard to speak. "You've done too much for me already, and I'm sure you have your own costumes to work on."

Lindy laughs, her voice echoing around the wagon. "Oh no, dear. Peter and I always go as the same thing. Our hawk and dove are famous! I'm working on Suze's peacock costume, but it's almost done. Really. It's no trouble at all."

"Thank you. I don't know what I'd do without you. You're so incredibly generous," I say, and I think my earnestness embarrasses the lot of them, because Suze helps herself to more meatloaf and Lindy titters on about how excited she is that I might be hooking up with Jack Fuller's son. You'd think it was her own daughter she was talking about, which makes me feel all gooey and warm inside, the embodiment of Ramón's sticky buns.

I've got to figure out some way to repay their kindness, or at least express my appreciation, since there's no way I can truly repay them for all they've done. I start by gathering the dinner plates when we're finished eating so that Lindy can enjoy the rest of her dinner without playing hostess.

There's a small wastebasket under the countertop, and I scrape the leftover crumbs into it before laying the dishes in the sink. Lindy's taken up a good portion of the tiny counter displaying a beautiful tea set. It's Robbie's handiwork; I can tell by the way the petals of the roses are shaped out of curving brushstrokes. On the window ledge, Lindy's propped up a few family photos (one of Suze as a toddler, enchanting in a tiny little Renaissance dress) and a cross-stitch that says HOME IS WHERE YOUR RUMP RESTS. Lindy has certainly made this wagon feel like home—with personal touches that show all the love and warmth they share.

Maybe if I want to thank them, I could bring my own personal touch to this place. Maybe I could make my own mark on the wagon somehow.

I think of the fading, cracked mural on the side of the wagon and know what I have to do: The Mulligans need a new mural, an updated one that includes Suze. I'll have to spend every minute of my free time to get it done before the faire closes for the summer, but it will be totally worth it. There's just one problem . . . there's no way I can keep it a secret. Not exactly.

I turn back toward the family. "Hey, Lindy, have you ever thought about repainting the mural on the wagon?"

Lindy frowns and her gaze shifts to Peter, and I wonder if I've brought up a touchy subject. "Well, honestly, we've been meaning to for years. But Robbie gets so busy during faire season, and everyone else is so expensive . . ."

Peter rubs Lindy's forearm. "We could always just put some red paint over it."

"No," Lindy says, and though it's not forceful, it's obvious she won't budge from that answer. "This wagon's been in your family for generations. It's got to say Mulligan."

"Would you let me paint a mural?" I ask, and all three Mulligan heads jerk towards me in surprise. "As a thank-you for all you've done. I totally understand if you don't want anyone besides Robbie to touch it, but I'd love to do it for you. You've done so much for me."

Lindy and Peter exchange a look that's then exchanged with Suze. Then, at the unspoken agreement, Peter stands and offers his hand. But before I shake it, I add an important condition to the deal.

"Wait. You have to promise me you won't look until I'm done," I say. "I'll cover it up each night and none of you are allowed to peek until it's finished. Deal?"

Lindy looks over at Suze, who has taken a sudden, intense interest in a floret of broccoli. "Suze, can you promise not to look?"

Suze bites down on the broccoli and chews, mumbling around the green, "You know I'm no good with surprises . . ."

"Suze . . . ," Lindy, Peter, and I say in unison.

"Fine," she says, swallowing. She holds up three fingers like a Boy Scout. "I won't look. Promise."

Peter and I shake on it, Lindy hugs me, and Suze gives me a bright smile, even though I know she's going to beg me about seeing the mural later, despite her promise. The air in the wagon is charged with elation, and as a bonus, Lindy suddenly remembers there's dessert waiting for us. She reaches into their small fridge and pulls out a strawberry pie that looks heavenly, and doles out whopping pieces for each of us.

We sit and dig in, picking up the conversation right where we left off.

"Did you know the Burkes are coming to the Revel, Peter? Won't that be fun?" Lindy says while scooping up a juicy strawberry. "Now, if only the Hansens and the Fullers came too, it would be like a circus reunion. We should invite them . . ."

Although Peter grunts at hearing the Fuller family name again, Lindy's excitement about a possible reunion is palpable, and it also seems contagious. I'd love a reunion with my own friends. It's been so long since I've seen them, or even talked to them, and I'm dying to tell them all about my summer and to hear what's going on with them as well. The Revel would be the perfect opportunity to do that, and they'd love getting all dressed up and seeing all the staff (mainly me) in period dress.

Plus, as an added bonus, if Meg and Kara and Brian can come to the Revel, I won't be alone when Kyle and Lacey make their appearance, and it might help make up for leaving them behind over the summer. I'll have to go into town to e-mail them an invite, but I'm sure I can find some time soon to sneak away.

I pick up my fork and dig into Lindy's strawberry pie, smiling so wide I can barely chew, and start to make plans.

18

WEEK 3—SATURDAY

The morning of the Fairie Queen's Revel, it seems as if the very air is buzzing with excitement.

King Geoffrey's Faire is closed for preparations, officially, but inside it might as well be Christmas Eve at the North Pole. Everyone (save for Ramón and his cooking team) has abandoned their usual posts and is busy readying the whole village with dazzling efficiency for Revel guests.

For a place that frowns on electricity during the normal season, it is surprisingly electric. Even in the sun's noonday brightness, the village glows. Some of the men, including Peter, are on ladders, hanging long strands of lights across the walkways and paths, connecting to outlets on poles and buildings. I never noticed the outlets before, but then, I never needed to. To make things even more festive, they hang garlands of bright greens, purples, and golds in between each string of lights. The vendors have gotten into the spirit too. They've decorated their doors and windows, and their wares are sitting outside their shops, displayed elegantly on tables, looking even more tempting than usual. I can only imagine that at night, when the sun is down, this place is going to look like a carnival—a strange, gorgeous Renaissance dreamland.

I'd help with the decorations, only I'm busy doing some of my own. For the past few days I've been working on Phase One of the Thank the Mulligans Project: painting their masks for the Revel. I asked to do that in addition to the mural after seeing the masks they were planning to wear. Although they were nice, they were starting to fade and crack, and I promised Lindy and Pete that mine would be better. To get it done away from their curious eyes, I'd been stealing time during the day at the face painting tent, at Robbie's sometimes, and at night too. In Will's tent.

Once I explained what I wanted to do for the Mulligans, Will was eager to help and offered his tent as a secret place to work on the masks. Unfortunately, the nearness of him also makes me hyperaware of how much I like him, and I have to bite my tongue when I want to tell him so. We don't talk about our feelings for each other, and we certainly don't mention the incredible kiss we shared, but despite these awkward land mines in our conversation, it feels comfortable with him. He's helping me hone all my ideas for the masks, and we seem to get a little closer every day. I guess we can be good friends, once I get over wanting more.

When I get to Will's tent, he's already working, my paints spread around him. He's decorating his mask too, in plain black and white with an interesting geometric pattern, but he refuses to tell me what it is.

"Some kind of jester," I say, making him jump in surprise.

"Even if that was it, which it's not because that's lame, I will never tell." He pauses his brushstrokes long enough to hand me my mask, which is almost finished. It's just as well I haven't told him what I'm going to be either. I actually can't, because Lindy hasn't even told me what she's dressing me as, but still, we're even. I pick up my brush, move the glittery gold paint closer to me, and get to work.

We're silent for a while; easy, comfortable silence, and while we work I try to convince myself it's for the best that he's not my date to the Revel. It'll be better if he's not there when Kyle walks in; that way he won't think it was all about getting back at an ex.

Which it might have been, with Christian. With Will it's so much more.

I look at him, melting at the way he's focusing so hard to get his lines right, his glasses slipping down over the bridge of his nose as he scrunches it in concentration. It's totally adorable, and I have to wonder again how I didn't see that right away.

I'm fighting the urge to try to kiss him again when Will says, "So, your friends are coming?"

I deflate a tad. "I don't know," I admit. "I e-mailed them

in town but I haven't been able to get back and check for a response. Maybe they won't want to, and I'd totally understand that. I ditched them for this place, you know? So maybe they resent it and would rather just stay home."

"I doubt that. They sound like they're too good of friends to be that petty." Will looks at me, his golden-brown eyes making my stomach do a somersault. "I'd like to meet them."

"Trust me, they'll want to meet you, too," I say. "And I hope you're right. You know, we've been friends since we were in elementary school."

"Friends like that are the best. Because they remember the times you ate paste in school or peed your pants at a sleepover or blew up your microwave by nuking Peeps until they got big." Will laughs at himself and adds, "In other words, they've seen you at your worst and are still friends with you in spite of yourself. Davis is like that for me."

"I didn't know you'd known each other that long."

"Yeah. His dad used to be the blacksmith here before he left and got a job in the real world. Davis stuck around for some reason. He's been torturing us with his presence ever since."

I laugh at that, and notice that Will is watching me instead of painting his mask. We both look away quickly. After a moment of nervous silence, he says, "Hey, you don't have to teach those Renaissance dances with Suze, do you?"

"No! I narrowly escaped that humiliation somehow. I don't think Suze wanted the torture of teaching me the dances first, so that I could teach the guests. But Grant wasn't so lucky. He's got to dance with Suze all night."

"Ouch. Painful." Will's paintbrush stops moving and he looks at me again. "I could teach you a dance or two if you want . . ."

It's all I can do not to jump to my feet and give a celebratory shout, but I manage to keep myself planted on the tent floor and tease him some. "You're risking broken toes."

"Some things are worth the risk."

"Yeah, I'm learning that," I tell him. The air around us has suddenly become far too warm and too thick, and I'm a little afraid I'll try to kiss him again. So I give his mask a very obvious glance and say, "Are you a zebra?"

"Not even close, Rainbow Ro."

As I approach the Mulligan wagon, a mere two hours before the Revel, the box in my hands is shaking because I'm so nervous. Not because of the dance, or seeing Kyle, or dancing with Will, but because I'm about to present Phase One of the Thank the Mulligans Project, and I'm not sure they'll like the masks.

Lindy sees me coming from the tiny side window of the wagon and flings the front door open, welcoming me in. Before I enter, because I just can't stand it anymore, I thrust the box at her and squeak out a pathetic, "I finished the masks."

So much for presentation.

As Lindy fumbles with opening the box while balancing it in her hands, I ramble on. "If you don't like them you don't have to use them. You're probably used to your other ones, but I just thought I'd try. You really don't have to wear them."

But then Lindy opens the box and breathes, "Oh, Ro. These are just gorgeous. Just *gorgeous*. Of course we'll use these. Peter, come and look!" and all the anxiety drains away.

Lindy carries the box inside and I follow a few beats later. The whole family is bent over the box in the kitchen, and Lindy pulls out hers and holds it up in the light. Hers is a light shade of gray with sloping streaks of black that combine with streaks of yellow on the nose to create a dove's face and beak. I've added accents of silver throughout the paint, not in a particular pattern, just enough to give the idea of feathers. Peter's mask is very similar, but with the brown, red, and white of a hawk. His has gold accents the same way, giving an impression of a hundred shimmering feathers.

Suze's is the best of all, and the one I had the most fun making. Instead of a beak for her, I altered one of my face painting designs. The whole mask is rich turquoise, with a set of peacock feathers that wind around the mask's right eye. Each plume is intricately drawn; I used my smallest paintbrush to make that happen, and each sparkles with a hint of glitter underneath each stroke. The eyes are outlined thickly, like Cleopatra, and I've drawn in eyelashes for a bit of drama. It's so beautiful that I had a hard time giving it away, but it was the least I could do for my newest friend.

My own mask is beautiful as well, and I'm proud of the work I've done on it. Lindy didn't give me much to work with, wanting my costume to be a total surprise, but she did tell me the basic color scheme: red and gold.

With only those two colors to go on, I knew exactly the kind of feeling I wanted to evoke: passion. I painted the whole mask blood red, and then, with a lighter shade of red and gold glitter, I created a curving pattern all around my eyes that looked like dancing flames. It's tucked under my arm, and when Lindy's done admiring her own mask, I hold mine out to her.

"Will this work for me?"

Lindy doesn't answer, but pulls me in for a crushing hug. She keeps me like that, pressed against her and jostling me from side to side, and when she finally releases her grip she looks like she's only a step away from crying. "Wait until you see your dress," she says. "We were on the same wavelength."

She pulls out a gown from the single closet in the Mulligan wagon and hands it to me, laying it in my arms, and I have to blink back tears. Lindy and I certainly were on the same wavelength, and the dress is perfect—not just because it's lovely and because of the design, but because of what it represents.

"Look at us, sniffling like complete fools when there's a Revel to get to," Lindy says, wiping her eyes and then straightening with new determination. "Try it on, Ro. We need to make sure it fits."

As it turns out, it fits. It fits almost too well. The corset-like top is certainly doing its job. When I check myself out in the mirror, I gape and immediately cross my arms over my chest.

Lindy stands behind me and winks at my reflection in the mirror. "Just a little help, dear."

"Thank you," I squeak out. I still have my manners to fall back on, even if my exact sentiments are somewhere closer to *Oh my god, my fairy godmother just gave me boobs.*

Then Suze grabs my hand, pulling me toward the door, and I have to leave my self-consciousness behind.

"Come on. It's going to take forever to get our hair right."

We scurry across the campground to our tent, laughing as we run awkwardly in our full skirts. She's painted her toenails green, and I've painted mine red, and we're both wearing flip-flops. Sure, it's not exactly a classy look, but we're going to ditch our shoes the minute we get on the dance floor, anyway. Besides, as Suze said, it's our final screw-you to Jeff. As I watch her run in her flip-flopped feet, I have to admit: There's no one I'd rather be breaking the rules with.

It takes a full hour for Suze to do my hair and her own, and then it's time. We walk together toward the tavern, following the paths of lights and garland through the village. A tent has been set up in the open field across from the tavern, and it glows with soft white and purple lights, blending seamlessly into the other lights around us and the stars over our heads. Though it's one of those tents designed for events like weddings, with several peaks instead of one big one like a big top, it could be something straight out of a circus. It's striped, alternating green, purple, and gold, and with the glow of the lights, it looks whimsical, even enchanted.

Suze and I pause at the main opening, taking it all in with a big breath. People turn, stopping mid-conversation or mid-drink to look at us, and a flush works its way from my face to my neck to my chest.

"They're staring at us," I whisper to Suze, but she shakes her head.

"Yes, they are. How awesome is that? Come on, let's go!"

Suze pulls me into the tent, out onto the wooden dance floor in the middle of the tables, and holds our joined hands up high. It's so like her introduction of me that first night at the campfire that I get choked up, and the crowd around me blurs.

"Lords and ladies, the peacock and phoenix have arrived!" Suze proclaims. "Now the Fairie Queen's Revel can officially begin!"

That gets a lot of laughs and quite a few people clapping. Suze and I do a short dance, turning each other once to show off our dresses. Her peacock dress is gorgeous, with a tight black bodice that flares out into a full skirt of layers of green, turquoise, and blue, making it look like feathers. Lindy's put some iridescent beads here and there, giving the dress a shimmering, crystalized look. It's breathtaking but, I have to admit, mine is even better.

My dress is bright crimson. One of my shoulders is bare

while the other has a thick strap covered with feathers in gold and all shades of red and orange. The feathers continue, with a smattering of gold beads, across my body and down to my opposite hip, where my dress is gathered to the side. The pattern of feathers and beads continues across my body again, down to my opposite foot, where the feathers and beads suddenly expand to cover the entire bottom of the dress. The dress flares out from my knees, mermaid style, so that as I spin it looks as if I'm standing right inside a fire, being reborn from the ashes.

Reborn. Transformed. Ignited. Those words are the closest I'll ever get to describing what happened to me this summer—my love of art, my friends, and Will.

When Suze spins me under her arm, several people whistle and clap, and as we're turning she spots Grant, who is looking dapper in a doublet and cape of black and white. It takes me a minute to realize that the pattern in his clothes is the stripes of a badger, his knightly mascot.

"I'm going to go, okay?" she says, and just then the music starts up from the band of faire musicians in the corner: lutes and fiddles, drums and sackbuts. "We've got to start teaching dances. Do you see him?"

It takes me a moment to realize she's talking about Kyle, when at first I thought she meant Will. I give a cursory glance around the tent, and I see Kyle and Lacey. He's in a suit I saw him wear to a lacrosse awards banquet, and Lacey looks great in a bright pink dress. They're holding hands. What's surprising is how much it doesn't hurt to see. I continue my search, finally finding the person I'm really looking for. Suze follows my gaze and her pretty face breaks into a grin.

"Good luck," she says, nodding in Will's direction.

"See you on the dance floor," I say, and we give each other's hand a squeeze before I start toward the cute whip cracker who stole my heart without me noticing.

"Ro!"

Before I can get to Will, a familiar voice makes me turn, and I have just enough time to hold my arms out before Kara flies into them. She squeezes me hard, and then shoves me toward Meg, who hugs me just as crushingly. When she releases me, I stand back, admiring their dresses. Kara obviously outfitted them from the place she works at in the mall; I remember seeing both their dresses there and drooling over them. Kara's in a teal color that makes her eyes really pop, and the dress shows off her long legs. Meg's in a sparkly coral dress that clings to her thin waist and shows off her beach tan nicely. Brian stands behind them, looking uncomfortable, either because he doesn't know what to say to me or because he's wearing a tie. He gives me a slight wave.

"I didn't think you were coming!" I exclaim to them. The music has started, all of the faire musicians playing a dancing song at once, and we have to raise our voices. "I was afraid maybe you didn't want to come."

"Of course we wanted to come!" Kara says. "We had to see how awesome this place was."

"Ha!" Meg says. "Just tell her the truth, Kara. We wanted to see the hot knight."

"Oh." It's clearly been too long since I talked to them last if they don't know that Christian's a jerk. "Well, there's some news on that end. Seems I can't help but fall for no-good cheaters." I glance at Brian. "Sorry. No offense. I know Kyle's your friend."

"None taken."

My friends look crestfallen, and Meg all but says so. "Damn. We were hoping the hot knight worked out for you and that you'd be totally over Kyle."

"Oh, I am," I assure them. "But it's not the hot knight I want. There's um . . . there's this other guy now. He does this show with a whip."

Meg blinks. "A whip? Right on. That could be super sexy."

Kara's shaking her head at me. "Only our friend Ro could find a job at a Renaissance faire and hook up with a dude who does whip tricks."

"And . . . ," I say, pausing for suspense, "I've decided I want to major in art."

"Wow," Meg says, breathless. "How awesome. We have an artist friend, Kara! We're totally the cool people who hang out with eccentric artists and whip people now. We've definitely moved up a notch in the social ladder."

"Agreed. All cool people have to have artist friends, right? Or at least a hipster friend."

"Yeah. I mean, the only way we could get any cooler is if we had a British friend, too. Or a celebrity friend."

I watch them, amused and a little flattered. They called me their artist friend, their eccentric friend. And I can't help myself: *I love it*.

Suze appears at my side, pulling Grant behind her and introducing herself without preamble. "You must be Meg and Kara. Wait, don't tell me. You're Kara and you're Meg."

She points to the correct friend with each name, and totally earns brownie points for me with Meg and Kara in the process, because now they know I haven't been able to shut up about my friends while I've been away. Suze chats with them as if she's known them forever, and while they talk, I scan the room for Will. He's moved, and now he's standing by the bar, a glass of ale in his hand (it pays to be friends with the bartender, I suppose), and he's searching the room as well. His gaze lands on me and stays there, steady, and my heart thuds hard against my ribcage. He was looking for me.

"Suze?" I say to my friend. She stops explaining how we get by without electricity to Meg and Kara and leans close so I can talk into her ear. "Can you entertain them for a while? I've got to take care of something."

"Sure thing."

Dodging around the gathering crowd, I make off toward the bar. Will sees me coming toward him and smiles, and some of my nerves die down.

"Looking for someone?"

A wolf steps into my path, and even though there's a mask and a whole lot of fur involved in the costume, it's still elegant and somehow fashionable, and I'd certainly know those broad shoulders anywhere.

"Not that it's any of your business, but yes," I huff. "Who are you here with? Cassie or your girlfriend?"

"I'm here alone," Christian says, removing his mask. His crystal blue eyes dart about the room. "Exploring my options."

He eyes me then, glancing overly long at my chest. "You know . . . if you still wanted to have a little fun before summer's over—"

"You have got to be kidding me," I say. I'm so disgusted that I actually taste it in my mouth, and it tastes a whole lot like orange juice that's way past its expiration date. "Just because you're good-looking you think you can treat girls like crap."

"I treat girls how they ask to be treated," he counters. "So before you go name calling, look at yourself. You said you wanted a fling. All I did was take you up on it."

"Yeah. While you had a girlfriend. You're a liar."

"I may not have told you about my girlfriend, but I didn't spend the night in someone else's tent and then claim to be just friends after."

I suck in a breath. "I wasn't lying about that. I told you. Will and I are just friends."

"Oh yeah? Is that why you were looking for him just now?" Unbelievably, Christian makes a tsking sound and shakes his head as if he's disappointed in my behavior. *My* behavior. "Three guys in one summer. Sounds like a slut to me."

I want to slap him. My hand twitches like it wants to, too, and it's just waiting on the order. But he's not worth it. Christian isn't worth the scene it would make, or any other words I could spit at him, and he most certainly isn't worth the ache I'd get in my hand when I smacked his thick skull.

I push past him, making sure I push hard enough that he stumbles back, and head toward the exit. I need to get outside, into the cool night air. I make for the tavern, plopping myself down on the back stairs by the kitchen with a loud thunk. Inside, Ramón's barking out orders to the wait staff and dishes and glasses clink together; out here with me is the whirring of the ventilation system and the smell of rotting food from the Dumpsters. It all somehow perfectly fits my mood.

As angry as I am, there's something far worse bubbling up beneath it. Hot tears fall down my cheeks, and though I wipe them away, they keep coming.

I know I'm not a slut. If anything, Christian's the slut, but that word still stings. I've never been called that before, at least to my face, but I've certainly used that word about others. I wonder if they felt like this, like they'd been hit with a stun gun and had no way of defending themselves. I wonder if Lacey felt that way when the whole school was talking about her and Kyle.

But maybe she wasn't either, really. Maybe Kyle hadn't told her about me. Or maybe she just really liked him and couldn't help herself. After all, Kyle was cute and charming, and maybe he fell for her, too. They seemed so happy that day when they came into the tavern. They seemed to have a lot more of a connection than we ever did.

Maybe sometimes you meet the right person while you're with the wrong person and that's all there is to it. It's nobody's fault—it just happens. But when it does, someone always gets hurt.

Unfortunately, in my scenario, I realized Christian was wrong and Will was right too late. The last thing I wanted to do was hurt Will, but I couldn't have known.

The sound of grass crunching mixes with the soft whirring of the ventilator and I realize I'm no longer alone. My thoughts disperse like heavy fog, and Will's standing there, watching me with concern.

I give him a half-hearted smile and take in his costume, which is a white tunic with a repetitive black pattern, paired with these awesome black leather boots that must have come from The Bone Needle. I have no idea what he's supposed to be. He can't be a badger; that was Grant's costume. Maybe a weird spotted skunk?

"Okay, you got me. I have no idea what you are," I say to him.

"I'm an ermine." When I only blink at him in response, he sighs heavily and explains. "It's the stoat, a weasel-type thing, and in winter its coat is white with a black tail. They used to sew a whole bunch of the winter furs together to create this pattern, which became a symbol of royalty. It's very historic."

I hold back laughter. "You're such a dork, you know that?"

"A hopeless case, I'm afraid." He sits next to me on the steps. We're silent for a minute, then he bumps my knee with his own. "Are you okay? I saw you run away from Christian."

I sniffle. "He called me a slut."

Will tenses, and I watch his knuckles turn white. "Want me to go in and beat him up? I mean, I've never hit anyone in my life but maybe I could just confuse him with big words or something."

I laugh, a big rumbling laugh that feels good as it breaks through my tears. "Thanks for the sentiment, but I'd rather you just stay out here. With me. He's not worth it."

I open up my hand, extending it out a little so he can see my waiting palm. There's a split second where I think he's not going to take it, he's going to leave me hanging there, but then he slips his calloused hand over mine and we fold them together on his knee.

"Have you seen Kyle?" Will asks. His voice is soft. Cautious.

"Yeah. He's here with Lacey."

"Want to go in there with me and make him jealous?"

I smile a small smile at that. "No. I don't want to go in."

Will's hand twitches in mine, but he doesn't pull it back. "Are you over him?"

I think about it, taking a long moment before I answer. "Kyle broke my heart. And I don't know that I'm over that. But I don't want to be with him anymore." I take a breath, and when I exhale it feels like I'm pushing out some of Kyle with it. "Besides, there's this other guy who I'm kind of falling for. He's smart, and funny. Dorky. And he's got great eyes. He's always there for me, even when I act like an idiot. And I really, really like it when he holds my hand."

Will's eyes are golden and bright, happiness dancing in them just as sure as the reflection of the hundreds of Christmas lights decorating the tavern.

"Really?" he asks. Will reaches toward me slowly, cupping my face. "Well, that guy would really like to kiss this girl right now."

I nearly pull away from him, I'm so surprised. "But you said 'some day,'" I say, confused. "I thought—"

"Today is some day, Ro. I just wanted you to be sure," Will says, and then he leans forward and presses his lips to mine.

It's just as magical as the first time, only this time he doesn't pull away. He pulls me closer instead, wrapping his strong arms around me so there's nothing between us except the fabric of our costumes. It feels so right in his arms, and for a glorious moment all I know is his warmth and his lips and his heartbeat against mine.

When we finally do part, it's with a sigh of regret from both of us.

"Can't believe I missed out on that all summer, and now there's only a week left," I say.

"Yes, but I have a feeling it's going to be a hell of a week," Will replies, and we both start to laugh. He stands, helping me up as well. "We should get back in there. Your friends are in there with Suze and Davis. Who knows what debauched, depraved things they're dragging them into."

"Who knows what debauched, depraved things we're doing out here?" I ask in my sauciest voice, and Will makes a whimpering sound before kissing me again.

When we finally pull apart, I take off running toward the tent, whooping and laughing as Will catches up and grabs me around the waist, twirling me through the air once like we're ballroom dancers before he puts me down. We kiss again, swaying a little in the grass, and we have to remind ourselves that we abandoned our friends and need to get inside.

Inside the tent, the revelers are getting serious about partying. Everyone is moving like one body on the dance floor, doing some crazy sort of Renaissance dance that looks a lot like some line dances I know. Suze and Grant are out in front, leading. Suze looks absolutely euphoric as she dances, the flush of exertion in her cheeks and laughter lighting up her eyes. Grant seems to be enjoying himself too, though he's a little self-conscious about his dancing. When he's not looking at his feet to make sure he's doing the right thing, he's looking at Suze, clearly enthralled.

Kara and Meg are right behind them and they've dragged Brian out there with them. Kara and Meg are in hysterics as they try to mimic Suze and keep bumping into each other, and Suze looks over her shoulder, laughing with them before she takes a step back and joins them, exaggerating her moves so they can keep up better.

I watch, completely enchanted as my friends dance

together. My two worlds have collided, and blended seamlessly. In fact, if I didn't know better I'd think Suze, Meg, and Kara have known one another for years. It warms me, and I squeeze Will's hand. He looks over at me, smiling, completely reading my thoughts, and squeezes back.

But when that song ends and a slow one starts, the first couple out on the dance floor is Kyle and Lacey and my stomach drops. They look right together, I have to admit. She fits into his arms like she was made for them. He spins her and pulls her close, just like Will did to me moments before, and when they look at each other, it's clear how much they care about each other.

"That's Kyle," I say, and I don't have to point. Will's looking at them too.

"Want to dance? Show 'em up?"

Although dancing with Will would be incredible, I shake my head. "Nah. I don't need that."

It's then that my friends notice I'm back, and they all come over, panting from their shimmying on the dance floor. Suze, Kara, and Meg all look down at Will's and my joined hands. There's a moment, a calm before the storm, in which they exchange glances, then they jump in with questions.

"Aren't you going to introduce us?" Kara asks.

"Yeah," Meg says, jerking her head at Will. "We need to meet the whip-cracking hottie."

Suze merely smiles for a moment and then says, "Congratulations, you two. Finally."

"You can say that again," I tell her, then I look straight at Will. "We need to make up for some lost time."

Will pulls me closer and his voice lowers to a purr. "Want to start now?"

I nod, half giggling, half breathless, and turn back to my friends. "I'm sorry, guys, but I'm going to take off. I, um . . ."

"Yeah, yeah, I know. Go lock it down," Suze says. She grabs me by the shoulders, turns me around, and practically shoves me toward the door. "Have fun you two. And don't worry. I'll entertain Meg and Kara."

I turn to wave to my friends, but Will and I can't make it to his tent fast enough. We're out of breath by the time we peel back the tent flaps and tumble onto his air mattress.

I don't know how much time passes after that because it all feels like a dream, like an out-of-body experience. Maybe it's because my head can't accept that this fabulous life, a life with art and beautiful dresses and strange characters and a wonderful guy, is really mine.

But it is. At least for another week, it is.

I pull away from Will, breathless, about to tell him my thoughts, when Davis stumbles into the tent. From the look of him, I'd say someone broke into the mead again. He stands there, swaying, his bleary eyes roaming over me and Will cuddled tight in Will's sleeping bag, our lips all swollen, and mutters, "Finally!" before walking back out.

Will cracks up, then plants a kiss solidly on my mouth.

"Sorry, what were you going to say before my smooth roommate so rudely interrupted?"

I look into Will's brown eyes, studying the flecks of gold.
"Just that I'm happy."

"Me too."

I give him a fake pout. "Good, but don't stop kissing me.
We only have a week!"

"Yes, my lady," Will says, and obeys my command.

19

WEEK 4—SUNDAY

I wake up with my head on Will's chest, rising and falling gently with his breathing, and snuggle closer to him. He stirs but doesn't wake, simply drawing me tighter against him. I press my nose to his skin and inhale, not caring how strange that is. His smell is masculine but sweet, and so deeply *Will*. I try to memorize it so I can recall it next week when we're in different cities, and all the weeks after that.

"Ro . . ."

I lift up my head to look at Will's face, but he's only mumbling my name in his sleep, and when I lie back down his hand winds itself in my hair.

I curse myself for probably the thousandth time that I didn't get to do this sooner, and I'm sure that by the time this week is over, I'll curse myself at least a thousand times more.

But there's nothing that can be done now. We have to enjoy the time we have, which is only a few short days. It's already the last Sunday, which means tonight will be the last bonfire and—

I sit up, swearing loudly. Will bolts up too with a snort that's cuter than it is undignified, and blinks at me. "What? What happened?"

"It's Sunday. The *last Sunday*," I say.

"Mmm hmmm," Will mumbles.

"My parents are coming to visit today! What time is it?" I ask, my heart pounding.

"Dunno," Will says. He starts to lie back down, his eyes falling shut. "Everyones sleeps in after the Revel."

"Will," I say in a tone that lets him know I mean business.

Will harrumphs and turns on his side to reach for his pocket watch. He squints at the tiny numbers and hands. "'s eight thirty."

I swear again. Then once more for good measure. Then I start to get up, gathering my shoes and mask.

"Where you going?" Will drawls. "Stay s'more. Sleep."

"You're not a morning person, are you?"

"Nuh-uh."

"Sorry, I have to go," I say, slipping on my flip-flops. I'm still in my phoenix dress, which means I'm a little overdressed for the walk back to my tent.

"So? The gates don't open until ten."

"No, but the Duncans will be here before the gate opens. To be on time is to be late," I say, quoting my parents, who use that expression nearly every time we exit our house.

Will groans. "Too early . . ."

I sit back down on his mattress and lean over him, my hair creating a tent around our faces. "It's not too early. It's the usual time. Maybe someone shouldn't have kept us up so late."

Will groans again, and this time it's not a sound of displeasure, but something far sexier. "You didn't seem to mind."

"Not at all." I lean down and kiss him, and he wraps his arms around me, the weight and warmth of them nearly persuading me to linger for a few minutes.

Nearly.

"I'm sorry. I've got to go. If I'm not at the gate to meet them, I'll get some kind of lecture, I'm sure."

"Fine. Ditch me for your parents." He gives me a lazy smile, and I decide then and there that it's his second best smile. Almost as great as the smile he gave me after we kissed last night.

"Duty and honor and all that." I stand, and our arms slide away from each other as if they're the last part of ourselves to surrender to separation. "And now to do the Ren Faire, Post-Revel Walk of Shame."

Will chuckles sleepily, and before I can even say good-bye, he's drifted back off into dreamland. I give him one last look, just a visual to keep in my memory for later, before slipping out of the tent.

I keep my head down and scurry like some woodland creature toward my tent, which proves to be harder than I predicted because my skirt is huge. It didn't feel so big and heavy last night when I had all the energy in the world, but this morning it's dead weight. I hike it up as best as I can and run, unladylike as can be.

I'm only a quarter of the way back to my tent when someone falls into step next to me.

"Suze!"

"Ah, I love that I have someone to slink back to the tent with in the wee hours of the morning. What a glorious day this is going to be!"

I gather that Suze also had a wonderful evening. By the time we reach our tent, we're both breathless. I sit down, gasping, and she collapses next to me.

"Why are you up so early?" I ask her.

"Because your parents are coming, silly. If you weren't back in the tent yet, I was going to wake you up."

"Such an awesome friend."

"I totally am," Suze teases. "When will they be here?"

"When the gates open."

"Oy." Suze makes a face that looks like she's about to hurl. "Okay, well, we've got to make you presentable. Your eyeliner's doing the raccoon thing, and your hair . . ."

Suze touches my hair, and just from the slight pressure I can tell that it's tangle city on my head. I grimace, realizing what that means. "I can't believe Will saw me like this . . ."

Suze looks like she's biting back a laugh. "Too late to worry about it now. At least your parents won't have a clue. I have makeup remover. And don't shampoo, just condition. A lot. Like. Twice."

I take her advice and ten minutes later I emerge from the shower, all traces of last night's fun times and adventures gone, with the exception of a small hickey right in the valley of my collarbone. Suze disguises it with some industrial-strength concealer, all the while grilling me for details of the night.

"There was a lot of kissing," I say, trying to keep it vague, as opposed to Suze's detailed descriptions. "A lot. Then we fell asleep in his sleeping bag, tangled together."

"So . . . you didn't . . . ?"

I'm sure all the industrial-strength concealer in the world can't hide my blush. "No!" I squeal.

"What? I'm just asking. It's not like I can judge." Suze swipes some concealer under my eyes for good measure. "That's cute. Going to really get to know him first?"

"Yeah. Well, that and . . ." I draw in a breath and force myself to say the next words. "He's going to MIT soon. Maybe he won't even want to see me then."

"I seriously doubt that," Suze says. She looks into my eyes, giving me a really convincing look while she also sizes up the circles under my eyes.

"I hope you're right," I say, but shove the hope down deep. "But today I have more important things to worry about. Like my parents coming. And I'm going to tell them that I want to major in art."

"You are?" Suze doesn't wait for me to answer and pulls me into a hug so tight that I'm wheezing for breath when she lets go. "I'm so proud of you! It's about time you listened to me. And my mom, I guess."

"It's about time I listened to myself," I say, but then shrug. "They aren't going to be happy . . ."

"They will be," Suze promises, then wrinkles her nose. "But just in case, better use some waterproof mascara."

I end up wearing the forest green Renaissance gown, which has become my favorite since the troubadour performance. With the lush green material and the gold trim at the edges, this one definitely stands out as the most romantic of them all. Plus, as a bonus, it has a higher neckline, which is never a bad thing when it comes to the Duncan clan. Proper and dignified, after all.

When I see Louise and Ted Duncan walk through the front gates of King Geoffrey's Faire and gape at the Renaissance village around them, I have to bite my lip to keep from laughing. The expression "fish out of water" comes to mind. Mom's wearing jeans and new blazing white sneakers, and clutches her large purse to her side as if afraid one of the Renaissance hooligans will snatch it. I see my father look at the signs that point in the directions of all our main events, and see him frown as he reads. No doubt he took in the words "belly dancers" and "sword swallowers."

"Mom! Dad!" I call, and my parents turn, doing a double take at their own daughter, who looks like a respectable Renaissance maiden. When I reach them, just for dramatic effect, I drop into a curtsey. "My lord, my lady."

Mom gives me a fluttering laugh and brings her hand to her chest in surprise. "Rowena! We hardly recognized you. You look so . . . so . . ."

"Old-fashioned?" I venture. "Mom, you can let your purse go. This is a Renaissance Faire, not a Dickens novel."

"Oh, of course." Mom lets her purse hang by her side, but her hands hover over it, just in case. "We're so glad to see you."

"Me too," I say, and it catches me off guard how much I mean it. "I took the day off, so I thought I could show you around a bit, take you to all the shops and the craftsmen. Then after, I'll take you to some of the coolest performances you'll ever see."

"That sounds like a wonderful plan, sweetheart."

"Good." I turn and wave for them to follow, which they do while they gawk at everything around them. I feel just as overwhelmed because I don't quite know where to start, but then I remember the way my first day at the faire started: Will introduced me to Ramón's sticky buns.

I turn and give my parents a huge grin. "I hope you guys are hungry . . ."

"We are!" my mother answers, and so I lead them toward the bakery.

Ramón isn't in, of course. He's too busy at the tavern this time of day, readying things for lunch, but Magda's there. She flashes her gap-toothed grin and I introduce her to my parents.

"Three sticky buns?" Magda asks, and I nod my head, though after my mom has her first bite she decides to get a whole dozen to take home.

We sit on the bakery steps, finishing the buns and licking our fingers clean in a way that is decidedly un-Duncan of all of us. Then, for the next few hours, we make our way around to all the vendors. My dad spends a freakish amount of time in the men's costume shop, asking questions about how chain mail was made and what it could protect you from, and my mother is absolutely enchanted with the teacups at Robbie's, and seems startled when I tell her I painted some of them.

Of all the shops we visit, though, Lindy's is by far my mother's favorite. Lindy seems to be a favorite as well, and she bends over backwards to charm my parents—as if they wouldn't have loved her anyway. Everyone loves Lindy. She even tries to convince my mother to buy a corset, even if she never wears it "outside of the bedroom," which makes my mother blush furiously and my father inquire exactly how much the corsets are.

Gross.

We arrive at the face painting tent right before the afternoon shift starts. I introduce them to Cassie, who acts so syrupy sweet that I almost go into a diabetic coma. I show them my station and talk a little bit about my routine, and they listen with interest. I can tell they're both wondering how to turn this experience into a college essay; I can see the gears grinding in their heads like an old rusty machine.

My parents see my Polaroid wall before I get the chance to point it out to them, and my mother turns to me, her hand on her mouth.

"Ro. You did all these?"

I nod and go to them. "I took a picture of almost every face I painted this summer. Just, you know, for posterity or something." I point to the upper left hand corner and then extend my arm to the right, then back to the left again. "They're in order. I like to think I got better as summer went on."

"Oh, you did," my mother says. She turns her gaze to my first Polaroids. "But the first ones are good, too. It's just that these, at the end . . ."

Mom doesn't finish her sentence but nods, as if agreeing with whatever she just said in her head.

"Well, it's different, you know? I had to get used to working on skin, and on a surface that wasn't flat," I explain. "It's different than working on a canvas. A lot of it is like you're just working with art that's already there. Like, if a person has great cheekbones or eyebrows or something, you can incorporate it into the design and highlight it."

"Sounds more like makeup than paint," Dad says. I

catch a whiff of disapproval, but I shrug it away.

"Sometimes." I think of Anna, the little girl I made into a butterfly princess, and Colin, my shy fuchsia dragon. "It can make people feel better about themselves. Make them feel beautiful. That sort of thing."

"I know," Mom says. She gestures to the wall of Polaroids. "You can see it in their faces."

My throat goes all dry and tight at that. "Wow. Thanks, Mom."

"Wouldn't that make a wonderful essay subject, Ted? Seeing inner beauty?" My mother gets a far-off look in her eye, like she's imagining some old college dean at Harvard reading my essay. "'The Beauty Within: My Summer at a Renaissance Faire,' by Rowena Duncan. Oh, that's just lovely."

My father turns suddenly, and I think he's going to agree or perhaps even comment on the value of my work, but instead he says, "Do you think we should see the joust now, honey?"

I deflate. He's not getting it, he doesn't see it at all. I'm going to have to make him listen and make him understand. The problem is I have no idea how to do that. My father's never been much of a listener when he's not on board with the subject, and I've never been one for keeping my cool when I feel like someone's not listening. The Duncan stubborn streak is too prominent in both of us.

"No," I answer him, resigned. "See the last joust of the day with me. Trust me, it's the best one. It's for all the marbles."

"Sounds like a plan, Stan," my father says, a strange little saying that takes me back to family vacations in my childhood. "Can we eat again? I'm starving."

"The two sticky buns you wolfed down aren't cutting it, huh?" my mother asks wryly.

Dad looks sheepish at that. "Hey, it's been hours since the sticky buns and I can smell turkey legs and potatoes from here. You can't blame a man for getting an appetite."

"I'm hungry too," I say, more to earn brownie points with my dad than out of actual hunger. "Let's go to the tavern. Suze can wait on us. She's my best friend here. She'd love to meet you."

I can't believe it.

I'm at Will's show with my parents, stuffed so full of Ramón's cooking we can barely stand, and my dad is *guffawing*.

Like, not chuckling, not a few polite laughs at the right time—guffawing. He thinks Will's act is hysterical. Which it is. I just never imagined that Will's over-the-top French accent, his painted-on mustache (which I still haven't helped him with), and his jokes that are as cheesy as Ramón's cheddar biscuits would be my father's style. But Dad gets really into it, even clapping along to the beat when Will does his awesome whip routine.

My mother doesn't find it as humorous, and after a while I notice that she's looking at me more than she's looking at the stage. I bite the corner of my mouth and try to stifle the pride for my almost-boyfriend that's making me grin like an idiot.

"He's kind of cute," Mom whispers to me, and with that small statement, I know that she knows Will is more than a friend. "Much better looking than Kyle, if you ask me."

"He is, isn't he?" I whisper back.

"Is he just as charming offstage?"

"More."

"Sounds pretty serious."

I shrug, my eyes focusing on Will, and try to force a smile. "Maybe. I'm not sure yet. I like him a lot."

Mom hums at that as if she understands everything that's packed into my few words. She rubs the center of my back. "I suppose I should meet this young man."

"I don't know. Dad might ask him for his autograph."

We both glance over at my father, who is bobbing his head to the rhythmic crack of the whip, and chuckle to ourselves.

I do take them to meet Will, who seems nervous for only a moment before turning on his considerable charm. He compliments my mother and spends a long time explaining his training and some behind-the-scenes stuff about his show to my dad. My dad asks him about a thousand questions, and Will keeps sneaking glances at me whenever Dad looks away for a second. Of course Mom notices this and leans in to whisper, "So is he your age?"

I shake my head. "He's going to college in a few weeks."

"Where?"

"MIT."

My mother seems impressed, thank goodness. She lowers her voice even more. "Should we tell your father that you're dating his new hero?"

I try to suppress a smile and whisper back, "Please don't. At least not until after you leave."

When Dad finally lets up, I thank Will for his time and hope my parents don't catch it when I mouth, "See you tonight," to him.

"Is it time for the joust yet?" my father asks. His voice is laced with excitement, and he's looking all around as if he's afraid he might miss something.

Huh. Seems like maybe Dad had some of ye olde Kool-Aid.

I laugh and sling an arm around his shoulders. "We have a few more hours yet. There are some other shows you need to see. My friends Patsy and Quagmire do this hilarious mud show, and the acrobats are incredible. Then I'll take you to see the animals in the menagerie. Suze's dad trains the birds . . ."

We pass the hours leading up to the joust so quickly, and with such great entertainment, that my father almost forgets to be impatient. Almost. By the time the bell tower chimes out the hour and hordes of people start to break for the jousting field, he's practically vibrating with anticipation.

Amused to no end, and feeling some of that excitement myself, I lead them toward the jousting field, right up to the fence line so they've got a great view of the whole ring. At the opposite end of the fence, the knights are suiting up for the final chapter of today's script.

I don't explain how jousting works to my parents; I want them to enjoy the illusion, even if my dad may see right through it. But I do try to sway them in the right direction of who to root for.

"The one in black is the good guy," I tell them. "The guy in gold is great too. Hopefully, they win the round."

As it turns out, King Geoffrey's kingdom is threatened by the mysterious knight in blue today, and the knight in black is chosen by the king to defend the realm, which means that Christian is about to get knocked off his horse. I can't believe my luck.

When Christian comes out, everyone in the crowd boos and I and my parents join in. Though I would like to think of myself as a bigger person, the truth is I hope he falls on his butt. Hard. And he feels it for a week.

The reality is as satisfying as I could have hoped, and Christian lands in thick mud, dirtying his fancy doublet. I at least have the decency to stifle a smile when I turn to my parents and ask if they enjoyed the joust.

"How does it work?" my dad asks in response, his eyes shining as he tries to work out the secrets in his head. "Is it cues that the audience can't see? Are they wearing a lot of padding under the armor?"

My mom and I exchange an amused glance, then I turn

my dad in the direction of Richard and Grant. "Go ask them. Tell them you're Ro's dad, and they'll talk with you all day if you want. But I should get ready for dinner. I'm not wearing this dress out."

"Sounds great, honey. Invite Suze to go. She's a lovely girl." Mom winks at me, then lowers her voice. "I'll go with him and make sure he doesn't embarrass you too thoroughly with your knight friends. We'll meet you by the gate in twenty."

I leave them at the jousting field and head back to my tent.

"They really want to take me?" Suze asks, flattered.

"Yes, but you're going to have to help me." Suze's face crumples in concern, so I tell her. "My dad was seriously unimpressed when I talked about art today in the face painting tent, so I haven't told them yet."

The look of pride on her face reminds me of Lindy, and it eases some of the fluttering nervousness in my stomach. Suze puts her hands on my shoulders and looks into my eyes.

"You're going to be fine, Ro. Just tell them how you feel. They love you. They want what's best for you."

"Yeah," I say miserably. "But what they think is best isn't what *I* want."

"Then convince them." Suze pulls me in for a tight, strong hug. "I know you can. I've seen you paint. You love it and you're good at it. Show them that."

Mom and Dad take us to Max and Erma's, which is a little ways down the highway, and Suze is so happy to get a cheeseburger that she talks about it most of the way through dinner. My parents ask us every question they can think of about the faire, and about our friends there, and Suze and I do an admirable job of regaling them with our tales of summertime adventure and doctoring them into a PG rating.

It's not until Suze and I are halfway through the sundaes we made at the sundae bar that the questions run out, and I realize it's now or never to talk about art school.

I clear my throat and push my sundae away from me. Suze, God love her, squeezes my hand under the table and kicks off the conversation for me.

"So, Mr. and Mrs. Duncan, have you seen Ro's Polaroids in the face painting tent? They're so good."

My parents nod, my mother punctuating it by saying, "I was quite impressed."

"Thanks." I swallow. "You know how I was talking about how I could paint things that might make people feel better, or highlight their good qualities? Well, I wasn't so good at that before. This summer has really helped me see the good in others." I pause to think about how I'd seen everybody at the beginning of the summer—Will and Christian, but even Kyle and Lacey too—and how I see them now. "I think art has changed me. It's helped me grow and learn how to be a better friend, and to look inside a person instead of just looking at the outside."

"All very good lessons," my father agrees, and raises his

glass of iced tea as if to toast. "And a fine topic for college application essays."

"Yes, but . . ." I struggle for the next words, but Suze squeezes my hand again, and that gives me courage. "I want to write this essay for art schools."

"Art schools?" my mom asks. My father, on the other hand, seems to be having trouble understanding.

"What do you mean, art schools?"

"I love painting," I tell them. "I do have a talent for it, but more than that, it's something I'm so passionate about that I have to paint every day or else I get itchy. Whenever I see a face that interests me, or a scene, the only thing I can think about is how to paint it so everyone else can see it like I see it, too. I've really fallen in love with it."

My father reaches for his glass and takes a giant gulp of ice tea, and I bet anything he's wishing it was the Long Island variety. "Rowena," he begins, "I'm sure you've had a fun time this summer painting faces, but it's not a way to make a living."

"I don't want to paint faces, Dad. I want to paint canvases. Real art. Like Monet, or Rembrandt, or Picasso."

My mother is shaking her head. "There's no money in that, sweetheart."

"It's not about money, it's about doing what I love to do." I blink back some tears that are starting to fill my eyes.

"But what about Boston College?" my father asks me. "Why this sudden change? It's very unlike you, Rowena."

"I never wanted to go to BC, Dad."

"But then why—"

"Because you wanted me to go and major in economics, like you did," I say. It's not angry; it's more like an apology. "You had my whole life planned out for me and I didn't know how to tell you it wasn't what I wanted. Even if you don't want me to go into art, I'm not sure I'm cut out for the business world. I'm sorry, Dad."

I swirl my spoon around the ice cream soup my sundae has become and stare at the Reese's Pieces and sprinkles as they dance around my dish, counterclockwise. Next to me, Suze is doing the same thing and I know the tension in the air and her nervousness for me killed her appetite. The waitress comes to our table and Dad asks for the check. When she's gone, I finally look at him again.

"Say something, please." I swallow. "I hate thinking that I'm disappointing you."

"We're not disappointed, Rowena," Mom says gently. She has her hand on Dad's. "We're just surprised, that's all. We've talked about Boston for so long, this is quite a shock."

"Yes, but I think it was us doing all the talking, Louise," my father says. He looks at me like I'm a puzzle and he can't figure out where the last pieces go. "Art, huh?"

I smile at him. "Art."

My mom lays her hand over mine. "If this is what you want, Ro . . ."

My father's face next to her is serious. "This is your future,

Rowena. You can't just jump into this, you need to—"

"Do my research, I know." We smile at each other, and I could swear there's pride there in his eyes, not to mention a few tears.

"A Duncan always does their research," Dad explains to Suze. "Our family motto, passed down for generations."

I turn to Suze. "Don't listen to him. He's full of it."

"*That's* our actual motto," Mom quips.

Suze finds this uproariously funny, and by the time we've left the restaurant, she's deemed my parents super cool. I shake my head at her, but I'm flattered that she likes them. And she's right: Maybe they're not so bad. It just took us way too long to talk honestly, and that's as much my fault as it is theirs. But they're letting me try art school, and we had a great, honest talk tonight, and I feel very loved and very relieved.

As my dad jokes with my mother about buying a whole suit of armor before they go home, I turn to Suze, shaking my head at them, and say, "Yeah. They're pretty cool sometimes."

Back in the tent, I plop myself down on my air mattress before taking out my sketchpad. I turn to the page where I've started putting together my thoughts for Phase Two of the Thank the Mulligans Project, something that will show Suze's family how grateful I am for all of their kindness to me this summer. I've been slowly piecing ideas together since I painted their

Revel masks, building on one theme to the next, and if I can pull this off, it's going to be amazing.

I look up at Suze, teasing, "I can't wait until you see what I'm doing for them."

"Show me."

"Nope. Remember the deal. Not until it's done."

"Ro . . ."

"No way."

Suze lunges for the sketchpad but I'm too quick. I dodge her and Suze ends up sprawled facedown on my air mattress, both of us giggling and snorting like hyenas.

"Uh, hi. Did I come at the wrong time?"

We look over at the tent flaps and Will is parting them, looking at us with an eyebrow raised to such an arch that it looks pointy.

"Not at all," Suze says, standing and smoothing down her hair. "I was just about to head out and see Grant. Maybe I'll just, um, stay with him. So, Indy, if you'd want to, you know, stay here tonight to make sure the bears don't eat Ro, well, that would be the gentlemanly thing to do."

Suze slips out of the tent, wiggling her eyebrows at us, and when she's gone, Will says, "Well. That was subtle."

"Suze and subtle don't belong in the same sentence," I say. Will chuckles and enters the tent, sitting on the mattress cross-legged so we're facing each other.

"How did dinner go?"

"Well. I told them I want to apply for art school."

Will looks both impressed and surprised. "How did they take this new information?"

"Better than I expected," I admit. "They realized Boston College was their thing, not mine, and said as long as I research my options and keep an open mind for other things, I can do it."

"That's so awesome, Ro," Will says. He takes my hand as he says it and the earnestness of it makes me flush.

"It is, isn't it?" I say, squeezing his hand.

As an answer, Will leans forward and kisses me. I want to sink into him and stay that way for a week, until we have to get in our cars and go to separate places. But he pulls away too soon, and I can't help but pout.

Laughing, he takes his pinky and pushes my bottom lip back in line. "I think your dad liked me," he says.

"He loved your act. The corny jokes really did him in." I twitch my nose at him. "Mom liked you too. She thought you were cute."

Will huffs hot breath onto his fingernails and polishes them on his shirt. "What can I say? I can't help being dashingly handsome."

I roll my eyes at him. "I don't know how she managed to see it with that God-awful mustache you draw on yourself."

"Hey, you promised me a better one but you haven't delivered the goods."

"That's true, I did promise." I lean over and grab my paints and a fine-tipped brush out of the pile of art supplies between the air mattresses. "Let me remedy that now, Jacques."

"Eh eh eh," Will laughs in a distinctly French way. "But o' course, zere ees one zing zat we must do first, no?"

"And what is that?" I ask, my mouth itching to break into a grin.

Will wiggles his eyebrows. "Zis," he says, and kisses me again.

I promised him a better mustache, and I will deliver. But for now, that mustache is just going to have to wait.

20

THE LAST DAY

The last morning of the Renaissance Faire, I eat breakfast with the whole gang: Will, Davis, Ramón, Quagmire, Patsy, and even Suze and Grant, because I insist and pull them to our table.

Quagmire and Davis try to outdo each other with jokes this morning, and I laugh in between sips of Ramón's black sludge excuse for coffee and bites of what will be my last sticky bun for at least nine months. Will takes my hand under the table, which Ramón notices and grunts his approval.

When we're finished eating and I set off to do the day's tasks, it's hard to say good-bye to Will even for just a few hours. We don't have much time left, and it seems like I'm aware of every passing minute. I feel them all slipping through my fingers as I try to catch them and latch on, but nothing stays.

But it's not just Will who deserves a good-bye. He's not the only one who's changed me this summer.

I walk toward the stables, taking the long route through the village. The place is busy like the day of the Revel, only this time instead of setting something up, they're tearing down. Striking for the season, Lindy explained yesterday when the whole process started. Yesterday we still had customers, and the place still felt alive with excitement. Today the energy is much different. Not sad, really, but subdued—the feeling of moving on.

I stop walking and watch. Robbie's inside her little shop, wrapping teacups in newspaper. There's a box marked RO next to her, and it's an impressively small box. Save for a handful of teacups, most of what I painted was sold. Magda's sweeping the porch of the bakery, and I notice that for the first time the smell of cinnamon and yeast isn't pervading the air. On down the row I can see Lindy talking to the guys from The Bone Needle and Davis saying something that's cracking her up. Everyone is packing their belongings and wares away. Soon, this place will look like a ghost town, an abandoned bunch of streets and buildings from the Renaissance, a time capsule from the wrong era.

It's kind of a shock that all of this won't exist after today. I've loved this place so much, grown accustomed to the smells and the sights and the sounds. I've even grown to love how crowded it can be, and the crazy people who wear elf ears, and the children who are longing to see dragons. Tomorrow it will just be empty, and quiet, and that is the saddest and weirdest thing in the world to me.

"Where do they all go?" I whisper to myself.

"Some go on to other faires." I jump, and then smile as I realize Robbie's come out of her shop and is standing next to me. "There's a Viking festival down in Pennsylvania that a lot of people go to. Some people have other jobs."

"And where do you go?"

"I, uh, I teach. Elementary school art." She shrugs like it's no big deal.

For a second I imagine Robbie surrounded by a bunch of six-year-olds, her instructing them on their finger painting or their construction paper shapes, and my whole face feels like it's cracking with my huge smile.

"That fits you."

"Thanks," she says, and looks legitimately flattered. "You should come teach an art class. Hell, take 'em off my hands the whole day if you want."

I laugh. "Deal."

We hug, and when I can't find the words to tell her thanks for her guidance and for the time she spent with me this summer, she just nods and says, "I know. Me too. I'll see you next summer, Ro."

After that I finally make my way to my original destination: the stables. Although Sage and I may have had a falling out, the pony she introduced me to is going to keep a considerable chunk of my heart when I leave, as well.

Jiffy lifts his head when he sees me, snorting his hello. I open his pen and take out a grooming brush. I take my time, combing out his mane and tail and really digging into the strong muscles that must get so tired when he carries me or the children down at the menagerie. I get lost in the repeated motion of it, finding calm and solace, my worries melting away.

I don't worry about Will and when we'll be able to see each other again. I don't worry about applying for art school or the other research I promised my parents I'll do. I don't worry about if I'll be able to finish my present for Suze and her family. I don't even think about saying good-bye to anyone, or how sad it was to work my last shifts in the tavern and the face painting tent yesterday. The pony is patient, as if he knows this is our last time. Then I take his big horsey face in my hands and rub along the middle of his snout.

"Bye, boy. Thanks for not throwing me off. Or getting me lost."

His big, wide-set eyes blink at me in understanding.

"I hope I'll see you next year," I say, and it's the God's honest truth. I couldn't imagine a summer without King Geoffrey's Faire now, but I don't say that. There are too many other factors I have to keep in mind.

I leave the stables before I get teary. My plan is to grab my supplies out of my tent and head over to the Mulligan wagon to finish up my final thank-you for them. As I round the bend, however, I see Ramón sitting on the front porch of the tavern, his legs dangling over the sides, and I realize he needs a good-bye as well.

As I get closer, I see he's in street clothes, which is unusual. Usually, even on off days, he's in a tunic and rustically sewn pants. But today he's wearing an old Grateful Dead concert T-shirt and a pair of khakis that have been cut off around his knees, revealing skinny, hairy legs. I try not to stare.

When he sees me he pauses, gives me a sour look, and says, "Go away."

I take that as an invitation and sit next to him, watching as he scrapes his knife against a nearly finished wooden troll.

"I'll miss you, Ramón."

"No, you won't."

"I will. I'll miss your sticky buns and your yelling and your good advice."

A tiny smile turns up the corners of his thin lips. "But mostly the sticky buns, right?"

"Mostly the sticky buns," I agree with a laugh.

Then Ramón holds up the troll to the sunlight, turning it as he inspects it. It must meet his standards because he nods at it, sets his knife down, and brushes off all the wood shavings. Then he surprises the hell out of me by handing it to me, looking hopeful and embarrassed at the same time.

"For me?" I ask dumbly.

He nods. "For you."

I look down at the little troll in my hands. It's different from the others. The eyes are bigger and detailed with lashes, the ears are prettily pointed, and underneath its hat, the troll has a mess of curly hair. Though it has a huge belly and Ramón's trademarked bulbous nose, it's clear who this troll is meant to be.

"You made a troll of me!" He nods at me, proud of himself. But my smile falters. "I hope you didn't cut your hands too badly."

Ramón flips his left hand over and points to a tiny red mark on his palm that's in the shape of a horseshoe. "It will help me remember you."

I grin down at my troll likeness. "I'll always remember you, Ramón. Thank you. I love it. You'll be back next year, right?"

"Yes. King Geoffrey's Faire is my home."

"Where will you go now?"

Ramón shrugs before closing up his knife and tucking it into his pocket. "Viking Festival. Celtic Festival. Wherever Magda wants to go."

"Magda. I see," I say, happy to hear that perhaps they've finally admitted they love each other.

"Will you come back?"

"I want to," I tell him. "But I don't know if I can. It will depend on my college choice."

"If you want to come back, you'll come back. You'll find a way," Ramón says, and it might just be his best piece of advice yet. We sit in silence for a moment. Off in the distance I can hear people calling out good-byes in the village. It makes my chest feel tight and achy.

"I have to get going," I tell him, standing. I tuck the troll into my pocket. "There's a project I have to finish before I leave."

Ramón grunts in understanding, and stands up too. Then, without warning and before I can prepare myself, he's wrapped me up in a bear hug that nearly cracks my ribs. I squeal and giggle, which makes him laugh-grunt in response, and when he unhands me I take a step back so I can look him in the eye.

"Thanks for this troll. And for everything, Ramón."

"Yeah. Get out of here. Before I get angry."

With one last wave, I round the bend and disappear into the woods.

I tuck an unruly curl behind my ear and concentrate on the final details of the Thank the Mulligans Project.

The mural, my surprise for Lindy, Peter, and Suze, is almost complete. It's taken me nearly all the free time I had (after work and time with Will, of course) to get it done before the faire closes, but it will be so worth it to see their faces when I pull the drop cloth away and reveal it to them.

The idea is simple enough. I played off their Revel costumes and used a dove to represent Lindy, a hawk to represent Peter, and a peacock to represent Suze. The hawk and dove rest in a giant oak tree at the center of the mural, both of them keeping a watchful eye on the beautiful peacock standing at the tree's roots. The roots stretch downward and look like they're growing right into the side of the wagon, and beyond the tree is the rest of the forest. In the distance, over the tops of the leaves, I painted the village bell tower and the opening gates, but I also included the points and stripes of a couple of big tops, to represent their circus days. On the other side are the tops of stables and a few animals, their brown and black forms barely more than shadows beyond the trees. A sign saying MULLIGAN'S FANTASTICAL CREATURES hangs on one of the stables. The sky above fades to black and the constellations are out in full force: Orion, the Big and Little Dippers, and Aquarius.

It takes me nearly an hour to finish the details I was saving for last: the gold and silver of the birds' wings, the shadowing of the trees that provides depth, the troll hiding behind the very first tree, and finally, my signature.

It's the first time I've ever put my signature on anything meant for someone else, and I take my time, giving the R and D of my name an extra curlicue, and adding one simple phoenix feather underneath it. When I'm done I step back, wiping my hands on the discarded drop cloth, and admire what I've done.

It's by far my best work, which is fitting, because the Mulligans have certainly brought out the best in me.

I take a deep breath and open the front door of the wagon. "Hey, guys . . . I'm done."

Lindy drops the dish she was washing back into the sink, Peter sets aside his book on rare eagles of the Northern Hemisphere, and Suze, who was apparently just pacing in agony at the wait, squeals out, "Finally!"

As they all exit the wagon, I step out of the way of the mural and motion to it, like the glitzy hostess of a game show.

"Rowena! My goodness. It's beautiful!"

Peter stands there looking at the mural. He doesn't say anything, but I hear him swallow, and when I look at him, his eyes are filled to the brim.

Suze falls in behind me and gasps too, sounding so much like her mother that I have to smile. "Ro. This is amazing! I mean, holy crap."

Lindy tucks me under her arm, pulling me in hard and tight. "What a career you're going to have."

We stand there in silence for a while, just looking. As they admire my work, I try to comprehend that I've made something that means so much to this family, this family who has come to mean so much to me. My heart is so full of pride it could burst.

"Thank you for this," Peter finally says. His voice is gruff and wavering. "We've never had anything like this before."

"Okay, everyone, group hug. Come on. It's far overdue," Suze says, and the entire Mulligan family crowds in around me until we're all squeezing and sniffling.

"Thank you so much for everything you've done for me this summer," I tell them. "I feel like I have a whole other family now."

"You do," Lindy insists.

"And a new best friend," Suze says, and we all pull apart reluctantly. "Seriously. We've got to hang out. Amherst isn't that far away. We could meet in between and go shopping or something."

Shopping with Suze? Yes, please. It would be so much fun to hang with Suze in the modern real world, even if it might be startling at first to see her work her Renaissance wench charms on innocent waiters or retail clerks.

"That sounds awesome, Suze. I mean, 'yea, verily!'"

Suze gives me a wry look. "I think it might be time to lay off ye olde Kool-Aid."

We're giggling at that when the village bells ring that it's the top of the hour, four o'clock to be exact.

"Oh my goodness. I haven't even packed yet," I say, horrified. We have to be out of the faire at six so Jeff can clean up the grounds and lock up for the season.

"I'll help," Suze says, and before we start off, I give Lindy another quick hug and wave good-bye to my surrogate family one last time.

Packing is easier than I thought it would be. Mainly because, except for my art supplies, I throw everything into my suitcase without any sort of rhyme or reason. The art supplies I pack carefully, each brush in its own little case, each tube of paint tightly sealed. Suze helps in her own way, which is to say she picks through her own stuff to make sure she hasn't accidentally stolen some of mine, and gabs with me.

I turn to her, holding up the three dresses of hers that her mother tailored to fit me. "What about these?"

"Keep them."

"But they're yours."

"They don't fit me anymore." She looks down at her chest and then at mine. "No offense. Besides, you'll need something for next year."

"But what if I can't come back next year?"

"You will," she says. "You've caught the Ren Faire fever. Even if it's just for a visit, you'll be back. Because I'll be here. And Indy."

I turn so she can't see my goofy grin. "Ramón says that if I want to, I'll find a way."

"He's a wise man, that Ramón."

"Tell me about it." I sink down onto my mattress, which has been deflating since I pulled the stopper out half an hour ago. It lets out a sad whine when I sit. "So what will happen with you and Grant?"

"Fairemances," Suze says, as if that's all the explanation needed. "It was a good season. Maybe next summer we'll hook up again. We had a good thing going."

"But you won't talk to him until then?"

"Nah, it's not that deep. We didn't have much of a connection beyond . . . well, you know." Suze's smile is downright naughty. "And who knows? Maybe I'll meet a guy at college who will sweep me off my feet."

"And if he's a history major specializing in the Renaissance, even better," I say, and Suze agrees, adding, "And shaggy hair and abs that could crack walnuts wouldn't hurt either."

Suze tosses my last article of clothing, the sandals from The Bone Needle, into my suitcase. I have to sit on it to get it to close and zip.

"What about you and Will?"

My heart flutters at his name, then sinks slowly as I think about leaving him. But I give Suze a smile and try to make my voice sound neutral. "We haven't really talked about it. He's coming to say good-bye later."

What I really want to tell Suze is that I don't know how I'm going to survive not seeing him every day, and that I'm going to sob my eyes out all the way back home after I tell him good-bye.

"Yeah, but you and Will . . . there's a real connection there. It'll happen, Ro."

Suze pushes herself up from my suitcase and hands it to me. It feels a ton heavier than it did when I first arrived, and it should. After all, now it has three Renaissance dresses, a couple of teacups, canvases and paints, and a whole set of Polaroids.

"Have room for one more thing?"

Suze and I turn. Will's standing at the entrance of the tent, holding up his IT'S ALL SO TRIVIAL sweatshirt. If it still smells like him, there's no way I won't be taking it home with me.

"Well, I'll let Will walk you out," Suze says, and pulls me into a hug. We squeeze each other tight, and when we part we're both teary. "Call me soon, okay?"

"Absolutely. Bye, Suze."

"Fare thee well, Ro," she says, her words soft and sincere, and she slips out of the tent with a nod to Will.

I take the sweatshirt from him and stuff it into the suitcase. A corner of the sleeve sticks out because the zipper won't close all the way. Will begins to roll up my air mattress, squeezing out the last pockets of air from it. It occurs to me that this might be the last time I'm alone with him, so I watch him work, the corners of my mouth turning up as he pushes his glasses back up on his nose. He's wearing jeans and a shirt with Einstein's face on it today, and he hasn't shaved. It's a look that is so completely Will Fuller that I have to let the image burn into my memory like one of the Polaroids I've taken this summer.

He folds up my air mattress and blanket, tucks them under his arm, and reaches a hand out for my suitcase.

I smile at him. "And I thought chivalry was dead."

"Only amongst the knights. The whip cracker still plays by the old rules."

I laugh and let him take my suitcase. We walk the worker route behind the village to the employee parking lot, which is just fine by me. I'm not sure I want to see the village empty, with none of Lindy's dolls and dresses in the windows, without the smell of Ramón's sticky buns, and without all the children running around playing swords. It's just not King Geoffrey's Faire without the people.

When we reach my car, Will lifts my belongings into my trunk and closes it. The sound of the trunk shutting and locking has a melancholy tone of finality to it, and a lump rises to my throat.

I swallow thickly. "Well, I guess this is good-bye, huh?"

It's like the words themselves break me, and the flimsy wall I've built comes crashing down. I've known good-bye was coming, that we'd leave this place and go our separate ways, but until now it seemed so far away. My eyes start to well up and I look down, letting my curls fall in my face so he can't see me cry.

"Hey," Will says, and takes both my hands in his. I screw up the courage to look at him, blurry as he is through my tears, and try to memorize him exactly as he is now. He looks at me intently, like he might be trying to do the same thing, and says, "I have something for you."

Will takes my hand and turns it over, then pulls a pen out of his jeans. On the ticklish skin of my wrist, he scrawls, "*crackerjacques@gmail.com*" in his slanted, pointy handwriting.

I stare at it, its meaning sinking in. All summer long, e-mail and the Internet and the technological world didn't exist, and now here he is, offering me a link to him on the outside. It's a promise, and as the ink dries, so do all my tears.

He's given me more than one summer.

"It's going to be hard not to see you every day," I say, finally looking back up at him.

"Well, if you miss me a lot, you can always find me on You-Tube. I don't mean to brag, but my whipping videos have a couple of thousand views."

"Ooh, a celebrity gave me his e-mail," I breathe, and feign swooning.

Will merely shakes his head at me. "I'll miss your strange sense of humor, Rainbow Ro. I'll miss *you*."

"I'll miss you, too."

"Then don't make me wait too long." He looks at me seriously. "E-mail me. I want to see you soon."

"First thing," I promise.

Will kisses me good-bye, and though it feels like he means it to be a short kiss, soon his arms encircle me and we're leaning up against my car door, lost in each other.

"Hmmm, I'll miss that, too," Will whispers as he pulls away.

"Yeah, I'm going to want to do that again," I say as I try to catch my breath.

"Then see you," Will says, and squeezes my hand.

"Soon," I agree, and get into my car.

Will is the last thing I see as I pull away from King Geoffrey's Faire. Well, Will and the small troll on the post that first directed me to this wonderful place—Ramón's troll. It's strange now to think of myself on that first day, taking a turn onto an unknown dirt road and ending up somewhere better than I could have ever imagined.

The whole summer feels like a dream—a dream filled with fairy-tale things like knights and pretty dresses, yes, but art and friends and new love as well. A dream filled with promises of great things to come. As I head back to reality, I can't resist giving the troll a wave good-bye.

I plug my cell phone into my car outlet and power it up for the first time in a month. I haven't missed the device at all, though I've deeply missed the people on the other end of it. There are three voicemails: one from Kara saying she wants to hang out tonight and celebrate my homecoming; one from Meg, who is asking if I'll get Davis's number for her, and one from my mother. The one from my mother is the most intriguing, for a few reasons, not the least of which is that it's about art school.

Rowena, this is your mother. I know we asked you to do the research but I couldn't help myself. Do you know there's a school for art in Providence? It's not too far away at all. The Rhode Island School of Design, it's called. The career paths are just lovely. Listen to this: They've got animation, graphic design, art history . . .

I listen to my mother ramble on about the prestige of being a graphic designer or an art museum curator and smile. Providence is only an hour away from Boston, where a certain whip cracker will be.

But right now, I have nothing but time. I turn off my GPS, not quite ready to be yelled at by a British robot. Instead, I dig the troll that Ramón made for me out of my purse and set her on my dashboard. She can guide me home.

ACKNOWLEDGMENTS

First and foremost, I want to thank Amy Rosenbaum for giving me Ro and King Geoffrey's Faire. You shaped this story into what it is, and your guidance was invaluable. Also, thank you, Amy, for your faith in me. It came at a time when I needed it most, and because of that, I was able to find faith in myself. Your support means the world, and I am so thankful that you noticed my writing.

To Navah Wolfe, my editor, thank you for your insight, for challenging me, and for taking this story to a new level. I learned so much from you, and you taught it all with patience, care, and enthusiasm. Thank you for jumping headfirst into this book and loving Ro and the gang just as much as I do.

A big thank you to the Ohio Renaissance Festival and all of their employees for answering my questions, letting me explore, and making me feel like an insider. I wanted to be a "lifer" after my experience there. A special thanks to Suzanne Robbie Hay, who let me watch her paint face after face while I did nothing but ask questions and gulp down turkey legs. You helped me bring Ro's job to life and provided a sense of realism that my nonartistic brain would never have imagined.

And, Laura Wills, thank you so much for tagging along and asking questions when I was too shy.

Thank you to Brent Taylor, who read this book in its first draft and whose continued enthusiasm never fails to keep me going and floors me at the same time. Thank you, too, to J. H. Trumble—a fantastic writer and a fantastic friend. Your advice is always right, and thanks for reminding me to take deep breaths and relax. I don't think I could survive without daily e-mails from the both of you.

I have a few friends who, over the years, have provided helpful feedback that has made me a much better writer. Ann Skinner, your keen sense of characterization strengthened my own greatly, and you always rope me in and help me keep the plot in line. I can't thank you enough for editing so much for me over the years. Kate Nondahl, your support, encouragement, advice, and grammar skills have helped me immeasurably. You've kept me going. Erin Sweeney, you've been a great cheerleader. We started this thing together, so hurry up and finish your novel! John Finck, you always manage to see my stories differently. Thank you for making me see them from new angles as well. It's your turn now.

Melissa Lawson, my partner in crime. Thank you for being a great listener, a great hand-holder, a great instigator of hijinks, and a great everything else. I know that if I ever show up at your door with a dead body, you won't say a word. You'll just go find a shovel and start digging with me.

To my parents, Nick and Ruth Pinnix, thank you for being so supportive of all of my dreams and for encouraging my imagination. Because of you, it is limitless. Thank you for sitting through stuffed animal weddings and for listening to all of their stories.

Finally, to my husband, Andy, you really are my hero. You're the guy who can always make me smile, who can always get me dancing, who can always make me laugh. You make me brave because, with you, I know there's always someone on my side. Thank you for picking up the slack when I daydream too much, and for looking out for things that might make me stumble while my head is in the clouds. I truly don't know what I'd do without you. Love you, baby. Always.